D0058196

A TALE OUT OF LUCK

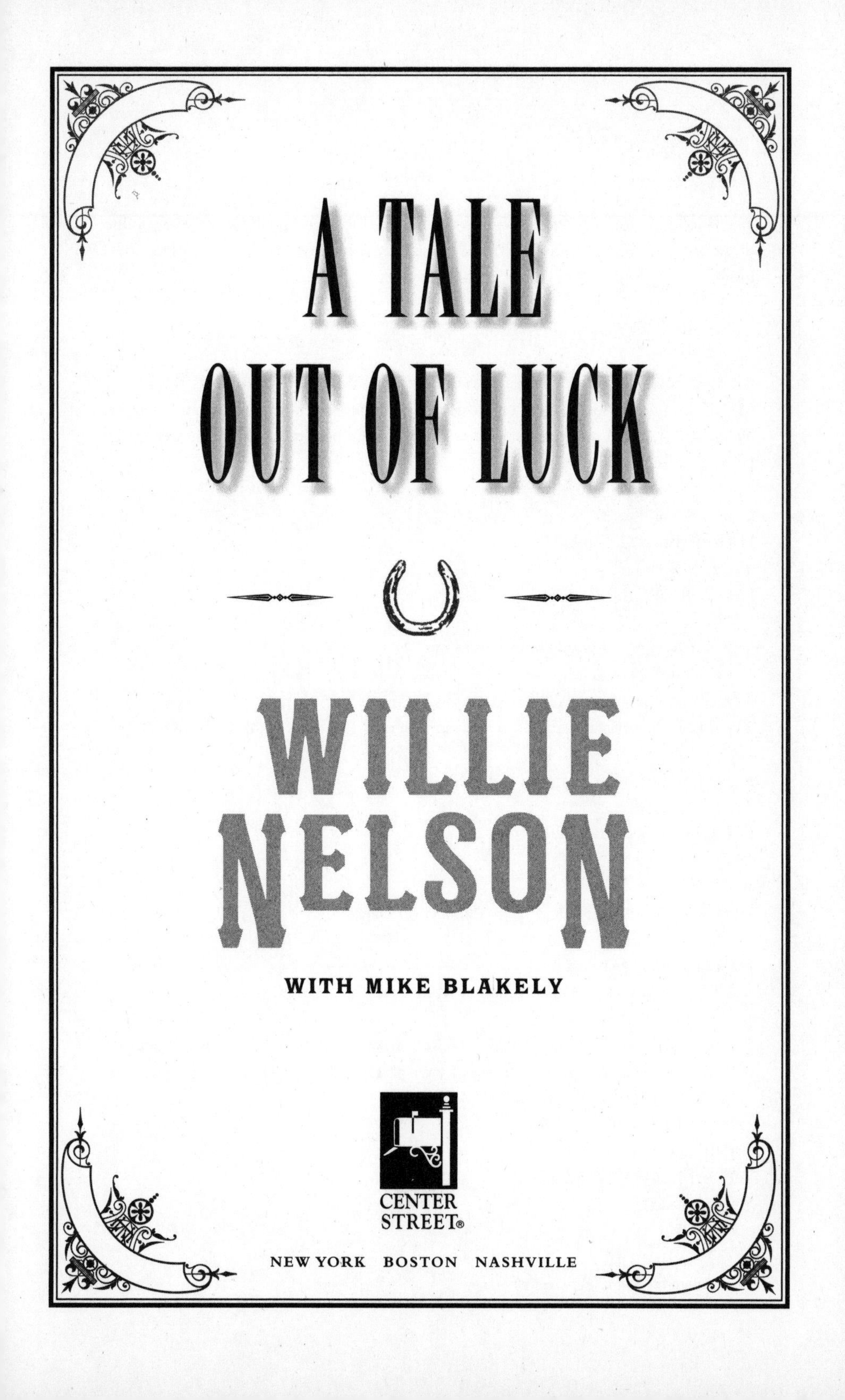

A TALE OUT OF LUCK

WILLIE NELSON

WITH MIKE BLAKELY

CENTER STREET®

NEW YORK BOSTON NASHVILLE

Center Street
Hachette Book Group USA
237 Park Avenue
New York, NY 10017

Visit our Web site at www.centerstreet.com.

Center Street is a division of Hachette Book Group USA, Inc.
The Center Street name and logo are trademarks of Hachette Book Group USA, Inc.

Printed in the United States of America

First Edition: September 2008
10 9 8 7 6 5 4 3 2 1

Library of Congress Cataloging-in-Publication Data

Nelson, Willie, 1933–
A tale out of luck / Willie Nelson & Mike Blakely. — 1st ed.
p. cm.
Summary: "Country legend Willie Nelson makes his fiction debut with an action-packed western set in the semi-fictional town of Luck, Texas"—Provided by publisher.
ISBN-13: 978-1-59995-732-6
ISBN-10: 1-59995-732-9
I. Blakely, Mike. II. Title.
PS3614.E44957W55 2008
813'.6—dc22

2007048747

Book design by *Ralph Fowler / rlf design*

1

HE CALLED HIMSELF, among other aliases, Wes James. Hunkered down now beside a fire of compact yet functional design, he made it a point to actually *think* of his name as Wes. The crucial thing here was to keep branding the current alias into his mind, as surely as he aimed to use his running iron, now heating in the coals, to do some quick branding of its own.

He whispered the assumed identity as he used a stick to pile gray-speckled orange coals over the tip of his running iron: "Wes James . . . The name's Wes James . . ." He glanced across the open top of the rocky hill where he had come upon the brindle yearling. As he turned the iron with his fingers, his wary hazel eyes swept the line of live oaks rimming the summit. He looked over his shoulder at his claybank cow pony, the gelding still keeping a taut rope on the lassoed brindle, the heifer securely hog-tied now on the ground.

"Howdy, ma'am, the name's Wes James."

The trick was never to react to one of the *other* aliases should some stock detective or brand inspector track him here to the limestone hills outside of the frontier town of Luck, Texas. In New Mexico, he had named himself Butch Smithers. He had styled himself Samuel Longstreet in Indian Territory. Elsewhere, he had variously announced his handle in saloons and recorded his identity in brand registration books as Joe Dudley, John Allen Roark, Shorty McDonald, Billy Ballard . . .

The alias was never random. It was always shaped around a brand Wes needed to register somewhere—a brand made by altering an existing brand on somebody else's livestock. Wes James—John Wesley James, to be more precise—was not without a measure of intelligence, a sense of creativity, and even a parcel of pride. What he lacked was ambition. He had no vision of the future, other than where he might find his next bottle of whiskey or woman of soiled virtue. His given name? The name of a father he never met? The name his mean stepdaddy had forced him to adopt? None of them mattered more than a plug of chew to one Wes James.

He looked up at the wisp of branding-fire smoke trailing off at an angle and dissipating into the slate gray of the evening sky. His identity here would fade like that smoke trail. He fanned it thinner with his hat. He didn't want anyone to see the smoke any more than he wanted to remember his past or visualize his future.

Wes James had gotten caught only once doctoring brands, in Omaha. Lucky he was caught in town, instead of out on the range where he would have been shot or lynched on the spot. Hard labor, mean guards, and meaner convicts were the consequences of carelessness that he didn't intend to suffer again, though he had fared better than men of lesser grit. Wes was six feet tall, lean, broad-shouldered, and tough. He wasn't given to violence, preferring to escape clean rather than fight his way out of a bind, but he could take care of himself, and would, with fists or firearms, if pressed into a corner.

He felt heat creeping up the running iron—a simple, straight rod no bigger around than his little finger. With it, he could "run" a brand with the same deft hand he often used to forge bogus bills of sale. He had employed this particular running iron for years—a short model that, after it cooled, slipped into a hidden pocket of his saddlebag. He knew from experience that when this end of the iron began to scorch his leathery palm, the business end was plenty hot enough to transfer possession of one brindle heifer to Wes James's ill-gotten ownership.

He lifted the iron from the coals and rose from his crouch, his knees and back aching a bit. Again his eyes swept his surrounds. He kicked some dirt on the coals, then hastened to the hog-tied brindle, the red-hot tip of his running iron leading the way, taking on the same shade as the setting sun.

The claybank was still leaning back on the rope. Too bad he couldn't keep this pony. He was a real good one. But Wes James never rode the same horse or wore the same crease in his hat for very long. The brindle thrashed on the ground as Wes approached, but the piggin' string held tight around the two hind legs and the left forefoot, and soon the beast rolled her eyes back in her head and lolled out her tongue in bovine stupefaction.

This was the moment of highest risk for a brand doctor—a rustler of beeves who specialized in modifying existing brands. It was impossible to explain away the act of doctoring another man's brand. Once altered, however, he would have his own brand registration papers showing title to the new design of the brand. No one would have reason to believe it had ever been altered. And, just to make sure no one saw the old brand in the new one, Wes would trail his rustled beeves far away to Jacksboro to sell to some unwitting British investors who had bought a large chunk of the Texas free range near there.

Selling his ill-gotten cattle too close to home was the mistake that had landed Wes in prison before. He had sold a small herd of rustled beeves at the stockyards in Omaha. After the sale, a sharp-eyed brand inspector had recognized the original brand, owned by a prominent area rancher, through Wes's doctored brand. They found Wes—George Brannigan as he called himself there—drunk in an Omaha saloon, a maiden of ill repute on his lap. He had always maintained that he could have jumped up and made a run for it, had the harlot not been so plump. He had leaned toward slender whores ever since, and suspected he could find one skinny enough to suit him up in Jacksboro.

Now the red-hot tip of the running iron descended on the brand of the Broken Arrow Ranch—two lines, roughly vertical, but closer together at the top than the bottom, intended to represent a broken arrow shaft.

/\

The brand, and the ranch, belonged to one Hank Tomlinson, a retired Texas Ranger captain of some renown. Tomlinson was not the kind of man Wes cared to get caught by, and that, in part, was what worried him now. On top of that, he had heard in town that a small band of Comanches had camped on Flat Rock Creek. Wes made a point of staying better mounted and armed than Indians, but the prospect of losing his scalp still raised concern.

Then there was that other matter. He tried not to think about that at all. In the past, he had always kept things simple and worked alone. He had always rustled for himself. He should have held to that policy.

His iron touched the existing brand, joining the tips of the two lines that made up the Broken Arrow brand, changing it to an inverted V. At the touch of the red-hot rod, the heifer bellowed and lunged against her bindings. Wes lifted the iron for a moment so the brand wouldn't smear an amateurish burn scar across the hide. He held the iron as an orchestra conductor would hold his wand, waiting to signal the strings, and he shushed the complaints of the heifer.

"Shhh . . . Hush, now, girl, I know it ain't fair."

And the beast seemed to listen. Deftly now, he added two more lines, expanding the inverted V into a W, all the while lifting his wand and shushing the piteous bellows when the brindle convulsed. He squinted past the odors of burnt hair and flesh as he added a J below the W.

W
J

This was the brand—the WJ—that Wes James had registered up in Jack County. This brand was, in fact, the reason for the alias, Wes James. As a final touch, he ran the hot iron over the scars of the existing brand, to freshen up the look of the entire brand and make it all appear newly burnt. If caught with this fresh-branded brindle somewhere between here and Jack County, he could claim that he was simply a mavericker working the free range—a poor cowboy trying to get a stake by roping and branding wild cattle owned by nobody.

A welcome sense of relief came over him. Now he could remove the piggin' string and let the heifer up. He'd leave her necked to a live oak overnight so she couldn't wander off. He'd camp nearby, catch some sleep. Before dawn, he'd be moving the heifer to that lonesome canyon where he was holding half a dozen more rustled beeves with doctored brands already penned behind a crude cedar picket fence. By daylight, he'd be on the trail to faraway Jack County. After that, he'd never again return to these ranges, ride this claybank, or use the name of Wes James.

Something sent a sudden alarm through Wes's nervous system. Had he heard it, smelled it, or just felt it? He turned. His eyes locked onto a figure at the tree line, fifty paces away, backlit by a western sky of red and purple. A feeling of dread chilled his guts. Then his eyes focused more clearly, and he knew he was in trouble. He gasped, and his heart throbbed in fear as he dropped the running iron and groped for his revolver. An arrow hissed toward him and thudded into his chest like a drumbeat before the running iron even hit the ground. He gasped and staggered back at the impact of the projectile. His fear overwhelmed him, and he could not find the handle of his weapon in the holster.

The pain and terror mounted now, and the last thing Wes James saw was a second arrow shaft protruding from his chest, just an inch from the place where the first one had struck. The colors of the sunset melted away, and Wes James hit the ground dead, his long, straight frame cooling alongside that of his trusty running iron.

From the east, swelling above the distant horizon, came the leading bulge of a full moon, thinly smeared with a tincture of blood.

2

SKEETER RODRIGUEZ stepped out of the bunkhouse and into the cool autumn evening.

"Mind them Injuns, Skeeter," came a voice from the bunkhouse, followed by a chorus of chuckles from the grown men inside. Skeeter smirked and slammed the door behind him. Already, he was regretting covering guard duty for Jay Blue. It was Jay Blue's night. Skeeter had gotten talked into taking the night guard in his stead so Jay Blue could ride into Luck and flirt with some barmaid who scarcely knew he existed. Agreeing to the favor had made Skeeter feel like a good friend at the time, but now it seemed like a bad decision, for the Winchester was heavy in his grasp, and he was already tired from a long day's toil around the ranch.

The headquarters of the Broken Arrow Ranch overlooked a broad bend in the Pedernales River, the pretty stream named a couple of centuries earlier, most probably for the remarkable flint arrowheads—*pedernales*—that the conquistadors had found and admired. Most of the Anglos who had since moved into the frontier region could not even pronounce the name correctly, and had bastardized it into a thing that sounded like "Perd 'n' Alice."

And so, the river enjoyed two pronunciations at the Broken Arrow Ranch, for the spread employed white cowboys as well as Mexican vaqueros. Skeeter Rodriguez was caught in the middle of it all, a little confused as to exactly where he fit in. He didn't remember his mother, a Mexican woman about whom no one would give him many details. He remembered his grandfather. His a*buelo*, a kind but strict old goat herder, had raised him to the age of six, dubbing him Izquierdo, meaning "lefty." Finding his grandfather dead in the pasture one day, little Izquierdo Rodriguez had walked to the newly founded town of Luck, Texas, not knowing what else to do.

Captain Hank Tomlinson, owner of the Broken Arrow Ranch, retired Texas Ranger, founder of Luck, and the most respected citizen of the Pedernales River valley, happened to hear of the orphan's plight and took Izquierdo in, giving him a home at the Broken Arrow Ranch and raising him alongside his own son, Jay Blue, who was only a year older than Izquierdo. The cowboys on the ranch—the Anglos, that is—could no more pronounce Izquierdo than they could Pedernales, so Izquierdo became "Skeeter." Skeeter Rodriguez.

Now, eleven years later, he spoke both Spanish and English with equal facility. It was as if he had half a dozen fathers, some Mexican, some white, for all the hands on the ranch liked Skeeter and looked after him. Yet, he had no father at all, and in fact had no clue as to the identity of the man who had sired him. Well, he had one clue. Skeeter's eyes were blue. That didn't exactly narrow it down a whole lot. Skeeter was just an orphan, and that's all there was to it. It lurked in the back of his mind as he trudged away from the warm bunkhouse.

He took a moment to admire the full moon rising across the river. It was the color of cream skimmed from the top of a milk pail. Its brightness almost hurt his eyes. He looked across the neatly organized grounds of the ranch headquarters. The road to town stretched downstream, along the rim of the bluffs overlooking the river, running under the sign reading Broken Arrow Ranch, suspended high between two tall, straight cedar timbers. His eyes swept across the wagon yard, blacksmith shop, toolshed, smokehouse, barn, and springhouse, to the two-story limestone home rising among venerable live oaks. There was one light on in a window upstairs, and Skeeter knew the captain was reading. Maybe the Bible, the mail, the Austin *Daily Statesman*, or a book of poems. Skeeter reckoned he, himself, ought to learn to read better if he wanted to be more like the captain. And he did.

He wandered to the circular corral where the ranch hands busted broncs. The captain's new Thoroughbred mare stood alone in this enclosure. Captain Tomlinson had traveled all the way to Kentucky to find and purchase this mare, hauling her back to Houston in a railroad stock car and leading her the rest of the way to his ranch on the frontier. Having gone into heat yesterday, she had been segregated here alone, out of reach of the studhorses. The captain had yet to choose and purchase the stallion who would enjoy the charms of this Kentucky mare, and in fact intended to race her a year to establish her fame before he let her breed.

The Thoroughbred saw Skeeter coming. She raised her head in a greeting. He leaned on a corral rail, and she came right to him, in contrast to the wilder ranch ponies of mixed mustang blood, who would usually shy away from a man afoot. Skeeter liked this mare for this reason. Her big doe eyes sought his face with curiosity, her long neck extending gracefully, her soft muzzle reaching between corral rails as if to kiss Skeeter on the cheek.

He smelled her sweet, warm breath; let her smell his. She nudged his face, with more anxious purpose now. He read her mind. *Where have you been? Let me out!*

The lantern light in the window shrank into darkness. Skeeter thought he saw the curtains move. He stood straighter, propping the Winchester on his shoulder. He felt the captain looking down at him.

"Guard what?" he said to the mare. "Guard *you*?" There hadn't been trouble around the ranch in years. Indians—Comanches, Kiowas, Lipan Apaches, and others—still passed through the valley on the way to Mexico, but they knew Hank Tomlinson's reputation as well as anyone, and stayed clear. The captain had a wild notion that rustlers were working the outlying extremes of his ranges, chiseling away at his ample herd, but Skeeter attributed that to the old Ranger's longing for the old days, when he had ridden roughshod through the haunts of outlaws, Mexican bandits, and renegade Indians, helping to wrest this whole broad swath of the frontier out of the grasp of the lawless wilderness. As far as Skeeter was concerned, he and this mare were as safe from depredations here on the ranch as Jay Blue was in town at this moment.

Jay Blue, who by all rights, should have been standing guard over the Broken Arrow Ranch precisely now, as a matter of fact. He heard a roar of laughter in the bunkhouse and knew he was missing out on a joke that nobody would remember in the morning. "Night guard, my *foot*," Skeeter said. Then he grew even more morose, considering how Jay Blue, the rancher's son, had talked him into this nonsense. "Your *ass*!" he said to the mare.

3

JAY BLUE could hardly wait to get inside Flora's Saloon, feeling quite sure that he was already missing out on an opportunity at this very instant. But his father, Captain Hank Tomlinson, had taught him to always take care of his horses before entertaining himself, so he let a few inches out on the latigo, loosening the cinch and allowing the dun to breathe deep while he stood tied at the hitching rail.

Thank goodness he had talked Skeeter into taking his watch. Jay Blue knew he wouldn't get much sleep tonight, but hadn't his father often ridden days without sleep in the old times? Jay Blue considered himself pure Tomlinson, as much so as his daddy. More importantly, it had been over a week since he had been to town, and he could feel his chances slipping away. He had to put in an appearance tonight or forever lose any hope of winning that girl.

He leapt to the top step of the boardwalk, his jinglebobs ringing merrily against his spur rowels, and shoved the double swinging doors aside, entering the saloon with something of a flourish. Those swinging doors squeaked to good purpose. Nobody stood anything to gain in a frontier town by letting anybody slip into a saloon unnoticed. Every eye turned to look at the new arrival.

There were an odd number of eyes, for old Gotch Dunnsworth was at the bar, and Gotch had lost an eye in the war. Dunnsworth owned the livery stable next door, and spent as much time in the saloon as anyone. But Jay Blue had not come here to see Gotch Dunnsworth.

Within a fraction of a second, he located the object of his sleepless nights of longing. Her name was Jane Catlett. She was the prettiest thing in this saloon, and perhaps in the state of Texas, as far as Jay Blue knew. Like everyone else, Jane glanced toward Jay Blue as he stood in front of the still-swinging doors. For a moment her indifferent stare brightened. But then she clearly smirked and rolled her eyes in such a lazy way that their gaze took some time landing elsewhere, and not anywhere near Jay Blue.

He smelled lilacs, or maybe it was lavender—one of those feminine fragrances. He glanced back over his shoulder to see Flora Barlow, the owner of the saloon, standing right behind him. She was old enough to be Jay Blue's mother, but that didn't much tarnish her desirability, or the popularity of her drinking establishment. If young Jane was the prettiest thing in Texas, Flora Barlow surely ran her a close second. She also exuded a vague essence of knowledge of things that would surely make a man very happy.

"I hope you don't have your sights set on little Janie," Flora said, her voice a tease and a warning all at once. "She doesn't like cowboys. At least not as much as I do."

Jay Blue turned to Flora and smiled. "Janie? Janie who? I just came in for a beer, Miss Flora."

Her hands landed naturally on hips accented by her corseted waist. "You rode all the way here from your daddy's ranch for a beer?"

"It's my ranch, too. Will be, anyway."

Flora smirked at him, crossing her arms under her breasts, and making it difficult for Jay Blue not to glance toward the low-cut bodice. "What would your daddy think about me selling you a beer? You're barely old enough to shave."

"I beg to differ, Miss Flora. I'm on my second straight razor. I wore the first one smooth out."

Flora smiled and dropped the mock interrogation. "Well, I guess one beer won't hurt you, then. But, just one, then you'd better make tracks for that ranch you intend to claim. If I know your father—and I do—he's not going to hand that ranch over to you just because your name is Jay Tomlinson."

"Jay Blue, ma'am."

"Oh, Jay *Blue*, of course. You're going to have to earn that ranch, Jay *Blue*." She sure made her mouth look attractive when she said, "*Blue*."

"Yes, ma'am."

"Harry, give this big-shot rancher a beer," Flora said to her bartender.

Jay Blue sauntered to the bar to collect his beer, nodding a greeting to Gotch Dunnsworth.

"You want to drink a whiskey toast to Dixie, kid?" Gotch said.

Jay Blue knew Gotch expected him to purchase said shot of whiskey. "I never touch the stuff, sir," he replied, lifting the beer mug to his lips and sucking in the warm, bitter brew.

"Don't know what you're missin'."

Jay Blue's eyes followed Jane across the room. "I'm sure you're right about that, Mr. Dunnsworth."

"Your daddy know you're here?"

"Not exactly."

"Well, your ass is gonna be *exactly* in a crack when he finds out." Gotch wheezed a volley of laughter.

Jay Blue smiled sheepishly, but then entertained himself with thoughts of what it was going to be like when Jane finally consented to being alone with him somewhere. He stood there at the bar—suffering through tiny sips of his acrid beverage and hoping Jane would again look his way, which she did not—until the squeaking hinges of the swinging doors announced a new arrival. A towering hulk of a man burst in, followed by five loud and dusty cowhands.

The big man was Jack Brennan, owner of the Double Horn Ranch, the closest thing the Broken Arrow had to a rival on the ranges around Luck. Jack possessed the size and muscle to strike fear into the hearts of most men, but came nowhere near Captain Hank Tomlinson in his command of respect.

The Double Horn cowboys spotted an empty table and went to claim it. Jay Blue knew them all by name, though considered none of them as a friend. The redheaded foreman, Eddie Milliken, led the way, followed by Joe Butts, Ham Franklin, Bill Waterford, and Johnny Webb. Jack Brennan stood his ground at the door for a moment, sweeping the room with his eyes. When he spotted Jay Blue, he drew back his head and furrowed his brow, then strolled over to the bar.

"Whiskey," he said to the bartender. "And you better send a bottle to them boys at the table, too." His big hand gripped the full shot glass hastily placed before him. He threw the shot back and seemed to get lost for a moment in some faraway place full of worry and sorrow. "Hit me again."

With his second shot in hand, he turned to Jay Blue, feigning surprise. "Didn't notice you there, Jay Boy."

"It's Jay *Blue*, Mr. Brennan."

"That's what I said. Did you see that thing outside?"

"What thing?"

"Looked like a cross between a ox and a javalina. I guess it was a ox-alina. Anyway, it had a saddle on it looked just like yours." He threw the second shot of whiskey past his teeth.

Jay Blue felt stupid for letting Jack Brennan set him up, once again, for an insult to his horseflesh. "I'll match Old Dunnie up to any cow horse in the country—" he began, but Brennan stepped on his reply as if it were nothing but a whistle in the wind.

"What the hell are you doin' here, kid?"

"Huntin' strays." Jay Blue kept his eye on Jane as she moved closer to the table the Double Horn Ranch cowboys had occupied.

"I know what kind of stray you're huntin'." Jack tapped the shot glass on the bar at the bartender. "Gotch, you want a whiskey? Harry, pour Gotch a whiskey, for God's sake. The man's a war hero."

"To Robert E. Lee!" Gotch said, lifting his glass toward Harry's bottle.

Jack looked down at Jay Blue. "Where's that little half-breed shadow of yours? What do y'all call him? Skinner? Scooter?"

"Skeeter. He's standing guard tonight."

Jack shook his head in disapproval. "Your daddy ought to know better than to put a boy out on guard tonight. I hear some Comanches are camped over on Flat Rock Creek. I don't reckon they'd steal one of y'alls' horses to ride, but they might want to eat one."

The comment galled Jay Blue, but not as much as the fact that the Double Horn foreman, Eddie Milliken, was clearly flirting with Jane.

"Daddy just came back from Kentucky with a new Thoroughbred broodmare."

"*Brood*mare, my ass. That's a racehorse. Ya'll think you can win the stake race on Texas Independence Day with that nag, don't you?"

"Well, we've got to prove her reputation around here if we're going to advertise her as any kind of a broodmare for our future. So, yes sir, Mr. Brennan, we're going to run her in the stake race, alright."

"One prickly pear sticker's liable to send that spoilt bitch limping back to the barn."

"On the contrary, I think we can win next year, Mr. Brennan."

"Ain't that what you said before this year's race?" Jack slurped at his third shot of bourbon.

"Next year will be different, Mr. Brennan. I'd bet money on it." Over the rim of his beer mug, Jay Blue continued to watch Jane. She was ignoring Eddie Milliken, but he was still saying something to her that Jay Blue could not hear. The foreman had a stupid grin on his face that Jay Blue did not like. Then, apparently, Jane said something that put him in his place, judging by the way the other cowboys laughed at their own foreman. But when Jane turned away, Milliken stood and grabbed her ass.

Jane wheeled to slap the foreman, dropping a tray of empty glasses as she did so. Milliken caught her right arm, then grabbed her left wrist as she tried to strike with that hand. Jay Blue was already advancing among the saloon patrons, arriving at the Double Horn boys' table in seconds. He hit Milliken in the side of the head, knocking him to the floor. But Milliken managed to hold on to Jane and dragged her down with him.

Jay Blue pounced on Milliken and landed another punch, but soon found himself swarmed by the cowhand's friends. A fist struck his jaw, a boot kicked his ribs. He wrenched his right arm free and hit somebody somewhere, but was soon restrained again. Something hit him in the mouth. He tasted blood. He could hear Jane screaming, "Stop it! Stop it!" He could hear the Double Horn boys cussing him as they laid on more blows. He saw too many fists and boots flying at his face to enumerate.

Jack Brennan watched the melee and chuckled until he heard

Flora call out to her bartender: "Harry!" The barkeep reached for a shotgun behind the bar, but Jack cautioned him with an open palm. "I'll break it up." He took three big steps to the pile of cowboys and began pulling his ranch hands off Jay Blue one at a time, tossing them aside like half-grown children. When he finally got down to Jay Blue, he lifted him to his feet and looked him over.

Jay Blue spit out some blood in the direction of Eddie Milliken. "That'll teach you," he slurred across a busted lip.

Jack laughed. "You ought to know better than to start a fight you can't win."

Jay Blue wiped the blood from one eye with his shirt sleeve. "Somebody had to take up for the lady."

"I can take up for myself, Jay Blue Tomlinson!" Jane grabbed him by the sleeve and dragged him toward the door. "Now you get on out of here and go home."

Before he knew where he was, Jay Blue felt the cool night air in his face and heard the hollow thump of the boardwalk under his boots. He turned and managed to catch a glimpse of Jane shaking her head at him before she disappeared back into the saloon. The beer and the beating made his head swim. He spit more blood out onto the boardwalk, then grinned into the flickering lantern light of the saloon. He grinned so big that it hurt his busted lip. He blinked and snorted, trying to clear his head, then turned toward the hand pump over the water trough in front of Dunnsworth's livery barn next door.

4

HE HAD HIS BARE FEET in the creek and the water was cold and crawdads were pinching his toes. Then he slumped sideways, gasping as he woke from the dream. Pinpricks of cold night air had crept through his worn boots, making him dream of crawdads in the cold stream. But now he was back at the corral, sitting on the ground, holding his rifle, leaning against a cedar post where he had fallen asleep on guard.

Skeeter jumped up and glanced toward the captain's bedroom window. He had been hidden in the shadow of the barn when he sat down, but the moon had risen over the roof now, bathing him in light. Thank God the captain hadn't seen him sleeping at his post.

He yawned and shivered. He was just so damned tired. It wasn't even supposed to be his night on guard. It aggravated the tar out of him the way he sometimes let Jay Blue talk him into things. Jay Blue was so blasted full of confidence and forty-dollar words. Right now he was probably telling a joke and winning a poker game, with some barmaid on his lap. Not the barmaid he wanted, though, because that girl—the pretty one—didn't have much use for Jay Blue. Still, he probably had one of the ugly gals on his lap, and he was probably drinking a beer near the woodstove at Flora's Saloon, and he was no doubt sneaking some glances at Flora's tits. She was always leaning over and showing them off.

Skeeter could actually hear men snoring through the walls of the bunkhouse. He had grown accustomed to that long ago, and in fact it sort of lulled him to sleep nowadays. Right now it just irritated him. Lucky bastards. Those old, stove-up, bowlegged cowpokes were slumbering like puppies right now. Crotchety old men. They were all over thirty. Old farts. Listen to them, snoring like nobody's business.

"I ain't gonna be worth a damn mañana," he muttered to himself. It would make more sense for him to sneak back to his bunk right now and get some rest so he could pull his weight tomorrow. Hell, yeah, who would know? That settled it, he was going to sneak back into the bunkhouse. Nothing was going to happen tonight. Nothing ever happened.

He was already at the bunkhouse door. He pulled the latch string and let himself in. He closed the door quietly, tiptoed to his bunk, and lay down on top of the covers, fully dressed. Ah, now that felt more like it. My God, they were snoring louder than a freight train! He stretched out, felt the knots shudder out of his skinny frame.

No more crawdad dreams. He was going to have that good dream where he found out that his father was really a rich rancher out yonder somewhere, and had been looking for him for years, and wanted him to come break horses and boss the outfit. And they were always eating fried chicken. Except for breakfast, when they ate scrambled eggs. Nice firm scrambled eggs, though—not jiggly the way Beto made them in a hurry every morning.

He yawned and closed his eyes. The snoring sounded like a sawmill.

And his daddy had blue eyes like Skeeter's and was the best shot in the county and rode the fastest horse, and owned the dry goods store in town where pretty girls came with their mothers to shop for cloth and buttons and . . . and the name of the town was not Luck, but it was Buena Suerte . . . and beautiful paint horses were just wandering around everywhere . . . no school . . . and apple pie . . . gold watch chains and pearl-handled pistols . . . and . . . saltwater taffy . . .

Jane Catlett finished rinsing the last of the beer mugs and shot glasses in the lean-to kitchen adjoining Flora's Saloon. She dried her hands and looked at her palms, red and soft right now due to the warm soapy water, but sure to dry and crack later. She wished she had some hand cream at home. You couldn't get anything nice like that in this little frontier town. It was a day's ride on a stagecoach to Austin, and she didn't have the time to make the trip or the money to spend on stagecoaches.

She heard laughter and a ridiculously loud holler of drunken joy through the thin partition wall between her and the tavern. She was hoping the Double Horn boys would have left by now, but they were still drinking and playing cards. She took off her apron, hung it on a peg, and quietly opened the door to the saloon.

She looked to the opposite corner of the saloon and saw Jack Brennan and his men passing a whiskey bottle and playing a game of poker. That Jack Brennan made her nervous. He was just so big and rough looking. The scar on his cheek was hideous. A saloon girl, Dottie, who had never been nice to Jane the whole time they had worked together, was sitting with the cowboys, sharing their whiskey. Flora was looking over Jack's shoulder. She seemed to sense Jane standing across the room, and looked up at her. Wordlessly, she dismissed Jane with a tilt of her head and a smile.

Thank God for Flora Barlow. Jane didn't have much, but she knew she'd be well nigh desperate without Flora.

Jane walked to the swinging doors and stepped outside unnoticed. She breathed a sigh of relief that blew a stray lock of golden hair out of her face. It was cold outside, and she had forgotten her shawl when she walked to work this afternoon in the warmth of the Texas sun. She embraced her own shoulders against the chill, as if hugging herself.

"Why don't you wear my coat?"

She gasped, then looked up to see Jay Blue Tomlinson in the moonlight, a saddled horse at his side. "Good Lord, are you still looking for a way to get your head stove in?"

He offered a nonchalant shrug. "Those rounders from the Double Horn don't scare me."

"Well, do me a favor, Jay Blue. Next time you knock one of them down, make sure he doesn't have ahold of me first."

"Sorry about that. How about if I escort you home?"

"I can escort myself just fine, thank you."

"But I insist. Here, wear my coat."

She hesitated, then grabbed the coat. She didn't really want to encourage him, but it was cold. He helped her put it on, as if he were a gentleman instead of a cowboy, and they began walking down the street, Jay Blue leading his horse. She almost thanked him for the coat, but thought better of it.

"It looks good on you," he said.

"It smells like a barn. I forgot my wrap, that's all. It won't happen again, so I don't want to find you lurking out here, waiting for me anymore."

"Waiting for you?" Jay Blue forced a laugh. "Have mercy, Janie, you think I was waiting for you? I was just stargazing. See, there's Pegasus. There's Pisces, and Cassiopeia." He was pointing every which way.

"Don't call me Janie. I hate that."

"Sorry. That's what Miss Flora calls you, so . . ."

"She's the only one I let call me that. My name is Jane."

They strode down the dirt street, Jay Blue's jinglebobs tinkering away like a carnival wagon. "Okay. Jane it is."

She glanced at him, her eyes fully adjusted to the moonlight now. "You look terrible."

He touched his split lip. "Of course I do, walking next to you. Helen of Troy would look like a mud fence walking next to you."

She tried not to show it, but she liked the way he put that. This Jay Blue tended to say things with his own flare. In general, she was sick and tired of being told she was pretty, but he always found an original way to say it.

When she was little, back in that East Texas town where she was born, Jane's folks told her she was pretty every day, and she had loved it then. But then her father joined the Confederate army when she was nine, and went away to war, never to return. Later, her mother took up with a freighter who started doing things with Jane that even she, at the age of thirteen, knew he was not supposed to be doing.

So she told her mother, and her mother shot the man in his sleep. Then it got worse. The county sheriff jailed Jane's mother. A lynch mob made up mostly of the dead man's family broke into the jail and hanged Jane's mother in her own cell. All this because Jane had turned prettier than she was supposed to be at the age of thirteen. No, she did not care for being pretty one little bit. She just didn't know how not to do it.

She still remembered clearly what her mother told her when she got to visit with her that one time in jail, before the lynching. Her mother hugged her and stroked her hair as if she were a little girl again, though she knew she never would be. She closed her eyes against the tears, and sniffed in the aroma of the pine forests outside. Then Jane had started to cry.

"Mama, what are they gonna do to you?"

"Listen to me, Jane. You're a very pretty girl. You've got to watch out for men who want that—men like that son of a bitch I shot. But you can use it to your advantage. Use it to find a nice man with money. You don't have to be in love with him, and he doesn't have to be young or handsome. Do you hear me?"

Jane nodded, but didn't understand why her mother was telling her all this right now. "But, Mama . . ."

"Hush, girl. Just listen. Go to my cousin Jenny's in Luck, Texas. It's out past Austin somewhere. You'll find it. Luck, Texas. Remember that. Go there and find Jenny and tell her what happened. Find a nice man with money. You promise me, right now!"

Jane had promised. She had come to Luck, but no one knew what had become of her mother's cousin, Jenny. Flora Barlow had taken her in, but Jane was still looking for that kind, not-so-handsome, rich man her mother had told her to find six years ago. Neither man nor boy had gotten close to her since her mother shot that freighter. She held them all at bay with an icy demeanor and a knack she had developed for keeping to herself.

Jane knew everyone thought of her as tough, but she just felt scared most of the time. The truth was, she was a little relieved to have a safe escort in the form of Jay Blue Tomlinson walking her home tonight. But he was not the man her mother told her to look for. He was just a cowboy.

"Her face launched a thousand ships," Jay Blue was declaring. "They started a war over her."

She realized he was still talking about Helen of Troy. "A thousand ships?" She surprised even herself with the depth of sarcasm in her voice.

"Can you believe that?"

"No, I can't. It's just a stupid old story." They had passed the blacksmith shop and the lumberyard, and Jane could now make out the adobe walls of the house she stayed in at the edge of town. It was just a vacant shell with a leaky roof, but no one objected to her staying there. "I can see my house from here," she announced. "You can have your coat back now."

"Not at all. I'll walk you all the way to the door. A gentleman wouldn't leave a lady out in the cold right here in the street."

"I've got a mean dog in there, so don't think you're coming in. He'll tear you to pieces."

"I didn't figure on coming in tonight." Jay Blue left his pony at the rail and accompanied her up the walkway to her front door.

"Not tonight or any night." She stopped at the door and started removing the coat.

"You want to put some money on that?" he suggested.

"As if you had money? Take your coat and go home. You're just a boy." She shoved the garment at him, feeling the cold night air envelope her again.

"I'm older than you are."

"You're older in years, maybe. But that's all. Good night, Jay Blue." She reached for the latch on the door.

"Hey, let me meet your dog," he said.

She slammed the door in his face, shutting herself inside the cold, dark room. Too bad he wasn't the one her mother told her to find. She kind of liked him. She felt very alone there in the dark. The old adobe smelled musty. She wanted to cry, but that had never gotten her anywhere, so she sniffed her childish sorrows aside and felt her way to the bed. Perhaps the lynch mob would stay out of her dreams tonight. She just wanted to go to sleep, and wake up to her mother's voice in her ears, and her mother's gentle hands brushing her hair back from her cheek.

• • •

Skeeter woke, briefly, from his dreams of girls in calico dresses and fried chicken on a Sunday afternoon. He thought he had heard something outside. A rattle of hooves, the squeal of a strange stallion. But there were so many different kinds of snores in this bunkhouse that they could sound like almost anything. That wheezing noise in Long Tom's nose must have been what had sounded like a stallion, and Tonkawa Jones's teeth popping together could have easily passed for hoofbeats in his sleep. Skeeter pulled his pillow over his head and went right back to sleep.

5

JAY BLUE still felt the percussion of the heavy door she had slammed in his face.

"Good night!" he yelled. He stood there awkwardly, as if he might hear a reply through the thick wooden slabs. He put on his coat. It smelled like her. It was warm. His chest ached. He fought an urge to knock on the door, deciding he had done enough damage. He turned, trudged to his horse, and mounted for the long ride home.

"Stupid," he said to himself. "You don't *meet* a dog."

He could have offered to carry some firewood in for her, but *let me meet your dog*? "Some sweet-talker you are, Jay Blue."

Maybe his skull was fractured from the beating he had taken. Maybe that's why he had made such an idiot of himself. It was hard to see the road in the moonlight because his left eye was beginning to swell shut. His lip was already as swollen as a snake-bit pup. His ribs were hurting like hell where one of those bastards had kicked him. He should have just taken his ass-kicking and left town.

But, he *had* stood up for her honor. That had to impress her, even if she didn't show it. And that bit about Helen of Troy was inspired. He smiled a little, but it hurt his split lip. He felt as if *his* face had launched a thousand ships.

What if the worst was yet to come? What if his father had found out that he had slipped off to town. You didn't want to see Captain Hank Tomlinson mad. He touched his bleeding lip. *Oh, shit.* Now the dread really sank into his stomach. His father would want to know what had happened to his face. He could lie about it—make up some wild story about falling out of the loft or something—but sooner or later somebody in town would mention the beating he had taken in the saloon at the hands of the Double Horn boys. Then he would be in trouble for lying on top of the unauthorized trip to town.

"You're in for it, Jay Blue. You stupid . . ."

His father was going to . . . He didn't even want to think about it. There was nothing worse than that old Ranger's wrath. Five hundred stampeding cattle didn't spook him as much. Maybe it was time to leave home. Go off on his own. He could write a note and leave it on the door.

But leave the ranch? Miss Flora was right. He would have to earn that ranch, and he couldn't do that by running off to avoid his father's rancor.

Jay Blue resorted to prayer. "I'm sorry, God. I'm so . . . gosh darn sorry. Help me out of this one, will you? I'll go to church someday. I'd give my left nut. . . . Let me retract that, Lord. I forgot who I was talkin' to. I'll clean up my act, if you'd just get me out of this one with my hide."

He had no idea whether or not God was listening.

What's he gonna do? Is he gonna take the ranch from me? Like old Gotch said, my ass is gonna be exactly in a crack when my daddy finds out.

When he finally rode under the Broken Arrow Ranch sign, he was tired, and his head hurt, and he just wanted to go to sleep, more so to forget the trouble he was in than to catch up on his rest. He would lie down awhile and wait for the beginning of the worst day of his life.

As he rode among the outbuildings, he didn't see Skeeter anywhere. He left his horse in the barn and trudged to the bunkhouse, where he usually stayed after guard duty. Entering quietly, he saw Skeeter fast asleep on top of his covers. Jay Blue could only shake his head. He pulled the latch string in so no one could enter from the outside. He went to the spare bunk and, like Skeeter, collapsed fully dressed. The snores sounded like the growls of a hundred grizzly bears. He'd rather face a hundred grizzlies than his father. He welcomed sleep. It held the only freedom from misery he was liable to know for a long, long time.

6

CAPTAIN HANK TOMLINSON possessed a rare reputation for vigilance. It was said that the wing beats of an owl could wake him from a sound sleep. The captain himself always dismissed the claim with a snort, for he knew owls' wings made little or no noise at all. He doubted even the owl could hear its own strokes cutting the wind.

"No, I can't hear the owl's wings," he'd reply, "but I can hear the mouse shit right before the owl catches him."

The truth was, Hank realized that his hearing was not all it once had been. He attributed that to too many hours spent practicing his marksmanship, testing firearms, and using them in hunting and fighting situations. A lot of gunshots had gone off in his ears, not to mention the occasional artillery blast.

But this morning, instead of waking to a noise, Captain Hank Tomlinson woke to the *absence* of one. His eyes flew open, and he gasped his first waking breath. A faint glow of almost-dawn filtered in through the curtains. His ears told him something was missing.

He realized that the stud horses had not screamed their desire for that estrus Thoroughbred mare for hours. The first half of the night, they had caught her scent every so often, each time singing their desperate love songs to her. He'd heard the stamping of hooves, too, as the animals looked for ways out of their enclosures. Then, at some point in the night, the lusty stallions had fallen silent.

He threw the quilt all the way off the bed, felt the morning's chill grab him. He winced at old wounds and aching joints on his way to the window. Though only a hint of daylight bathed the grounds outside, one look told him the mare was gone.

"There'd better be an explanation," he muttered.

Two minutes later, dressed and armed with his Colt, he reached the bottom of the steps. He caught a glimpse of himself in the mirror, all bowlegged, with his long gunfighter's hair jutting every which way. He pulled his hair back, Indian-style, jammed a felt hat down on his head, and burst out onto the porch.

"I did not give orders for that mare to be moved," he grumbled aloud.

He was beginning to get mad, and that was a bad way for Hank Tomlinson to start his day. For all of the qualities he knew he possessed, and all of the improvements to his character that he constantly strove to refine, Hank admitted that he had a bad temper.

He took a few deep breaths and then stalked toward the barn. He was hoping one of his men had put the mare in a stall, but a quick search proved the Thoroughbred was nowhere to be found.

He was growing seriously angry now, in spite of every effort to control his temper. Perhaps there was an explanation, but his hunches were telling him otherwise. That mare was gone. He could feel it. There was a great dearth of her being all around him. Whoever should have been standing guard last night had messed up on a grand scale.

Captain Hank Tomlinson turned on his heels and locked his glare onto the door of the bunkhouse. He began to stomp toward it. On his way to the old plank door, he noticed that the latch string had been pulled in. He wasn't in a mood to knock. His pace quickened, his body leaning, building momentum. As soon as he got to that bunkhouse door, somebody was going to catch something that would make hell seem like a Sunday afternoon church social.

The latch on the bunkhouse door was of hand-carved wood. Inside the door, two old boot soles had been nailed on to hold the plank door to the log wall. With one mighty kick, Hank splintered the wooden latch and ripped the makeshift boot-sole hinges clean off the log wall. Among the surprised men inside, he saw Jay Blue and Skeeter sitting upright in their bunks, still dressed, right down to their boots. His voice came out as a roar.

"Which one of you *girls* had guard duty last night?"

Jay Blue pointed toward Skeeter's bunk, but when he looked, he only saw Skeeter pointing back at him.

"It was your night," Skeeter said.

"You said you'd cover it for me!"

The argument ended there as Jay Blue's father reached for the nearest culprit, and that was Skeeter. But Skeeter was quick when he was scared, and he ducked aside, hurdled the broken door, and escaped with the foot speed of a cottontail rabbit.

Jay Blue saw his father descend on him next. He rolled off the mattress as the ex-Ranger pounced. Landing on the old puncheon floor, his ribs and his head flared with pain from last night's scuffle. Under the bunk, he could see daylight through the open doorway, so he rolled that way under the bed frame, avoiding his father's next attempt to grab him. Once on the other side of the bunk, he sprang to his feet, ran right over Long Tom Merrick's shins, and burst outside into the gray light of the morning.

He saw Skeeter duck into the barn and thought that was a good place to grab a horse and skedaddle.

Behind him, he heard Policarpo Losoya, the ranch foreman: "*¿Que pasa, Capitán?*"

Then the roar of his father: "Somebody stole my mare!"

Jay Blue stopped just inside the door to the barn, his father's announcement sinking into his brain. Skeeter had been trying to saddle a horse, but he had heard the captain, too, and now he was just standing there with his mouth open. He looked toward the empty corral where he had left the mare the night before, then back at Jay Blue. "Oh, shit!" he said.

"Hell's bells, Skeeter!" This was even worse than Jay Blue had imagined. He was in deep enough trouble for sneaking off to town—but the loss of that mare . . . His father might kill him. Well, okay, he wouldn't literally kill him, but right now Jay Blue was almost wishing he *was* dead.

"She was there when I went to sleep," Skeeter said.

"Christ almighty!" Jay Blue grabbed a bridle. "We've got to get her back, or we're dead."

Skeeter nodded as he went back to saddling the pony. "*Seguro que sí*. Even worse than dead."

The captain stormed into the barn just then, and both Jay Blue and Skeeter had to quit everything in order to climb the railings into the adjoining corral, staying just out of the captain's reach. Skeeter hid behind a trough as Jay Blue kept the horses between himself and his father.

"Come out of there and face the music, damn it!" The angry rancher was working the outside perimeter of the corrals, trying to catch sight of the boys. Jay Blue managed to stay hidden behind the moving horses in the corral, but lost track of where Skeeter had gone. As he played hide-and-seek with the most dangerous ex-Ranger in Texas, Jay Blue heard Policarpo giving orders, in a rather low tone of voice, to some of the other cowboys: "Saddle those boys two mounts so they can get out of here. Tonk, come look at the tracks around the mare's pen with me."

Jay Blue hoped his father, who had gone a bit deaf, might have missed all that. He was well winded from hiding behind the moving horses by the time Policarpo called out to Captain Tomlinson: "*¡Jefe!* You better come look!"

Under the bellies of the horses, Jay Blue watched his father break away from the barn corrals and stalk over to the circular bronc-busting pen. "Skeeter!" Jay Blue hissed in a loud whisper. "Now's our chance. Where the hell are you?"

Skeeter dropped from the loft into the barn corral. Crouching with Skeeter, Jay Blue caught his breath as he peered between the corral rails at the foreman, the captain, and the captain's trusted Indian scout, Tonkawa Jones—known as Tonk. Policarpo had pulled on some pants, but was still barefooted. Tonk wore his moccasins and a nightshirt. They were all studying and discussing the evidence on the ground around the mare's pen.

Jay Blue heard Policarpo talking to his father: "Tonk says one horse circled her pen. No shoes."

"Indians?" the Ranger growled.

Jay Blue didn't wait around to hear anymore. "We better *p'alla*," he suggested.

"*Vámanos*," Skeeter agreed.

They crawled between cedar rails, back into the barn, where they found two cowhands, George Powers and Beto Canales, cinching mounts for them.

"You boys better git," said Powers. "Never seen the old man this mad."

Beto only shook his head at the boys in disapproval.

Jay Blue mounted. As he spurred his horse out of the barn, he heard a curt little whistle and saw Long Tom Merrick in his long handles at the bunkhouse door, two hats and two gun belts with holstered six-shooters in his hands. Jay Blue reined his pony over to Long Tom, took his six-gun rig, and put his hat on.

"*¡Mira!*" said Americo Limón, stepping out of the bunkhouse. He tossed a Winchester to Jay Blue, and another to Skeeter. "*¡Corran, pendejos!*"

Jay Blue took the advice. Spurring his mount, he looked over his shoulder at his father, still standing at the bronc pen. The captain's stance said he was still hopping mad. The Ranger saw the boys making a run for it, and he shouted, "You little turds better get back here!"

Jay Blue could only think of one reply. "We'll get the mare back, Daddy! I promise we'll get her back!" It was only then that he remembered how seriously his father took a promise.

The galloping gait of the horse made his battered skull and rib cage feel as if someone had dropped burning coals into them, and yet the power of the animal coupled with the relief of his narrow escape filled him with an unexpected euphoria. Skeeter came up beside him, all wide-eyed with the confusion of the whole rude awakening. Jay Blue couldn't help it. He flashed Skeeter a grin. A second later, a wild yelp of joy burst from his lungs. Skeeter answered it with his own *grito*, and the boys galloped away down the river valley toward town, hollering like liquored outlaws after an all-night spree.

• • •

Hank Tomlinson stood back at the mare's pen with Policarpo and Tonk, watching the boys ride away. "Aw, hell, now what have I done, Poli? Over a damn horse."

"They'll come back, *Jefe*. Anyway, they're going the wrong way. Tonk says the mare jumped the fence. You believe that? Whoever took her, ran her off to the west."

Hank had a bad feeling about scaring the boys off. His eyes caught sight of the door he had kicked in, and he felt foolishly ashamed of himself. "Well . . . tell Beto to whip us up some breakfast, then we'll follow her tracks. And, for heaven's sake, get Long Tom to fire up the smithy and forge some hinges and a latch for that bunkhouse door."

7

JAY BLUE looked back over his shoulder again, scared half to death he'd see his daddy galloping up behind him at any moment, building a loop with which to lasso him right out of his saddle. He and Skeeter had let their mounts slow to a walk, but the horses were still prancing on account of the cool morning and the exciting start to the day.

"I can't leave you to do one simple thing," Jay Blue said, a scathing accusation in his tone.

Skeeter was just now getting a good, long look at Jay Blue's new facial features. "Looks like one simple thing busted you upside your head—about seventeen simple times."

"I ought to bust you upside your simple head for sleeping through your guard duty."

"*Your* guard duty. Anyway, it's a good thing I went to sleep."

"What? Why?"

"If I had been out there with that mare, those Indians would have scalped me."

"What Indians?"

"The ones who stole the mare."

"Tonk said just one horse circled the pen."

"Okay, one Indian. It only takes one to scalp a man."

"Well, you chickenshit, you should have been awake and on guard, and maybe you wouldn't have gotten scalped. Maybe you would have saved the mare."

"No, *you* should have been awake and on guard. It was your night."

Jay Blue glanced over his shoulder again. "I had things to do."

Skeeter rolled his eyes. "What the hell happened to you, really?"

"I was taking up for Jane. One of the Double Horn boys made ungentlemanly overtures toward her."

"Overtures?"

"He grabbed her ass, so I kicked his ass."

Skeeter laughed. "It looks like you got *your* ass kicked."

"There were seven of them. Maybe eight. I got in my licks."

"No shit? Eight of 'em?"

"Yeah, and that ain't all. Jane let me walk her home."

"Bullshit."

"I'm not kiddin'."

"Did you get inside?"

Jay Blue glanced at the road behind them. "She ain't that kind of gal."

"That's not what I heard."

"Shut up, Skeeter. I mean it."

"Okay, *hermano*. Damn. You're cranky this morning."

Jay Blue could only glower through his one unswollen eye. "I'll tell you who's cranky. The old man. I've never seen Daddy that mad."

"Hey, don't complain."

Silently, Jay Blue mouthed Skeeter's oft-spoken words along with him.

"At least you've got a daddy." Skeeter sighed, like he always did after the lamentation, and slumped in the saddle in abject sorrow.

"Oh, come on, Skeeter." He slapped his adoptive brother on the shoulder. "Don't get all blue on me. I need you to help me get that mare back, or I won't have a daddy who will claim me, either. Let's trot on into town and get some supplies for the trail."

They spurred up to a trot as Jay Blue told Skeeter all the heroic details of his eventful night. By the time he had told the whole glorious tale, the town of Luck was in sight, so the boys let their mounts finish the last leg at a walk.

The road led right past the walkway to Jane's door, where Jay Blue suddenly pulled rein. "Wait here," he said to Skeeter. "I've got to tell my sweetheart I'll be out trailin' that mare, and she may not get to see me for a while."

He ignored Skeeter's disapproving groan, dismounted, and strutted up to the door. He looked back at Skeeter with a confident smirk, then knocked. He waited. He heard Skeeter choke back a chuckle behind him. Jay Blue knocked harder. His embarrassment was about to set in, when he heard the latch rattle. The huge plank door opened slightly and he saw Jane's sleepy face looking cautiously outside, squinting at the early-morning light.

"Mornin', Janie." He dragged his hat from his head. "I mean, Jane."

Her voice croaked. "What in the devil's name are *you* doing here?"

"Well, I've got to go after a horse thief and I just wanted to tell you I probably won't be able to stop by and see you for a while. I'll be out there on the trail of a dangerous—"

The door slammed abruptly in his face. Slowly, he replaced his hat. He dreaded turning around. Instead, he spoke as if Jane could hear him through the door. "Okay, darlin', I'll miss you, too." He tried to put on a grin when he turned, but he knew he had to look as ridiculous as he felt. He avoided Skeeter's eyes and got back on his horse.

Skeeter could no longer keep his mouth shut. "She sure seemed tore up about it." He broke into a fit of laughter.

"Shut up, Skeeter. She's just shy, that's all. She would've been all over me if you hadn't been there."

"Does she sleep all day?" Skeeter asked, a note of disapproval in his voice.

"I told you she was up late with me last night, didn't I?"

"She seems kinda lazy, that's all."

"She's not lazy. Why do you always have to bad-mouth everybody? Anyway, you don't even have a girlfriend."

"Oh, and you do?"

They argued their way on into town and looped their reins on the hitching rail in front of Collins General Store. Sam Collins, the store owner, was also Luck's justice of the peace, the postmaster, the coroner, and—because he stocked buckets in his store—the chief of the local fire brigade. He was just unlocking his door from the inside as the boys stepped onto the boardwalk.

"Good morning, boys," he said. "Ouch, Jay Blue, you look worse than I heard."

"You've heard?" He looked at the clock on the wall. "It's not even eight."

"I just had coffee with Gotch at Ma Hatchet's Café. What brings you boys here so early?"

"Indians stole the captain's mare," Skeeter announced.

"Skeeter," Jay Blue groaned, "we don't know it was Indians. Somebody on a horse that wasn't shod."

"Sounds like Indians," Sam said. "So, what did the captain send you to pick up?"

"He didn't," Jay Blue said, hitching his gun belt a little higher over his hip. "I told Daddy I'd handle this one myself."

Sam looked at Jay Blue over the lenses of his glasses. "That so?"

"It was Jay Blue's night to stand guard," Skeeter added.

"Skeeter!" said Jay Blue through gritted teeth.

Sam took his spectacles off to polish them, all the while shaking his head and making tsk-tsk sounds with his mouth. "Oh, Jay Blue, tell me you didn't . . ."

"There were circumstances, Mr. Collins."

Collins nodded. "Yeah, Gotch told me about *her*, too."

Jay Blue decided to redirect the conversation. "We're gonna need some grub for the trail, Mr. Collins."

"On the Broken Arrow tab?"

"I'll need to start my own account, Mr. Collins. I'm not sure I work on the Broken Arrow anymore."

Sam Collins sighed. "Looks like you really got your ass in a crack this time, Jay Blue."

Jay Blue nodded. "Exactly."

"Well, everybody deserves a second chance. I'll start you your own account."

"Thanks, Mr. Collins." Jay Blue roamed the store and grabbed as much as he thought his and Skeeter's saddlebags would hold. Salt pork, beans, flour, salt, coffee, a small iron pot, and two canteens.

"And some saltwater taffy," Skeeter said.

"Not on my tab," Jay Blue argued.

"It's okay," Sam said. "I'll throw in the taffy."

As Collins figured up the charges, Skeeter gnawed on his taffy and watched the town wake up through the window. "Hey, Jay Blue," he said, "look just down the street. Mr. Brennan and the Double Horn boys are crawling out of the saloon."

Jay Blue stepped to the window. "Didn't figure that bunch of drunks would be up this early."

Skeeter turned to reexamine Jay Blue's black eye and swollen lip, then jutted his face back toward the window as if to get a closer look at the Double Horn crew. "I don't see one of them boys that looks anywhere near as busted-up as you."

"I got my licks in. You just can't tell from this far away."

"So, by 'licks' you mean you actually *licked* 'em with your tongue while they were beating the ever-lovin' shit out of you?"

Over at the sales counter, Sam Collins laughed out loud.

"I'll *show* you what I mean if you don't shut up," Jay Blue warned.

"No, you just keep your tongue off of me, thank you very much."

Sam Collins burst into guffaws.

Skeeter continued: "And you said there were eight of them."

"Seven or eight."

"There's only Mr. Brennan and five cowhands." Skeeter grabbed his chin studiously. "Still, that's a lot of lickin', I reckon."

Jay Blue lunged, but Skeeter was quick, and managed to stay on the other side of a hogshead full of sugar as Jay Blue took jabs at him with his fists.

"Here, now, boys!" Sam Collins shouted. "Jay Blue, come sign for this merchandise."

Back outside, while packing their goods in their saddlebags, Skeeter asked, "Well, do you have some kind of a plan or something?"

"Of course," Jay Blue said. "Don't I always have a plan?"

8

LO QUE HACE DE NOCHE, *aparece de día*," Policarpo Losoya said, gesturing toward the mare's pen.

Hank understood: What is done in the night, shows up in the day. He had cooled off, settled down, and eaten a good breakfast. Now Long Tom Merrick was saddling three horses while Hank, Poli, and Tonk took another look at the evidence around the bronco pen.

"The gate was never opened, *Capitán.*"

"How do you know, Poli?"

"I was the one who put the mare in there, like you told me. I always latch that gate chain the same way, like a snake around those rails, and I always put the fifth link on the nail."

"And Tonk's sure she jumped over that rail? That high?"

"Bigger than shit, *Capitán.* Look at the tracks where she landed."

With Poli, Hank walked around the outside of the pen to where Tonk was crouching, his fingers touching the place where the full weight of the mare had come down on her front feet, gouging fresh soil up from the earth.

Hank had been too damn mad to read sign earlier, but now he let his trained senses go to work. All the old tracks around the pen seemed to fade from view and the fresh hoof marks, the ones on top with keen edges not yet smoothed by wind and gravity, rose to meet his eyes. A lone horse had come from the west, shoeless. It had circled the pen, making the mare frantic enough to actually jump over the rails. As Hank's eyes took in the marks left on the hard-packed dirt, he began to picture the strange horse. He could see the animal making its sharp cuts; he could judge its size and weight and strength.

"Hell of a ride," he said, trying to imagine who could have stayed on a horse making such starts, stops, and lunges.

Tonk looked up at him and smiled. "We go see," he suggested, shifting his gaze down the trail the mare and the horse thief had left toward the west.

Long Tom led three horses out of the barn for them, and the trio of men mounted. The captain and Tonk rode on either side of the trail, both reading the sign. The trail showed the strange horse chasing the mare at top speed, cutting off every attempt she made to return to the ranch.

Now Hank pulled leather as he spotted a long black horsehair snagged on an agarita thorn near his stirrup. A few feet farther downwind was another. "Son of a bitch bit her tail," he said. "What do we have here, Tonk?"

"You tell me," Tonk said.

"*¿Que es?*" Poli asked. But neither tracker answered.

They continued to follow the trail until, a mile from ranch headquarters, even Poli noticed the marks of many more horses—a whole herd of unshod ponies.

Hank gawked at his old Tonkawa scout. "Do you mean to tell me?"

"Yup," Tonk said.

"Incredible."

Tonk nodded. "Uh-huh. Beats all."

"*¿Que pasa?*" Poli demanded. "Help a blind man see!"

"That mustang stallion," Hank said. "The one we've heard about . . ."

"El Grullo?"

"Yep. The Steel Dust Gray. He drove his mares to this point right here, and made them wait. He smelled that Thoroughbred in heat. He charged her pen, alone, and impressed upon her the virtues of freedom. After that, he was on her ass like a duck on a June bug, driving her into his herd, and back out yonder."

Poli shifted in his saddle. "A *horse* took your horse?"

Hank smiled. "Took her breath away and stole her heart."

"*Increíble*."

"Beats all," Tonk repeated.

Hank turned toward Poli. "Who had guard duty last night?" he said.

Poli frowned. He disliked informing on the men, but knew there was no choice. "Izquierdo went out at dusk. But he was covering for Jay Blue."

"And Jay Blue?"

Poli smiled; he shrugged. "Muchachos will be muchachos."

"He went to town."

Poli nodded. "From the looks of his face this morning, he had a hell of a good time."

Hank looked east toward town, then back out to the west, whence the Thoroughbred had run away with the wild ones. "You've done some mustanging, right, Poli?"

"*Seguro que sí, Jefe.* Plenty."

"What are the chances of us getting that mare back?"

"From El Grullo?"

"Yes, from El Grullo. The famous Steel Dust Gray. The mare stealer. The uncatchable ghost. What are the chances?"

Poli narrowed his eyes and looked westward for quite a while, calculating odds. Finally, he set his jaw the way he always did when he knew he had to give the captain the cold, hard truth. "It would be easier—and probably cheaper—to go back to Kentucky and just buy another one."

9

SKEETER HAD JAY BLUE'S plan figured out by the time they took the Fort Jennings trail off the Colorado River road. He was going to ask the U.S. Army for help in finding the stolen mare. Leaving the Pedernales River valley behind, they rode over high ground, through open grazing lands dotted with oak motts, the denser cedar brakes holding to the draws.

The four-hour ride brought them to the cool, clear waters of Cypress Creek. Rounding a bend in the creek, they came within view of the Stars and Stripes flying high over the fort.

They encountered a black soldier guarding the road, as they expected. The Ninth Cavalry garrisoned Fort Jennings. Except for the officers, all the soldiers in the Ninth were black—"buffalo soldiers," as they were known. Skeeter had been told that the Indians likened the hair of the black recruits to the shag on the humps of the buffalo, hence the name.

"What do you want?" the sentry demanded.

"We want to talk to the post commander," Jay Blue said.

"You have an appointment?"

Jay Blue shot a glance at Skeeter. "You don't think we'd ride all this way without an appointment, do you?"

The soldier laughed. "Just joshin' you, son. You don't need no appointment. What's the password?"

"Password?" Jay Blue said.

"That's it! How'd you know?"

Skeeter slapped his knee and burst into laughter. "That's a good one. He got your goat, Jay Blue." He could tell Jay Blue did not see the humor in any of this.

"Seriously, what's your business?" the soldier asked.

"We had a mare stolen by Indians," Skeeter answered.

The soldier looked the two riders over for a few seconds, then spit on the ground. "I'm gonna take a chance and let you two desperados on in." He gestured grandiloquently with his hat, showing them the way up the road.

"Obliged," Jay Blue said, trying to tip his hat with equal sarcasm.

"The colonel's campaigning up the Brazos," the private shouted as they rode on. "Major Quitman is the acting post commander."

Skeeter waved a gesture of thanks for the information.

Coming up to the brink of a slight elevation, Skeeter saw the grounds of the fort open up before him on a broad, level plain. A flag-pole ascended from the center of a large, rectangular parade ground. The thirteen stripes and thirty-seven stars fluttered gracefully on the breeze. All around the edges of the parade ground stood lines of buildings constructed of sandstone. Some were barracks for the soldiers. The two grandest structures housed the post commander and the junior officers. The remaining buildings included the hospital, the chow hall, the armory, the stockade, the sutler's store, and the quarters for the laundresses and other civilian employees.

Suddenly, a cheer rose from their left, and the riders looked to see a number of soldiers bunched around the corrals at the stables. One of the soldiers clung to the back of a horse that was bucking furiously inside a corral while uniformed spectators looked on.

"Damn," Jay Blue said. "That son of a gun can sure 'nough ride a bronc! Let's go watch!"

Skeeter trotted over to the corrals with Jay Blue for a closer look. A soldier noticed them, and elbowed the man next to him, who in turn slapped the shoulder of the next man until each soldier, one by one, ceased his cheering and turned away from the exhibition of bronc busting to regard the cowboys with suspicion. When the crowd had grown quiet, even the horse quit bucking, and the rider himself looked at the young civilians as if he had never seen such a sorry sight in his life.

"Hell of a ride!" Jay Blue said.

One of the soldiers pointed across the parade grounds. "Headquarters is over yonder, cowboy."

"I'm aware of that, soldier. Just thought I'd watch the fun."

"This is government business. You go on and check in with the commander over yonder."

"Come on," Skeeter said, reining his horse around and cutting between Jay Blue and the soldiers. He could see some of that Tomlinson temper swelling up in Jay Blue's neck, and figured it was best to go talk to the commander as suggested.

Nearing the post headquarters, Skeeter noticed one of the buffalo soldiers sitting in a chair that had been pulled out into the sunshine just off the edge of the porch. The man wore an immaculate uniform with the stripes of a first sergeant on the sleeves.

Farther back on the porch, leaning against the wall, sat a brown-skinned man dressed in a mixture of Mexican and Indian garb—moccasins, buckskin leggings, white cotton shirt, embroidered vest, red silk scarf around his neck. A sombrero lay on the porch at his side. His features were leathery and severe, his eyes set on nothing in the sky.

As the boys walked their mounts up to a hitching rail, the first sergeant casually rose from his chair, giving the tails of his tunic a crisp yank to smooth his uniform. With every movement of his arms, those stripes on his sleeves bulged as if he had bulldogs in there. "Howdy, gents," he said.

Skeeter had never heard a voice so deep. He touched his hat brim.

"First Sergeant," Jay Blue said. "We need to see Major Quitman."

"You sure about that?" The first sergeant smiled, then leaned closer to speak in a lower tone. "He ain't in the best mood today."

"Well, that'll fit in fine with the way this day has gone so far," Jay Blue said. "Anyway, you're the only soul we've met on this post who understands hospitality."

The first sergeant shrugged. "Fort Jennings ain't the most popular choice of duty stations in this man's cavalry. Tends to sour the disposition of soldiers and horses both. The fleas and bedbugs seem happy enough, though."

"We'll take our chances with the major."

"Better get down and light a spell, then." He waited for the boys to dismount before extending a welcoming hand. "I'm First Sergeant July Polk."

"Izquierdo Rodriguez." Skeeter felt as if he were looking straight up at that flagpole in the middle of the parade ground.

"Jay Blue Tomlinson." Jay Blue shook the big hand and glanced at the other man sitting on the porch.

"That's Gavilan Gutierrez, our post translator. What shall I say is your business here, gents?"

"We had a horse stolen."

"By Indians," Skeeter added.

"Maybe," Jay Blue scolded.

The first sergeant did not look surprised or even interested. "Wait here." He went inside.

Skeeter said, "*¿Como esta, señor?*" to the translator sitting on the porch, but the man only slid off the porch, donned his sombrero, and disappeared around the corner. Skeeter looked at Jay Blue and shrugged.

Polk came back out and whistled at the cowboys, motioning them inside with a tilt of his head. Inside, Skeeter found a bald man attacking a piece of paper with a pen. The man looked up from his desk, his glaring black eyes blazing at the cowboys over the lenses of wire-rimmed spectacles.

"Who are you?" he demanded, by chance addressing Skeeter first.

"Izquierdo Rodriguez."

"Mr. Rodriguez," he answered with a nod. "I'm Major Ralph Quitman. And you, sir?"

"I'm Jay Blue Tomlinson."

The major put down his pen and took off his spectacles. "Tomlinson? As in Captain Hank Tomlinson?"

"That's my father."

He seemed suddenly intrigued. "What brings you here, gentlemen?"

"Well, sir, last night, a mare disappeared from our ranch. We found some tracks made by an unshod horse. We figured it was probably an Indian. I hear there are some Comanches camped over on Flat Rock Creek."

The major's hardwood and leather office chair squeaked as he leaned back in it. "I know very well where the Comanches are camped, Mr. Tomlinson." He laced his fingers together and placed them atop his middle-aged paunch.

"Yes, sir. Of course. Well, we were wondering if you had heard . . . or seen . . . or if you wouldn't mind going to take a look . . ."

The major raised his right palm to silence Jay Blue. Slowly, he leaned forward in his squeaky chair. "Now, let me make sure I understand this. Your mare 'disappeared,' as you put it."

"Yes, sir," the cowboys said in unison.

"Would this be your father's new Thoroughbred mare from Kentucky?"

"Yes, sir."

The major stood. "So, your father's Kentucky Thoroughbred *disappears*, and Captain Hank Tomlinson, the most famous Indian fighter in Texas, sends his peach-fuzzed son to the U.S. Army for help!"

"Oh, he didn't send us," Skeeter said, honestly trying to clear things up. "We're lucky he didn't kill us. You see, sir, Jay Blue was supposed to be on guard—"

"Skeeter!"

"First Sergeant Polk!"

In an instant, Polk had entered the office and snapped to attention. "Sir!"

"See that these cowboys are escorted off the post."

"Yes, sir. And, Major, sir . . ."

"What is it?"

"Jubal's back."

"Who?"

"Jubal Hayes, sir. The mustanger. He's leading six horses in."

10

GET THESE BOYS out of here," the major repeated. He grabbed his hat on his way out the door. "And appropriate the funds to buy the remounts."

"Yes, sir," Polk said.

Jay Blue followed the major out onto the porch. "But, Major, about that mare . . ."

"Boy!" the commander fumed. "Go home and face your father! First Sergeant!"

"Coming, sir!" Polk stormed out of the office, stuffing some currency he had gathered up from somewhere into his pocket. "You boys lead your horses and come with me. I'll detail an escort to see you off the post."

"But . . ." Jay Blue began.

The big first sergeant, who had been so friendly, now cut Jay Blue off short. "You heard the major. You will be escorted off the post."

With no choice left to them, the cowboys grabbed their reins and led their mounts across the parade ground, toward the corrals, on the heels of the major and the first sergeant. It was only now that Skeeter looked across the parade ground to see the mustanger Polk had announced. The man was riding toward the Fort Jennings corrals, in the lead of six wild-looking horses. Two strange things immediately struck Skeeter about this man. First of all, the six horses followed him untied. They plodded along behind him as if mesmerized, not a rope nor a halter among any of them. Second, the mustanger wore a scarf across his face, like a bandito, and in fact had every square inch of his flesh covered, from the tips of his gloves and boots to the top of his dusty felt hat.

"Hey," Jay Blue said. "You ever seen anything like that?"

"*Nunca*," said Skeeter.

A soldier at the bronc-busting pen ran to open a separate corral, then backed away to give the mustanger and his followers plenty of room. The strange man led the loose stock into the corral. They followed him in there as if under his spell.

"Do y'all have to break mustangs to ride at this post?" Jay Blue asked the first sergeant.

"The colored regiments don't get the money other regiments get. Mustangs is about all we can afford. We break 'em ourselves."

"Who's the man in the scarf?"

"Name's Jubal Hayes. He catches mustangs for a livin'."

"Catches 'em? Looks like he just sweet-talks them into following him around like pups."

"Why's he wearing that scarf?" Skeeter asked.

Polk didn't answer, but looked over his shoulder at the cowboys and bared his teeth in a deep chuckle that sounded intentionally wicked to Skeeter.

By now, the masked man had slipped back out of the corral and shut the gate on the mustangs. He dismounted, left his horse at the corral, and began walking toward the captain. As they all came closer together, near the bronc-busting pen, Skeeter heard one of the buffalo soldiers, a corporal, speak up.

"Hey, whitey!"

At first Skeeter thought the corporal must have been taunting Jay Blue, then he saw that other soldiers were backing away, clearing the ground between the mustanger and the corporal.

A hawk cried, making Skeeter glance at the sky. There was nothing in that sky but the raptor and one lonely cloud.

"Are you talkin' to me?" said the growling voice of the mysterious Jubal Hayes.

"You're the whitest son of a bitch here, ain't you?"

"First Sergeant," Major Quitman warned.

"I'll break it up, sir." Polk quickened his pace.

Jubal drew a blade—a bowie knife that came from a belt scabbard. "Alright, this is how we'll do it."

The smirk on the corporal's face dropped from view. "I ain't got no knife."

"Then use your sharp tongue."

"Fists," suggested the corporal, a hint of a plea in his voice.

"Alright." Jubal threw his knife, sticking it in a corral post between two buffalo soldiers. Sunlight glinted on the blade until that one lonely cloud in the sky floated in front of the sun, casting its shadow on the knot of men at the bronc pen, softening everything with kindly shadows. Major Quitman and First Sergeant Polk were now trotting toward the scene.

Suddenly, Jubal pulled his scarf down and tossed his battered felt hat aside. Skeeter's eyes bulged. Jubal Hayes was like nothing he had ever seen or heard of. His facial features were similar in form to those of the buffalo soldiers, but his skin was of a hue so pale that blue blood vessels could be seen running just under the surface of his powdery white flesh. And he wore spectacles like the ones Major Quitman had worn in his office, except that the lenses to Jubal's glasses were dark as a colored bottle. His hair had the shaggy texture of the great buffalo—like that of the buffalo soldiers around him, except that Jubal's hair was golden! And, unlike the soldiers, who kept their hair trimmed short, Jubal had let his go do whatever it wanted to do, and it had matted together in places and formed snakelike protuberances, mossy appendages, and comet-tail projections.

The corporal kept his fists in front of him.

Now Jubal Hayes pulled his tinted glasses off, dropping them in the dirt, revealing one last unusual feature. The light gray color of his eyes was such that a person could only look *through* them, instead of into them. And as Jubal Hayes made a glance his way, Skeeter thought he saw the eyes actually turn red for a brief instant.

"Only thing is," said Jubal Hayes to his would-be opponent, "you better watch out. It's *catchin'*. If I touch you, you'll end up lookin' just like me." He made a rush toward the corporal, who screamed and ran away like a frightened child.

"Mr. Hayes!" scolded the major, finally arriving, out of breath, at the scene of the confrontation. "First Sergeant, catch that corporal!"

"Yes, sir!"

Jubal Hayes began laughing, until that one cloud in the sky moved away from the sun, and then he shrank under it like a slug under a handful of salt thrown down by a mean little kid. He ran for his hat and pulled his scarf up. He scrambled for his shaded glasses, blowing the dirt from the lenses before he returned them to his face. But when he turned to collect his knife from the corral post, he found that Jay Blue had already retrieved it and was offering it to him.

"Here you are, Mr. Hayes."

"Give me that!" Jubal Hayes looked so insulted that Skeeter thought he was going to cut Jay Blue's throat with that shiny blade, but Jay Blue did not appear to be afraid.

Skeeter stood gawking, fifteen paces away, where he had been compelled to stop. What was Jay Blue doing with that strange man's knife? The man said it was catching, for heaven's sake. *Why did we even come here? Oh, when is this bastard of a day ever going to end?*

11

JAY BLUE was studying his own reflection in the lenses of Jubal Hayes's glasses, noting that bruises covered a good portion of his face. He improved upon his image as much as he could, drawing himself up into a slightly bolder stance. He was hoping the mustanger might be of some assistance to him in recovering his lost mare, since Major Quitman had showed no inclination toward helping. If Jubal could charm the wildest of horses right into a cavalry corral, certainly he could track down a single stall-raised Thoroughbred.

But before he could broach the subject, the rattle of a wagon attracted his attention. He turned and saw a buckboard coming, five horsemen following at a trot. Instantly, he recognized the Double Horn Ranch crew, led by big Jack Brennan. As the buckboard came closer, Jay Blue saw that the ranch foreman, Eddie Milliken, was driving the vehicle behind two mules. Then he noticed some odd-shaped object in the bed of the wagon, covered by a wagon sheet.

First Sergeant Polk was dragging the offending corporal back by his collar as the buckboard rattled right up to the acting post commander. Milliken's shoulders lurched in a silent chuckle when he saw Jay Blue's face. Jay Blue snarled back.

"What is this?" the major demanded.

Jack Brennan ignored the major, his eyes bouncing back and forth between Jay Blue and Skeeter. "What are you two whelps doin' here?"

"Jay Blue was supposed to be on guard and Indians stole the captain's Thoroughbred," Skeeter claimed.

Jay Blue heard Jubal Hayes make a horselike grunt that said he knew otherwise.

"I'll ask the questions here," Quitman scolded. "What have you got in the wagon?"

"Evidence."

"Of what?"

Brennan shrugged. "The government's failed Indian policy?"

"What is that supposed to mean?"

"Why don't you take a look and see," Jack Brennan suggested.

"First Sergeant!" The major waggled his index finger at the wagon.

Keeping one big hand clamped tightly on the corporal's collar, Polk stepped forward and threw the tarp aside. The corpse of a man lay in the bed of the wagon, six arrows protruding from it at odd angles. Jay Blue approached close enough to look over the sideboards. He saw the lifeless face of the man staring heavenward, but only from one eye, as the other was missing. He grimaced at the sight of the bloody skull where the scalp had been torn away.

"We found him up on Shovel Mountain," Brennan announced.

"Who is he?" Jay Blue asked.

"Hell, I don't know. I saw him once at Flora's Saloon."

"What happened to his eye?" Skeeter asked.

Brennan pointed at the buzzards circling overhead.

"These are Comanche markings," Major Quitman claimed, studying the intricate designs in red paint on the dogwood arrow shafts. "We'll need to ride over to Flat Rock Creek and question those Comanches about this. First Sergeant, secure one of those arrows to bring with us, and get a section of men mounted."

"Section Two, Red Platoon, Company K!" Polk barked.

The buffalo soldiers made like a covey of quail, the men running to choose and saddle mounts. Polk looked at the corporal he still held in his grasp—the one who had started the trouble with the albino mustanger. "Well, Corporal Cornelius, if you're so full of fight, you can ride at the head of the column." He shoved the corporal toward the stables.

Jay Blue heard a chuckle of satisfaction from Jubal Hayes.

With one powerful hand, First Sergeant Polk yanked an arrow from the corpse. The sound of the barbs on the war point ripping flesh sent a chill down Jay Blue's backbone.

Jack Brennan had gotten down from his horse to address the post commander. "Me and my boys will go with you, Major. I've been missing a couple of horses, and I'll just bet that those red devils have got 'em."

"I'll bet they've got our Kentucky mare, too!" Jay Blue sang. "Skeeter and I will ride with you."

"No," the major said. "I will not be responsible for getting Captain Hank Tomlinson's son killed. You youngsters stay out of this. Go home. Mr. Brennan, your men can ride with me to identify your stock as long as you agree to act only under my orders."

Jack Brennan turned to Milliken. "Take the dead man into town. The rest of you men will come with me and the major." He looked at Skeeter, then Jay Blue. "You two whelps do what the major says and let the men handle this."

"But . . ." Jay Blue began.

"Don't try to follow us," the first sergeant added.

"But they've got our mare," Jay Blue insisted.

Jubal Hayes slapped Jay Blue on the shoulder with the back of his hand. "Them Indians don't have your daddy's mare. Do as you're told and go home. First Sergeant, who's gonna pay me for those horses I led in?"

Polk took the money from his pocket, handed it to the mustanger, then turned for the stables. The major was marching back to his headquarters, for his weaponry, Jay Blue assumed. Eddie Milliken was busy cussing at his mules to turn the buckboard around, but took the time to aim one of the cuss words at Jay Blue. Jack Brennan was remounting with a curious grin.

Jay Blue turned to the mustanger. "What did you mean, Mr. Hayes? If the Indians don't have our mare, who does?"

Jubal Hayes finished counting his money and tucked it into his shirt pocket. "I cut her trail this morning. Shod all around, long-legged, running with a herd of mustangs. That stallion got her."

"What stallion?"

"The wildest of the wild. The Mexicans call him El Grullo. White men call him the Steel Dust Gray."

Skeeter had walked up within earshot, though he still seemed leery of the albino man. "They say he's uncatchable."

"That's right," Jubal agreed.

"How could a mustang steal our mare right out of her pen?" Jay Blue argued.

"Was she in heat?" Jubal said through his scarf.

"Yes, sir," Skeeter replied.

"Then that stallion took her," Jubal insisted. "That mare is gone as a goose in spring, boys. You wouldn't even know where to look to find her."

"I was hoping you might guide us," Jay Blue suggested.

Jubal shook his head. "Not interested. Go home and face your daddy." He marched back to his pony, stepped up into his stirrup, and turned west.

Twenty-four buffalo soldiers had formed up with their mounts. First Sergeant Polk ordered them into a column of fours as Major Quitman marched back to the stables with his saber and his Colt revolver belted on. A corporal brought Quitman his horse and held it while the officer mounted. Within a minute, the major gave the order to ride, repeated by First Sergeant Polk at the top of his bellowing lungs. Jay Blue could only stand there with Skeeter and watch the column move off to the east while Jubal Hayes continued to trot away to the west.

"Maybe they're right," Skeeter said. "Maybe we should just go face the captain. You can't believe that crazy-lookin' mustanger. He didn't actually *see* our mare. That could have been anybody's shod horse running with the wild ones. We don't know if the Indians have got her, or El Grullo, or somebody else. We don't know any more right now than we knew this morning."

"The gate was closed, Skeeter."

"Huh?"

"The gate to the mare's pen was closed this morning. Didn't you notice?"

"I was a little busy dodging the captain, hombre."

"That mare jumped over the rails. What horse thief would open the gate, steal the mare, then close the gate back? She jumped, Skeeter. She's running with the Steel Dust Gray."

"Then we'll never get her back now. You heard that mustanger. He said not even he could get her back."

Jay Blue smiled, even though it hurt his lip.

"Uh-oh. I don't like that shit-eatin' grin. What are you thinkin'?"

"I'll bet Mr. Hayes can do it if we help him."

"You crazy? Didn't you hear him say it was catchin'?"

"The man's an albino, Skeeter. You're born with it. You can't catch it. You saw him lead those mustangs right into the corral like he was a mother duck. And that's working on his own. If we help him, I'll bet we can get the mare back, and maybe catch El Grullo, to boot. I say let's follow him. We'll catch up to him and talk him into it."

Skeeter frowned. "Well, what about this Indian trouble? Do you want to end up like that scalped man?"

"We've got good horses and plenty of ammunition. We'll watch each other's back, like we always do. Like brothers. Anyway, like Daddy always says, a man who fears Indians is liable to get snake-bit, and a man who fears rattlers is liable to get scalped."

Skeeter frowned. "What does that mean?"

"Hell, I don't know. Are you coming or not?" Jay Blue mounted his horse.

Skeeter sighed in resignation and put his foot in the stirrup. "I guess I'll take my chances with you and the mustanger," he said, settling into leather. "The captain would just kill me if I came back without you."

"He's liable to kill us both if we come back without that mare."

12

FLORA BARLOW'S SKIN smelled of her lavender bath oil and her patchouli perfume, but when she came down the steps from her bedroom and opened the back door to the saloon, the odors of tobacco smoke and spilt beer cut through the more feminine aromas and assaulted her nostrils. She didn't really mind. It smelled like a pretty tolerable living to her.

Looking to her right, back into the corner, she saw that the Double Horn boys had left a few shot glasses and empty bottles strewn around. One chair was knocked over. She had watched them play poker until about three o'clock, and then she had gone to bed alone. Dottie had stayed up with the cowboys, drinking and who knows what all. Flora did not run a whorehouse here, but Dottie was a big girl and if she wanted to make some extra pay that way, that was her business. Apparently, the Double Horn boys had all passed out and slept on the floor. She didn't see or smell any vomit. Someone—surely Jack—had left five silver dollars on the table.

Flora straightened up the mess in the corner, then walked to the double front doors with the glazed glass panels. Unlocking them, she swung them inward, propping each open with a brick waiting on the floor for just that purpose. Now only the swinging barroom doors stood between her and the street.

Luck, Texas, was going about its normal midday routine. A few pedestrians strolled the boardwalks. A farmer and his wife drove by on a hack loaded with a month's worth of supplies. The farmer looked longingly at Flora, then turned his eyes forward at the behest of his wife's bony elbow. He cussed the mules and shook the reins. Flora smiled. She loved being the unattainable object of desire. Way down the street, past the farmer's wagon, she could see three men riding into town. They were too far away to recognize, but they sat their horses like cowboys.

The day had warmed up nicely following last night's chill, so Flora decided she'd open all the windows and air the place out. Muscling the panes up on the west side last, she saw that those three riders had stopped to talk to Sam Collins in front of his general store, and now she recognized them very well. It was Hank, along with his top hands, Tonk and Poli. Her heart made a little skip, and she was glad she had her doors open in case Hank wanted a drink, as was his custom. She didn't know how Captain Hank Tomlinson could get her all worked up just by riding down the street. She'd had her share of men, and she should have known better, but she couldn't help herself when it came to the captain.

She watched him for a moment. He was shaking his head as he listened to Sam. She could just imagine what the conversation was all about. She didn't recall Sam being here last night, but the story of Jay Blue's beating would be all over town by this hour. She straightened the chairs around the poker table in the corner until she saw the silhouettes fill the doorway.

Hank and Poli came in, but Tonk stayed outside, like he always did. Hank turned to invite him in. "Tonk, come on in and have a sup of branch water. It's only Miss Flora in here, anyway."

But Tonk just shook his head and took a seat on the bench outside.

When Hank turned back toward her, Flora put on her prettiest pout of apprehension. "I've halfway been expecting you."

He flashed that familiar smile at her. "I'm halfway thirsty."

"I'm the other half," Poli said.

Relieved by their smiles, she moved into position behind the bar. "Beer? I'll bet it's still cool from last night's chill."

"Well, then, we'd better warm up a mug or two," Hank said.

She poured the beer, then leaned across the bar toward Hank, batting her eyes apologetically. "Hank, I'm so sorry about what happened to Jay Blue last night. It all happened so fast. He was taking up for my hired girl, Janie, and those boys from the Double Horn jumped him before I could—"

Hank silenced her with a wave of his palm. "Muchachos will be muchachos."

"Hey, you stole that from me," Poli complained.

"That's not why I'm here," Hank continued.

"Why, then?"

"Well, mostly for a drink—and to lay my eyes on the prettiest sight in Texas—but I also came to ask you a favor."

"Anything, Hank. And you know I mean *anything*."

Poli choked on his beer. "You want me to wait outside with Tonk?"

Hank ignored him. "That Kentucky mare of ours ran off last night while Jay Blue should have been on guard."

"Oh, no, Hank. She's gone?"

"*Más* gone than gone," Poli said. "She ran off with El Grullo."

"Who?"

"The Steel Dust Gray."

"The mustang? He really exists? I thought he was just a wild tale—an excuse for the fainthearted so they wouldn't have to chase down horse thieves."

"I wish he was just a myth. He chased off my mare, and Jay Blue or Skeeter was supposed to be on guard and neither one of them was, and . . . I got a little riled over it this morning."

"A little riled?" Poli whistled.

"Jay Blue ran off, Flora. Skeeter, too. They said they were going after that mare."

"Well, what do you want me to do, Hank?"

"Just keep your ears open for me. You hear all the daily gossip here first. Let me know if you hear where they went or what they're up to. I've trailed them as far as Sam's store, but I don't know where they went after that."

"Sure, Hank, but what about those Comanches camped over on Flat Rock Creek?"

"Tonk rode out the other day and looked them over from a safe distance. It's just a hunting party under old Chief Crazy Bear. They're not wearing paint. I wired the reservation in Indian Territory and found out that Crazy Bear has a pass from the Indian agent to lead a hunt."

"So, they won't cause the boys any trouble?"

"Not likely. I fought Crazy Bear in the old days, but he's been on the peace trail now for years. His warriors won't start anything unless some hothead riles 'em up first."

"If I hear anything, Hank, I'll make a note of it. If it's urgent, I'll send a rider out to your ranch. I'll ride there myself, if I have to."

"Well, now, there's a welcome thought." Hank winked at her, and drained his mug.

Flora grabbed the mug and opened the tap on the wooden keg.

Poli gulped his beer so he could have a refill, too. "Aw, those muchachos have got more sense than you think, anyway. They can ride hard and shoot good. And I'll guarantee you one thing, *Capitán*. After this morning, those boys will never miss guard duty again."

13

AS FIRST SERGEANT JULY POLK cantered his mount back toward the troopers Major Quitman was leading across the low rolling hills, he couldn't help but think what a pretty sight it was—the column of fours riding toward him, sunlight glinting on saber hilts and polished buckles. Only the cowboys from the Double Horn Ranch seemed out of place riding in a disorganized cluster to the major's right.

Polk thrived on army life, especially here on the frontier. He believed in the army way. He saw in the federal cavalry service a rare opportunity for himself and his fellow black men. Some of those soldiers had been born into slavery, and look at them now! They wielded weapons and rode half-wild horses across an open landscape, serving the union that had almost torn itself apart to set them free. This nation had a long way to go before it could live up to its claim of all men being created equal. But this was a start—this regiment of black soldiers. First Sergeant July Polk was a proud part of it.

As he slowed to a trot, he saw the major call a halt so that they could confer.

"Report, First Sergeant!" Quitman was plainly throwing his weight around a little more than usual for the benefit of the cowboys.

"The camp's still there, sir. Right where it was before."

"And their number?"

"Same as before, sir. Not more than two dozen men, women, and children. I'd figure on eight warriors, ten at the most."

"And their attitude?"

"Everything looked casual, sir."

"If I'd have scalped a white man, I might be a little nervous right now."

Jack Brennan let out an impatient sigh—almost a growl.

"Maybe it wasn't them, sir. Maybe it was some renegade band passing through. Or, on the other hand, maybe they just didn't expect anybody to find the body so soon."

The major used the arrow he had carried along with him to point at the first sergeant. "I'll find out, won't I? Did you go undetected?"

"They never seen a hair on my head, sir. Their hosses didn't even smell me. I scouted downwind."

"Sentinels?"

"Just some boys watching their horse herd."

"Well done. Give the order to march."

"Yes, sir. But, if I may, sir . . ."

"What is it?"

"The best trail is from the southwest, sir, because—"

"First Sergeant, remember your place!" the officer snapped. "Give the order to march!"

"Column of fours!" bellowed Polk. "Forward, *march*!"

Polk hoped he had made his point about moving in from the southwest. Comanches always set their tepees up with the lodge doors facing east. If the company rode in from the southwest, they would remain out of view of anyone who might be lurking inside one of those tepees.

If Quitman had had any Indian fighting experience, he would know this, but Polk happened to know that the major had no combat experience at all, having served throughout the Civil War as a commissary officer behind the lines. As a quartermaster he was quite efficient, but Polk feared he might be leading the men into dangers he didn't understand.

Another hour brought the column of fours over a rise that afforded a view of the Comanche camp. And, as Polk had feared, Major Quitman rode in from the southeast, where he could be seen by potential shooters inside the tepees. Polk dropped back to ride next to Corporal Cornelius.

"Good thing you're in a fightin' mood today, Corporal. You may need that mean streak any minute now."

"I ain't scared," the corporal growled.

The Comanche horse herd was some distance from the camp, being tended by some mounted boys. The animals had grazed their way into a position that put them between the soldiers and the Indian camp as the cavalry unit rode in. One of the boys rode at a gallop to the camp to spread the alarm, while the other boys bunched the pony herd and moved it away from the approaching cavalry.

"Look there!" said Jack Brennan, riding up to the major. "That sorrel and that bay. Those are the mounts I'm missing. You'll see my brand on their left hip. And that claybank! Do you see it?"

"What of it?" asked the major, examining the horse herd when he should have been keeping his eyes on the Indian camp.

"That's the mount the dead man rode."

"How do you know?"

"I told you I saw the man once at the saloon in town. That claybank was tied at the rail outside. You don't forget a horse like that."

First Sergeant Polk had to agree. That was some piece of claybank horseflesh. But those two mounts Brennan claimed—the sorrel and the bay—were the sorriest-looking animals in the herd. He wondered why a man would even want them back. He saw all this at a glance, as his main concern was the movement of Indians in the camp, and they were all astir.

The major was still distracted by the big rancher. "There are procedures to follow, so don't think you can just ride in here and claim your property. You'll get your stock back in due time."

"Due time, hell, Major! They've got the claybank! They scalped that poor bastard we found! We should attack before they can get organized."

"Nonsense. I'll question them, and we'll get to the bottom of this."

Brennan spat on the ground. "You just made a big mistake, Major. I can tell you don't know shit about an Indian."

Polk continued to analyze the movements in camp. He saw women dragging children and carrying babies to hide behind tepees on the far side of the camp. Several warriors were easing toward the near edge, but none held a weapon in his hand. Indians ducked in and out of the lodges, and it was hard to watch it all at once, but Polk sensed that not all the warriors were coming to the edge of camp to parley. A few, he feared, were watching from the shadows inside those lodges. He groaned under his breath and glanced at Major Quitman, sitting haughtily in his saddle.

Now the first sergeant saw an aged warrior walking toward the near edge of the camp carrying a stick festooned with a white flag, and the striped and star-spangled banner of the U.S.A. Five warriors came with him. They were strolling to the southeast edge of the camp, luring the soldiers into the line of fire from the lodge openings. The troopers splashed across the ankle-deep waters of Flat Rock Creek.

"Gutierrez!" the major shouted.

The translator, Gavilan Gutierrez, spurred ahead. Polk knew his story. An Indian captive as a boy, he spoke the Comanche language well.

As the soldiers rode right up to the edge of the Comanche camp, Polk got a close look at the chief. He wore a single eagle feather in his hair, deerskin breechcloth, and leggings. He went bare-chested and sported a huge scar right where an army officer in dress uniform would wear his medals. A young warrior trotted up to his side, clearly taking the position of lieutenant. He looked barely twenty. He wore a quiver on his back, but his bow remained in the quiver, unstrung. The old man carried no arms at all. Not even a knife could be seen.

"Ask him his name," the major ordered.

The translation came back from Gutierrez: "Crazy Bear."

"Who's the young man beside him?"

"His grandson," Gutierrez said. "He is called the Wolf."

Now the Comanche leader held up a folded piece of paper, wrinkled and soiled from travel. The translator took it and handed it to the major, who read it.

"They have a pass from the reservation authorities. They're hunting."

"Hunting poor white bastards to scalp," Brennan growled.

The major handed the folded paper back to the translator, who returned it to the chief. "Ask him where he got those horses. The bay and the sorrel. And the claybank."

Gutierrez made the inquiry and listened to the reply. "He says the horses wandered up. He says he doesn't want them, and you can take them."

"Lyin' horse thief," Brennan said. "Murderer."

"Ask him if this arrow belongs to any of his warriors."

The arrow was handed from the major, to the translator, to the chief. The old man looked at it. His eyes widened. He handed it quickly back to Gutierrez. It seemed to Polk that Crazy Bear couldn't get rid of that arrow fast enough. He seemed to fear it the way Corporal Cornelius had feared catching albinism earlier that day.

"He says it does not belong to any warrior in his camp."

"But he recognized it, didn't he? Ask him."

The translator had an exchange with the chief. "He said he will have all his warriors give you one arrow to show that the designs are not the same. He said they are not even carrying war points, only hunting points."

"He's avoiding my question. Ask him again if he knows who this arrow belongs to. Tell him the owner of this arrow killed the owner of that claybank horse." Major Quitman pointed toward the Indians' pony herd. "Ask him again who owns this arrow."

"He says he cannot speak the name."

"Or *will* not." The major drew himself up into his most authoritative posture. "Tell him every warrior in his camp must ride back to Fort Jennings with us for further questioning. Order each man to bring his arrows."

As Gutierrez made the translation, Crazy Bear frowned. But he and his grandson, the Wolf, began talking things over, and it looked to Polk as if they were about to give in to the major's demand. Until that big rancher, Jack Brennan, rode his horse into the Indian camp.

"Hey!" Brennan said, charging in among the tepees. "What the hell is this?"

Crazy Bear and his followers turned in anger at the disrespectful invasion of the camp and glowered as the big white man leaned sideways on his mount, low enough to snatch up a fine, tooled saddle in an impressive feat of strength.

"This is the saddle I saw on that claybank at the saloon! Tell me that don't prove they killed the son of a bitch." Then Brennan dropped the saddle and drew his Colt. "That one's armed!" he shouted, and fired at some target that Polk could not see behind one of the lodges.

Skittish cavalry mounts dodged in every direction with the first gunshot, and the Double Horn cowboys opened fire on the camp. As Polk had feared, muzzle blasts flashed from inside the nearby lodges, and Corporal Cornelius flew off the rump of his horse, the back of his head having become a pulpy mass of bone, brains, and blood. As warriors scattered, firing bullets and arrows, the cowboys charged haphazardly through the camp.

Polk's horse wheeled, and he caught sight of the major. The officer's hat had flown off, and blood was trickling down into one eye. Then the major drew his revolver and blindly pulled the trigger without aiming, his shot hitting Chief Crazy Bear in the stomach. The chief dropped his peace flags. The Wolf still stood beside him, stringing his bow.

Another blast came from somewhere in camp, hitting Major Quitman square in the chest, killing him before his body could hit the ground.

In this chaos, Polk noticed that Gavilan Gutierrez had charged off with the cowboys, who were riding in different directions through the camp, firing everywhere. Forcing his startled pony to face the camp again, Polk saw the Wolf notching an arrow. It flew before Polk could swing his pistol barrel around, and the arrow hit the first sergeant in one of those bulging stripes on his sleeve. Polk fired back, but only managed to cut the buffalo sinew string on the Wolf's bow.

The Wolf looped old Crazy Bear's arm over his shoulders and dragged him away from the soldiers, ignoring the crossfire from the cowboys and a few soldiers who had gotten control of their mounts and begun to shoot without orders to do so.

"Hold your fire!" Polk shouted. He yanked at the arrow in his arm, but the point was stuck in the bone. Adrenaline shot through him and he pulled as hard as he could until the arrow came cleanly free. He took note of the hunting point before he threw it down on the ground.

"Dismount!" Polk ordered. He knew he had to get the men off of those gun-shy mustangs. "Every fourth man, hold the horses here! Wounded men stay here with the dead. The rest of you form up on me! Form a skirmish line!"

By now the cowboys had run all the Indians to the far end of the village, where they were scattering as fast as they could, most on foot, a few on horses they had managed to mount as the Indian boys arrived with the horse herd.

"Form a skirmish line on me!" Polk repeated.

In the middle of the camp, he saw a mounted Indian warrior riding toward the Wolf and Crazy Bear, leading a spare pony. With precision swiftness, Crazy Bear was lifted on behind the rider, and the Wolf mounted the spare horse. Then the Wolf turned his mount on the cowboys, who were firing on the fleeing Indian men, women, and children. As his mount galloped, the young warrior reached low to pluck a stick of firewood from the ground. With this, he attacked the cowboys, clubbing the nearest one as he attempted to reload.

"That's a brave man," Polk said.

He watched, amazed, as the Wolf, armed only with the stick, bludgeoned away at the cowboys, distracting them from their murderous work. He winced when he saw Jack Brennan's Colt belch smoke, sending a bullet through the Wolf's torso.

"Sons of bitches," Polk muttered.

He watched the Wolf escape, badly wounded, into a stand of cattails along the creek, barely clinging to his mount.

A few shots came from the cover along the creek where most of the Indians had fled, driving the cowboys back toward the safety of the skirmish line Polk had established. They rode back, yelping idiotically, driving with them about two dozen mounts captured from the

Indians' herd. Gavilan Gutierrez returned with them, an arrow shaft protruding from his hip. He seemed to take little notice of it.

Jack Brennan galloped right up to the dead body of Major Ralph Quitman. "Now, *that's* the way to handle Indians!" he said to the corpse. He looked up at First Sergeant Polk. "Lucky we're not all dead. I told him we should have charged. If I hadn't seen that warrior drawing a bead on me, we would have been completely surprised—ambushed and massacred."

Polk looked back at the dead and wounded. "They were comin' in to the fort until you started shootin'."

"I defended myself! I had stock stolen from me."

"Consider yourself under house arrest," Polk said. "Go back to your ranch and stay there. The captured horses will go back to the fort with me as evidence."

"Aren't you going to mount your men and chase those red devils down?"

"I've got wounded soldiers to get back to the post hospital."

"Kiss my ass," Brennan growled. "Your damn translator has got more sand than you!" He spurred his horse and ran away with his men.

First Sergeant July Polk shot a glance at the translator. Gutierrez only shrugged, and pulled the arrow out of his hip without so much as a flinch.

The Wolf opened his eyes and saw the cattails rising above him to the sky. He placed his hand on his wound and felt blood coursing hot between his fingers. Thinking of his people, he summoned all his strength, rolled over, and began to crawl. One glance told him he was leaving a blood trail, but he hoped the white men would be too stupid to find it way down in the cattails.

Somehow, he knew his grandfather was already dead by now. Sorrow and worry consumed him. He scrambled on his hands and knees as fast as he could, and then he actually stumbled from weakness, though he was just crawling around like some lowly kind of four-legged. This was shameful. He decided to stand and reveal himself to his enemies and fight to the death with his bare hands. He was already good as dead anyway, judging from the way the blood ran from his belly wound.

He tried to stand and turn all at once, while drawing in a breath for his death song, but all this shocked his core with perfect agony, and Mother Earth lurched under his feet, sending him toppling, rolling down a mud bank, sliding into a cold pool of water like a snake. There was a dead willow tree here that had fallen into the creek from an undercut bank on the opposite side. The Wolf dragged himself in among the branches and pulled his head in like a mere turtle.

He held to one hope: that he would not die here without weapons in his hands, that he would not enter the Shadow Land without so much as a flint knife, that he might survive this awful wound and live to fight another day, that he, the Original Wolf, would one day stand again to avenge this injustice.

He remembered his vision quest, when the great wolf had spoken to him. The Original Wolf. The spirit-warrior who had fathered the Noomah nation, then turned into an immortal four-legged. He remembered what the Original Wolf had told him in his vision.

Now, you are as I was. You are the Wolf. The Original Wolf. Your time will come to howl.

He felt his conscious thoughts slipping away, and wondered in which world he might awake next.

14

A SPONTANEOUS PEAL of laughter shook the saloon as Flora served up Hank's fourth beer and slid a shot of whiskey into place beside the full mug.

"... and I don't think this kid had ever been five miles outside of San Antone in his whole life, but he wanted to cowboy," Hank said, continuing his yarn.

Several of Flora's best customers had drifted in as word spread throughout Luck that Captain Tomlinson was feeling talkative down at the tavern.

"We had about two thousand head of cattle we were drivin' to Kansas," Hank recalled, "and for the first few hundred miles, the kid learned fast and made a pretty good hand. The boys started callin' him the San Antone Kid. He turned stampedes and swam flooded rivers. Nothin' much spooked him. But, then, we crossed the Red River into Indian Territory and a bunch of howlin' renegade Kiowas attacked our camp at dawn, stampeded the cattle, and shot an arrow through the crown of the San Antone Kid's hat. Parted his hair! We rallied and chased the Indians off, but we spent all day roundin' up the cattle ..."

Hank held up a finger and paused to gulp his beer, clearly relishing the silent anticipation of the men around him. "Well, we started the herd north again, all except for the San Antone Kid, who I saw headin' south. So I rode up on him and said, 'Kid, where the hell are you goin'?' He said, 'I'm goin' to get my pistol.' I said, 'Well, where did you leave your pistol?' He said, 'San Antone!' "

The men burst into laughter again, and Hank threw back his shot of whiskey.

"Another?" Flora asked.

"Oh, I don't know, Flora. I mean, not unless these gents want to have one with me and drink a toast to Texas!"

A cheer rattled the windowpanes, coins hit the bar, and Flora began looking forward to turning a better-than-average afternoon profit. She was wishing Jane might show up a little early for work to help her and Harry deal with the drink orders, and just then, she heard Jane's voice.

"Flora! Captain Tomlinson! Y'all better come look!"

Flora turned and found Jane holding one of the double swinging doors open. Through the open doorway, Flora saw a buckboard wagon pass down the street. She couldn't see what was in the wagon bed, but above the sideboards, she clearly saw the feathered ends of several arrow shafts shaking like rattlesnake tails as the buckboard clattered down the rutted street. It stopped in front of Sam Collins's store.

Flora and Hank went to the door, followed by half the men in the saloon. The other half crowded the windows for a better view.

"Did you see inside the wagon bed?" Hank asked.

"No, sir," Jane answered.

Could be anyone lying back there, Flora thought. She remembered that Jay Blue and Skeeter were out there somewhere, and she knew Hank must be worried half to death right now, though a glance at his face showed no emotion.

She walked with Hank across the street, followed by the entire population of the saloon. Poli and Tonk fell into place right behind Hank. The driver of the buckboard had stepped from the wagon to the boardwalk to beat on the door of the general store, for Sam Collins served as the coroner in Luck. Flora recognized the wagon driver as Eddie Milliken, the Double Horn Ranch foreman who had started all the trouble with Jane the night before.

Though she dreaded it, she resolved to walk right up to the wagon with Hank. If one of those boys was in there, she didn't want him to see it alone. Fearing the worst, she peeked over the edge and saw the body of a more mature man, and felt a moment of something like relief, though the corpse full of arrows hardly set her mind at ease. She didn't look at the face long, for the top of the poor man's head was a horrible sight, and one of his eyes was missing. She turned and rested her cheek on the back of Hank's shoulder, half hiding from the dead body until she could get hold of herself.

Jane had not had the stomach to even look. "Is it?" she asked.

Flora shook her head. "Some stranger."

With her cheek still on Hank's shoulder, Flora felt his arm reach forward, and wondered why on earth he would want to get any closer to touching that ghastly corpse. She looked around his shoulder toward the wagon and saw Hank's gnarled fingers stroking the red markings painted on one of the arrow shafts. Her eyes swept up his arm, to his face. She had never seen such a look in the Ranger's eyes. She couldn't tell if it was stunned disbelief, or fear, or a combination of the two. She had never known Hank to fear anything before.

The door to the general store burst open as Sam came out to stand beside Eddie Milliken on the boardwalk across the wagon from the saloon crowd. He grimaced as he took in the sight of the one-eyed cadaver, then looked at Milliken. "Well?"

Milliken had pushed his hat back on his head and was standing hip-cocked on the boardwalk as if he was showing off some prize buck deer he had killed and hauled to town. "The boss found him on top of Shovel Mountain this morning."

Sam looked down at the body, the revulsion plain on his face. "Anybody know who it is?"

Milliken spoke up again. "Jack says just some drifter he recognized from the saloon."

"Did you ever see him before?" Hank asked Flora.

She set her jaw and took another look at the man's face. She nodded and looked away. "He said his name was Wes. Wes James. He rode a tall claybank horse. He fancied himself a mavericker."

"You're sure about all this?" Sam said.

Flora nodded. "I remember him well. He made Dottie mad because she went to sit on his lap and he told her she was too fat."

A group of men let out a whiskey chuckle, until Hank's disapproving gaze silenced them.

"What were you boys doing on Shovel Mountain?" Hank asked.

"We were huntin' strays we might have missed, and noticed the buzzards circlin'. Jack rode up on top of the mountain to see what was dead, but he was a little too late to save that eye."

Flora had noticed the bedrolls and skillets under the buckboard seat and judged the claim of a late-fall cow hunt logical enough.

Hank continued his interview. "Where's Jack and the rest of the outfit now?"

"We drove the dead body over to Fort Jennings. Major Quitman took some buffalo soldiers over to that Indian camp on Flat Rock Creek. Jack and the rest of the boys went with the cavalry." Milliken spit a brown stream of tobacco juice on the boardwalk. "Your boy, Jay Blue, was there. And that kid, Skeeter."

Hank's eyes flashed up from the arrows sticking out of the dead man. "Did they ride with the soldiers, too?"

Milliken smirked and shook his head. "The major wouldn't let 'em. He told 'em to go home."

Hank breathed a sigh of relief, but then set his glare on Milliken. "Were you one of the boys that ganged up on my son last night?"

The cowboy almost swallowed his quid as Hank's eyes drilled him. "I don't know what the hell you're talkin' about."

"He was the one who grabbed Jane and started all the trouble in the first place," Flora said.

The cowboy took a step back. He looked nervous under the glare of half the leading men in town.

"It's a lot different when you stand alone, ain't it? No rowdy ranch hands to back you up when you insult the virtue of a lady."

"I didn't do nothin'," Milliken argued.

Hank took a step back to stand beside Jane. "Take your hat off and apologize to this young lady."

"It's not necessary," Jane said in a quiet voice.

"It's necessary to me. Do it, son, or I'll shoot that hat off your head myself."

Sam Collins leaned away from Milliken and took a slow step aside.

Milliken faltered for a moment, but then jutted his chin. "The Texas Rangers have been outlawed by the Reconstruction government, and replaced by the new State Police. You ain't the law here no more, old man."

"This isn't between you and the law. This is between you and me. I'm giving you one last chance to take your hat in your hand and apologize."

Milliken sneered. "I don't believe I will."

Hank's Colt came out of the holster with a hiss and flashed fire and smoke before Milliken could flinch. The bullet caught both the upturned brim and the crown of the cowboy's hat, blasting it from his head. It also pierced the window front of Sam's store, creating a hole that sprouted an instant spider web of cracks.

Sam groaned.

"Now that I've tipped your hat for you, you might as well go ahead an apologize," Hank said. His hammer was cocked behind the next round in the cylinder, the sights set between Millken's eyes.

Milliken's hand was shaking near the grip of his revolver—as close as he had gotten to using it. He moved the hand away from the weapon. "I apologize," he said.

Hank reholstered his Colt. "If you ever bother this girl again, I'll aim lower."

Milliken turned to pick up his hat. "I gotta git this wagon back to the ranch," he said, unable to look Sam Collins or anyone else in the eyes.

"Some of you men help me carry this body inside," Sam said.

Several men immediately turned back to the saloon, but three stayed to lay hold of the corpse and drag it from the wagon bed.

Flora watched Hank step up on the boardwalk as Milliken shook the reins of the mule team and trundled away, shooting one last glance of hatred over his shoulder. Hank spoke low, but she heard him.

"Sorry about the window, Sam. Put it on my account. And, Sam . . ." He leaned closer. "Pull those arrows out of the body and stash 'em somewhere safe."

15

MERCIFULLY, the sun dimmed to a warm orange glow as Jubal Hayes rode through the gap that led to the rough canyon country he called home. He pulled his scarf from his face and enjoyed the cool air that rushed unfettered into his lungs. He took the shaded spectacles from his eyes and placed them carefully in a pocket of his worn jacket. This was his favorite time of day, when he could bare his flesh and sensitive eyes to the dying sunshine like any normal man. The money in his pocket made this particular evening just that much sweeter.

There was a trail here, to the left of the gap, that led up to a bluff. From the bluff, a man could see a good forty miles to the east. Jubal's mustang pony made the climb without hesitation. At the top, the mustanger dismounted and looped his reins around a hackberry sapling. He took off his gloves and reveled in the cool air that slipped between his fingers. He fished around in his saddlebag until he felt the telescope.

As the dying light of the setting sun painted his wild shocks of golden hair a shade of orange, Jubal slid his telescope over the rocky summit of the bluff to search his back-trail for trouble. It took only moments for movement to catch his eye.

Closer behind than he might have expected, he saw those two boys from the fort—the ones who had lost the blooded mare. It surprised him that boys so young could have followed his trail so quickly, but then again he had given little attention to covering his tracks. He watched them as they crossed Honey Creek at the same place he had crossed less than a half hour ago.

He collapsed the telescope and groaned. He could easily lose them. Now that he knew he was being trailed, he could hold to the rocky places that left no sign. It was almost dark and he was almost home. They'd never find his place. The slave hunters had tried, before the war, and had never gotten close.

But, judging from that corpse he had seen in the buckboard back at the fort, there was Indian trouble brewing. He wouldn't want to live with the knowledge that he had left those boys in the wilderness to get scalped. He shook his head as he rolled onto his back and saw the first star of the night twinkling in the gray sky above.

How the hell did I get stuck wet-nursin' two fool cowboys?

He rode down from the bluff and waited at the gap. Within a few minutes, the cowboys appeared.

"You boys lose your way?" he asked, his voice startling them. They only shrugged at him, not knowing how to explain themselves.

"We need your help," the one called Jay Blue finally managed to say.

"I'll help you keep your scalp tonight. Then you can be on your way tomorrow. But you've got to promise me you'll never tell a soul where I live. I don't like company."

"We promise!" said the one called Skeeter.

"Agreed," Jay Blue added.

Jubal scowled at them. "Come on, we're runnin' out of daylight."

Staying on the heels of Jubal's mustang pony, Jay Blue let his mount watch the trail as he took in the grandeur of this hidden canyon—a place beyond all previous explorations of his home surrounds.

Cliffs two and three hundred feet tall rose among rugged hills and craggy draws on every side. Spring-fed rivulets twined through heavily timbered ravines. Freshwater dripped among mosses and ferns in places that seldom saw sunlight. Soon the canyon opened into a wider basin surrounded by steep hills and sheer cliffs, and Jay Blue noticed Jubal bearing to the right, onto a faint trail that led through thick brush.

Once they had trotted through this brush, they came to a hidden side canyon that opened wide at the mouth, but narrowed toward the head the way the flare of a bugle curved inward as it swept toward the mouthpiece. He also noticed that someone had built a stout fence of cedar rails across the belled opening of the canyon. The fence and the canyon walls enclosed a fine pasture, watered by a spring creek that meandered through it. And up toward the narrow head of the canyon, a few hundred yards away, Jay Blue could see a good set of corrals, clearly meant to hold and train wild horses.

Yet there was still no cabin in sight.

As Jubal continued on at a trot, the trail began to cling to the right-hand canyon wall in a gradual ascent. Leaning toward the cliff on his right side, away from the void to the left, Jay Blue noted that places on the cliff wall looked almost polished, as if this were a very old trail, brushed by the touch of many a traveler.

Risking a glance toward the more dangerous side of the trail, he could now look down into the canyon and the stout corrals. The horses in those corrals noticed the riders, threw their heads high into the air, and whinnied a welcome.

And the trail went higher still as the canyon wall pinched inward toward the opposite cliff face. Soon, Jay Blue could look down into a chasm only twenty feet across, and a hundred feet deep. Here, the little stream tumbled over the head of the canyon in a sparkling thread of water and frayed into white froth before it hit the canyon floor.

As he looked back in admiration of the gossamer waterfall, his mount wheeled around a dogleg to the right just as something groaned a hideous guttural strain in Jay Blue's ear. He wrenched his neck around, shocked to find the huge snout of a camel staring at him.

"God Almighty!" he cried, his pony shying a bit at the strange beast.

"That ain't God, boy. Just ol' Thirsty."

As they passed by the hindquarters of the camel, Jay Blue noticed a CSA brand, but his question about how a camel with a Confederate brand might end up in the Texas hills got caught in his throat as he looked beyond the animal to the high shelf extending above the head of the canyon. There was a whole hidden pasture up here—as big as the one fenced in on the canyon floor, and rimmed all around by its own cedar-rail fencing, beyond which were wooded peaks and limestone outcroppings. The spring creek that fed the waterfall snaked through this level pasture like a torpid water moccasin.

Sweeping around to the right, his eyes now caught sight of some smoke coming from a small earthen dome, and then he saw a woman tending a loaf of bread inside the oven. This sight shocked him even more so than the camel. She was a small, trim-figured woman, brown-skinned, with black hair, somewhat younger than Jubal.

"God Almighty!" Jay Blue repeated.

"Save a few God A'mighties," Jubal suggested. "You're just gettin' started."

The woman had noticed Jay Blue and Skeeter now, and looked even more astonished than they did to see Jubal bringing company home.

"It's alright, honey," the mustanger said to the woman. "They're just muchachos."

Beyond the woman, and the earthen oven, Jay Blue saw that the sheer canyon wall had followed the trail around the dogleg to this high, hidden pasture, and now he noticed the cave sunk into the side of this cliff face. An adobe wall and a grass-thatched, lean-to roof expanded the cave into a domicile of respectable space, especially considering the possibility that the cave might extend quite some distance into the rock. A low, exterior wall of neatly stacked stone enclosed a yard that included a good-sized Spanish oak, the tree having shed most of its leaves for the coming winter.

"Might as well light and turn your horses into the pasture to graze," Jubal said.

Jay Blue and Skeeter followed his advice as the sky darkened, revealing a legion of stars.

"We've got grub with us," Jay Blue said. "We'd be glad to cook some up."

"Fair enough. Bring what you've got into the kitchen."

The woman had taken the loaf of bread from the earthen oven

and gone into the cave. Now Jay Blue entered, followed by Skeeter. Looking around the cave, and the adobe wing that expanded it, Jay Blue had to admire the way the albino hermit lived.

The adobe lean-to extension served as a kitchen and dining area. There was one small wooden table, handmade, and only two chairs. An adobe fireplace near the entrance included iron fittings to facilitate the hanging of cooking vessels over the fire. Where the cave joined the kitchen addition, a large, stuffed buffalo hide served as a couch or daybed, flanked by typical household odds and ends—a butter churn, a candlestick, a stack of split firewood, and a keg of flour. A dark passageway led deeper into the cave, presumably to the sleeping chambers.

"Boys, this is my wife. Her name is Luz."

The cowboys put their foodstuffs on the table, dragged their hats from their heads, and greeted the woman. She smiled shyly and nodded.

Speaking Spanish, Skeeter offered to help Luz get the cooking started. An hour passed pleasantly enough as the four unlikely dinner companions cooked and ate. Jay Blue didn't see any need to ruin a good meal with an argument, and he could sense that Jubal was not going to agree to chasing the mustang that had stolen his daddy's mare without some persuasion. So, it wasn't until Skeeter offered to help Luz clear the table that Jay Blue broached the subject.

"About us goin' home," he began.

"Yeah, tomorrow," Jubal repeated. "You had no business followin' me in the first place."

"Well, I was thinkin' maybe I could offer you a business proposition."

"Business?" Jubal laughed. "I live in a cave. What the hell use do I have for business?"

"Horse business," Jay Blue added.

"You can forget about that mare."

"How would you like to have the first colt out of that Thoroughbred mare?" He watched Jubal's eyes as he made the offer, and he could have sworn he saw a momentary flash of interest, though it was hard to tell with those empty gray eyes that shot flashes of pink and red when the light danced across them just right.

"You're awful free with your daddy's horseflesh, son."

"He won't mind. As long as he gets her back."

"Well, he's gonna mind plenty then, 'cause he ain't gettin' her back. She's gone."

"You don't understand, Mr. Hayes. If I don't find that mare, I can't go home!"

"No, *you* don't understand, son. *I don't care*."

In his frustration, Jay Blue bolted up from his chair. "What do I have to do to make it worth your while? What do you want? Just name it."

Jubal gawked at him. "You are as dense as that rock wall, son! You've got to get it through your head. That mare is *gone*. She's a shootin' star. She's gone as Grandpa's teeth. You'll catch up to *yesterday* before you catch up to that mare. If she's runnin' with that silver stud, she can't never be caught."

"Why not? Why is it so impossible?"

"Because he'll spirit her away to the wildest edges of his ranges, and you'll never find her."

"But you can. You're the best there is, Mr. Hayes."

"I ain't a fool, son. You can't flatter me. I know that stallion. He's a ghost horse one day and a demon the next. He ain't natural. He can be wilder than a deer at high noon and meaner than a cornered bear at midnight. I ought to know. I'm part mustang myself when I'm out there among 'em. I tried for years to catch him, and . . . well, I never did."

"But with Skeeter and me helping you, you'll have a better chance." Again, a glint in the mustanger's eyes told Jay Blue that his argument appealed.

But then Jubal shook his head emphatically. "I said *no*!"

Skeeter and Luz sensed the argument heating up, and turned from the tub of warm water they were using as a washbasin.

Jay Blue felt as if he would explode. It wasn't often he ran up against somebody every bit as hardheaded as he was. "Fine, then. We'll do it without you."

Jubal laughed in ridicule. "Son, you got no experience mustangin' and there's Indian trouble brewin'. You don't know what you're up against. Forget about that mare. You lose things in life that you can't get back. That's part of livin'."

"With all due respect, Mr. Hayes, I've got to go after the mare."

"You'll just get yourself scalped. And your friend, too."

"Maybe Skeeter won't even go with me, but I aim to get that mare back or die tryin'. I'm not gonna have one stupid mistake hang over my head the rest of my life."

"It's liable to be a short life, hardheaded as you are."

Jay Blue shrugged and sat down on the stuffed buffalo hide couch. "If nobody wants to help, I'll do it myself."

"Well, I guess that settles that," Jubal said.

A cold sadness seemed to well up from the depths of the cave and settle around the inhabitants like quicksand. Skeeter and Luz slowly turned back to the dishes. Jubal sat at the table, his jaw set. Jay Blue flung himself back on the couch, throwing his arms out in exasperation, like a man crucified. But as the fingers of his left hand extended beyond the cushions of the hand-stuffed couch, they fell against something that answered his touch with a familiar twang.

Turning his head to the left, he saw what he had missed before. Leaning back in a natural crevice of the cavern wall, obscured by the butter churn, he recognized the strings and frets of a musical instrument. Leaning his head forward for a better look, he counted four tuning pegs on the headstock, and knew he was looking at the neck of a banjo. He grabbed it, lifted it, and rested it on his thigh.

"Hey, put that down," Jubal warned. "You can't play that thing."

Jay Blue answered with a cold, businesslike tone: "With all due respect, sir, I beg to differ." Strumming the strings, he found the instrument in tune. He made a chord and strummed it. He wasn't in much of a mood for anything jolly, so he sang a mournful verse that suited his temperament, changing chords as he strummed.

Max Welton's braes are bonnie where early falls the dew
And 'twas there that Annie Laurie gave me her promise true
Gave me her promise true, which ne'er forget will I
And for bonnie Annie Laurie, I'd lay me down and die

"By God, you *can* play a little."

Jay Blue saw something almost childlike in Jubal's face, and hope took hold in his heart once more. He gave the second verse a bit more tempo, and sat up so he could sing it better.

Her brow is like the snowdrift, her throat is like the swan
Her face it is the fairest that e'er the sun shone on
That e're the sun shone on, and bright blue is her eyes
And for bonnie Annie Laurie, I'd lay me down and die

Jay Blue never bragged about it, but he could outsing anybody in the lower Pedernales Valley, and he could see that his voice had gotten to Jubal. After all, the mustanger had been up here for Lord knows how long listening to that camel bray.

Skeeter spoke up from the kitchen, anxious to lighten the gloom in the cave. "He's pretty good, huh, Mr. Hayes? Jay Blue can play about anything with strings on it. Comes by it natural from his daddy. The captain plays a guitar real good."

"Do tell," Jubal said, proceeding cautiously. "I don't guess you know 'Camptown Races'?"

"Know it?" Jay Blue blurted. "That's the first song I ever learned!" He switched keys to D, and set to fingerpicking to the gait of a trotting cow pony.

Oh, the Camptown ladies sing this song
Doo-dah! Doo-dah!
The Camptown race track's five miles long
Oh, doo-dah day!

As he played and belted out the old standard, Jubal rose from his chair, urging Jay Blue to continue with nods of his head and graceful swirling motions from his fingertips. He dashed into the bed chambers and came out two chord changes later with a fiddle and a bow. He blew dust from the instrument, plucked the strings, tuned one, and put the chin piece under his jaw.

Gwine to run all night!
Gwine to run all day!
I'll bet my money on a bobtailed nag
Somebody bet on the bay!

"Take it, Mr. Hayes!" Jay Blue shouted, hammering out a steady rhythm for the fiddler to follow. Jubal attacked the strings with his bow, and to Jay Blue's joy and surprise, the albino turned out to be a fine fiddle player! Before too long, Luz and Skeeter were dancing hook-in-wing in the kitchen, Jubal was tapping his toe while playing, and Jay Blue was singing the last verse, his voice ricocheting off the stone walls. There was a turnaround and a tag at the end of the tune that both musicians nailed as if they had rehearsed it, and—as players unaccountably do after the final stroke of a lively number—both the fiddler and the banjo picker busted out in spontaneous laughter for no reason at all.

Jubal took the fiddle out from under his chin and laughed right up at the ceiling. He turned and grinned at Luz. "I'll be damned!" he said. "I ain't had so much fun in . . ."

He failed to finish his sentence when he saw Jay Blue returning the banjo to its hiding place behind the churn. "That *was* fun," Jay Blue agreed. "But, like you said, I guess that settles that." And he donned the most cocksure smile he could muster, for he knew that if his case was not won now, never would it be.

Jubal lost his hold on his smile, grasping the fiddle and bow pleadingly in his hands, glancing between Jay Blue and the languid banjo. Stillness and silence hung in the cave for an uncomfortably long while. Then Jubal heaved a sigh of surrender.

"Shit," he groaned. He pointed with his bow. "Pick up the banjo, boy. Then we'll talk horse business."

16

THE MUSTANGER and the cowboys had put the musical instruments aside and retired outside to the small rock-fenced square that Jubal referred to as his courtyard. He had lit a kerosene lantern and a corncob pipe, and motioned for his visitors to sit on the two chairs they had carried from the kitchen. Jubal himself sat on a flat rock that crowned a stretch of the low stone enclosure.

The camel, Thirsty, came to stare at them.

"Mr. Hayes," Skeeter asked, "where in thunder did you come by a camel?"

"He just wandered up. He's a good watchdog, so I let him stay. The U.S. Army experimented with camels to cross the desert from Texas to California, back before the war. The Confederates captured the herd, and branded 'em with a CSA, but never knew what to do with 'em. I guess they just turned 'em out. The Indians think I'm a ghost and ol' Thirsty's a demon, so they stay the hell out of our canyon."

"And what about the Steel Dust Gray?" Jay Blue said, anxious to get down to business. "Some say he's a ghost, too."

Jubal puffed on his pipe thoughtfully. "We both come to this country about the same time," he began. "That stallion and me. The first time I saw him, he was a three-year-old, I'd guess. He wore a hackamore and had bloody gouges in his side, so I knew some mean son of a bitch had tried to break him. Most mustangs fear men. That gray—he hates 'em. And I don't blame him.

"Next time I saw him, he'd rubbed that hackamore from his head and had gathered a few mares. He had come here lookin' for his freedom—like me. He had escaped, and had to hide to keep from being caught and whipped—like me. But I wanted to catch him—a beautiful horse like that. I guess I thought we could help each other. Maybe I was wrong." Jubal struck a match on the rock wall and cupped his hand around it to relight the tobacco in his pipe.

"Were you a slave, Mr. Hayes?" Skeeter asked.

Jubal nodded. "Born lookin' like this, you can imagine my master wasn't too happy with my folks. An albino ain't fit for work in the fields. So that slave master sold my folks to two different buyers. I never knew 'em."

"You're an orphan, like me," Skeeter said.

Jubal looked at him. "Maybe you understand a little, then. But I was a slave, too. Like I said, I couldn't work in the fields, but they kept me around as a curiosity and put me to work tendin' horses. I became a good jockey, and my slave master bought me my shaded spectacles so's I could race. We had a big race in San Antonio, and I escaped there, and run off to hide in these hills. That seems well nigh a lifetime ago."

"So that's when you first saw the Steel Dust Gray?" Jay Blue asked, trying to get the conversation back on track.

Jubal nodded. "The story come up through Fredericksburg that the Steel Dust Gray was caught in the wild as a two-year-old colt, and killed a man tryin' to break him down around Bandera. Some German settlers I sold horses to over on the Pedernales told me to leave him be, or he'd kill me, too, but I still thought I could catch him.

"I taught myself and trained my horses to rope by watchin' the vaqueros, but I never could get close enough to that stallion to throw a loop at him. So I learned to charm these mustangs."

"How do you charm a wild animal?" Skeeter asked, amazed.

"You boys know what a horse whisperer is?"

Skeeter put his hand in the air, as if he were in school. "You mean like when your voice gets hoarse, *and you try to whisper*?" He rasped the last few words.

Jubal shook his head, a look of disgusted disbelief on his face. "I'm amazed you two scatterbrains put up with each other. Just listen, will you? There are men who can whisper in a horse's ear—in some kind of secret horse language—and the horse will just do whatever the horse whisperer says to do."

Jay Blue smirked. "Are you tryin' to tell us you're a horse whisperer?"

"Me? Hell, no, son, I'd be lyin' to you if I told you that. I've tried whisperin' to 'em, and it don't work for me. Even when I talk right out loud to 'em, they don't understand me right off. But sooner or later, I get my meanin' across to 'em. No, I ain't no horse whisperer. I'm more of what you'd call a *mustang mumbler*."

Smoke billowed from Jubal's mouth in the lantern light as he busted out in laughter and slapped his knee. Skeeter joined him, and even Jay Blue had to chuckle.

"Mustang mumbler! That's a good one!" Skeeter declared.

"What I learned to do was go out and live among 'em. I become one of 'em. After a while, they'll accept me into their band, and they'll learn to trust me. They'll follow me anywhere. That's how I led that string into the corrals at Fort Jennings today. You saw me.

"So, anyway, after charmin' and pennin' many a mustang, I went after El Grullo's herd. Took a long time, but every day he'd let me get a little closer to the herd. I was camped real close one night when I woke to the feeling of the ground shakin'. Ol' Steel Dust was on me in no time. He stomped my head pretty good, and bit me once or twice. I tried to get up and run, but he whirled and kicked. Broke my arm right here between the wrist and elbow—I heard it crack. He drove me out of my own camp where I couldn't even get to my gun to fire it and spook him off. I got behind a mesquite tree, and managed to stay away from him. But he wasn't done. He turned back to my camp and stomped everything that smelled like me. Broke a good Winchester rifle. Then he went after my gelding and spooked him so bad that he set back and broke his lead rope and run off, leavin' me busted up, afoot, and without a gun, a long way from home. Turned out it was one of the best things ever happened to me."

"What do you mean?" Skeeter said. "Sounds like your luck was runnin' even lower than ours has."

"Good luck comes in mighty peculiar packages sometimes, gentlemen. While I was limpin' home with a busted head and a busted arm, I stumbled across a camp of Comanches. They had been on a raid, and had a captive." He pointed toward the entrance to the cave with his pipe stem. "It was Luz. Don't ever ask her about it, because she don't like to think about it, much less talk about it.

"It was dusk. They were makin' camp. Luz was tied up. So I waited until almost dark and gave 'em my demon-on-furlough-from-hell routine." Jubal began to laugh. "I walked into their camp half naked, painted with dried blood, howlin' like a peacock. They lit out of there so fast that they left Luz and all kinds of handy things behind—bows and arrows, food, knives, buffalo robes . . . They didn't even bother to round up their spare horses, so I caught a few. Me and Luz rode home in style."

"Wasn't she scared of you?"

"You can only get just so scared, son. She was already scared well-nigh to death when I found her. Once she figured out I wasn't a ghost, we got along just fine. She set my broken arm and nursed me back to health. If that stallion hadn't attacked me that night, I never would have found that woman, and I'd be one lonely hermit to this day."

"I don't see our streak of bad luck turnin' out that way," Skeeter said. "At least not with Jay Blue in charge."

Jay Blue rolled a lazy look of disapproval Skeeter's way, but said nothing.

"Well, don't worry, Jay Blue ain't in charge," Jubal declared. "I am. I swore I'd never go after Steel Dust again, but maybe it's time. You boys can rope, so we've got one shot at catchin' that mare, and maybe even El Grullo himself, if he don't kill us all. I know where he's headed with that mare. I know his patterns. He's goin' to one of his favorite little canyons. I've got a mustang trap built in that canyon. If we can get a couple of ropes on him, we can pen him there."

A smile had begun to form on Jay Blue's face. "We can do this, Mr. Hayes. I told you, we could help you." He stood and rubbed his hands together, as if he was ready to get started that very moment. "Daddy's sure gonna be surprised when we ride back with that mare!"

"Don't start countin' chickens just yet," Jubal warned. "We got some hatchin' to do first." He stood and gently tapped the ashes out of his pipe, onto the flat rock atop the stone fence. "We'd best get a few hours of sleep if we're goin' mustangin' tomorrow. We'll be up by three thirty and mounted by four."

"I've got a good feelin' about this," Jay Blue said, nudging Skeeter as they returned to the cave.

"Oh, crap," Skeeter replied. "That's what you told me about goin' to town to see that barmaid, and my life's been a bad dream ever since."

17

BEFORE HE EVEN FOUND the strength to open his eyes, the Wolf felt himself wake from sleep. A great burning mass tortured his midsection. Another glowed through his eyelids. But in spite of the balls of fire inside and out, he felt chilled.

He forced his eyes open and saw the sun on the horizon. Was it rising or setting? He hoped this was not the eternity of the Shadow Land. The missionaries on the reservation had promised it would be free of pain, but this was like no misery he had ever felt. He closed his eyes again.

Visions, dreams, and memories intermingled until he could not tell one from the other. He thought he remembered having awakened before, in the cold water where he had hidden himself like a wounded varmint. He had dragged himself out of the water. But when? How long ago? And how far had he crawled?

Again, he opened his eyes. The sun had risen a bit, having broken free of the horizon. Dawn. Now he recalled the battle. He had fought well at first. He had shot that big soldier in the shoulder with an arrow, then dragged his grandfather, Chief Crazy Bear, away. He had picked up a stick and fought with that. Then his medicine had gone bad, and now he lay here, helpless—useless to his people. Had they escaped? Where was his cousin, Crooked Nose? His friends? The women and children? The soldiers?

He felt the gaze of Father Sun upon him, shaming him for lying there like a coward. He had to get up. Summoning all his strength, he pushed his body from the ground until he was on his knees. The pain in his torso was horrific, but he choked his groans of agony back down his throat. He tried to look around, but the images swam. He could focus only on the ground from which he had risen, finding it stained with his own dried blood. He refused to look at his wound.

Trying to rise to his feet, the Wolf stumbled back down to his knees. The scraping of his palms and knees in gravel and thorns was nothing compared to the torments of his fevered wound. Then he saw a slender tree limb lying on the ground—one that had been swept down the stream in times of flood and deposited here. He crawled toward it. Taking the piece of driftwood in hand, he found it strong enough to support him.

By leaning on the stick, he was able to rise to his feet and look around him. His vision blurred the distant landscape, but he could see the ground under him well enough, and the rising sun gave him his bearings. He began walking, using the stick like an old lady, keeping the sun over his right shoulder. He didn't know what else to do. He was not going to just lie there and die, in shame and defeat.

Before the fight, Crazy Bear had told everyone in camp that if they were attacked, and had to scatter, they would meet up again where the two big rivers came together—the ones named the Colorado and the Llano by the Spaniards who had come long before the Americans. He knew that campground was to the northwest, so he plodded along in that direction.

Neither time nor distance meant anything to him anymore, and so he could not say how far he had walked when he tripped. In straining, trying to catch himself upon his walking stick, he tore open the wound where the bullet had ripped out of his body over his right hip bone. His knees hit and he pitched forward onto his face. He felt the warmth of his own blood running down his side.

Was this how he would die? Bleeding to death, facedown in the dirt, too weak to sing his own death song? Father Sun's glare drilled mercilessly into him, and the Wolf knew that any hope he had of surviving would have to come from the spirits now, for he was no more able to help himself than a motherless infant. He felt very thirsty, and his eyes closed.

• • •

"Hey, *Jefe*, when do I get my next raise?" Policarpo asked, riding along at a trot beside Hank on the road to Fort Jennings. Tonk was riding ahead, as if he was still scouting for the Texas Rangers. They had stayed in town last night and had ridden home to the Broken Arrow Ranch after dawn. Failing to find Jay Blue and Skeeter there, they figured they'd better ride on over to Fort Jennings to inquire after the boys.

"A raise?" Hank said, scoffing at the idea. "I defy you to find another ranch foreman in Texas as well paid as you."

"But I need more whore money."

Hank appreciated the honesty, but didn't buy the argument. "You ended up with that plump gal from Flora's last night, didn't you?"

"No," Poli insisted. "She ended up. I was standing flat-footed."

Hank grinned, and shook his head. "You're liable to rot something off proddin' around in the wrong place. Then you damn sure won't need a raise."

"I'm serious, *Capitán*, I ain't so young anymore. I gotta make hay while the sun shines, if you know what I mean."

"You got plenty of time. Look at me." He shot a grin at his foreman, and felt the twinkle in his eye from last night at Flora's.

"Ah-ha!" Poli blurted.

"Ah-ha, what?"

"Forget about the raise, you just told me what I wanted to know."

"I didn't tell you a damn thing."

"How was it?"

"How was what?"

"Come on, *Capitán*, is the prize as good as the wrapping paper looks?"

Hank frowned. "None of your business. Let's lope on into Fort Jennings."

They caught up with Tonk and the three of them hit a canter that lasted until they came to the sentry on the road. Gaining entry to the post, they rode to the officer's quarters and found First Sergeant July Polk sitting in his favorite chair, leaning back against the porch in the sun. He was out of uniform, shirtless, his left arm bandaged and in a sling.

"Hello, Captain Tomlinson," he said as Hank and his two ranch hands trotted up. "I've been expectin' you."

Hank nodded a greeting. "Have we met?"

"Not exactly," Polk explained, "but I know who you are. I saw you here on the Fourth of July, for the festivities, but we didn't get a chance to howdy and shake." He rose from his chair as Hank dismounted. He offered his hand to the retired Ranger. "First Sergeant July Polk."

"Pleasure," Hank said, shaking the man's massive hand. "Why would you be expectin' me?"

"Your son was here yesterday. Thought you might be on his trail, with the Indian trouble and all."

"I don't exactly consider just one corpse full of arrows Indian trouble."

Polk frowned. "So you haven't heard?"

Hank felt that simmering feeling of dread trying to come to a boil. "Maybe you better enlighten me."

"We had a fight with the Comanches yesterday on Flat Rock Creek. . . ."

Hank listened intently to the account of the skirmish. According to the first sergeant, who painted a clear picture of what had happened, the Indians had suffered the worst of it, although Major Quitman and two troopers had been killed. Polk seemed neither proud nor ashamed of any of this, and Hank felt inclined to believe his story.

"What about the boys?" Hank asked.

"I'd hoped they'd do as the major ordered, and go home," Polk said. "But I asked around to make sure. A couple of privates who stayed behind at the fort yesterday remembered seeing your boys ride off to the west. It looked like they were on the trail of that mustanger."

"What mustanger?" Hank asked. He spent the next few minutes listening to what First Sergeant July Polk knew about one peculiar individual by the name of Jubal Hayes. This was a bit harder to swallow than the story about the Indian skirmish, but Hank still tended to give credence to Polk's account.

"Who's in charge with the major killed?"

"I guess I am," Polk admitted. "The colonel is way up on the Brazos. The captain took sick and was sent to San Antone. The lieutenant is on leave."

"You look like you can keep order among the men." Hank smiled.

"I can handle 'em, sir."

"Which way did the boys go?"

First Sergeant Polk pointed. "That way. To the right of the corrals. But the trail's a day old, and it's been windy."

"Don't worry about that." Hank stepped back up on his horse. "Between me and Tonk, we'll find 'em." What concerned him was *how* he might find them, but he didn't intend to bother Polk with his worries. "I thank you for your information, First Sergeant."

18

JAY BLUE eased his borrowed mustang pony up to the brink of the overlook, Jubal indicating with minuscule movements of his gloved fingers that the boys should approach with all possible caution.

"There they are," Jubal said in a whisper.

Jay Blue's right stirrup brushed Jubal's left as Skeeter stepped up to the mustanger's off side. Jay Blue removed his hat, stood in the stirrups, and peeked over the rimrock through the thorny-leaved cover of an agarita bush clinging to the precipice. Along the unnamed creek that took the form of a series of pools—like a string of pearls haphazardly cast aside—wild horses grazed and drank, meandering in and out of the cover, which included oak and elm trees, and several large, onion-shaped cedar bushes.

The sight filled Jay Blue's heart with more hope than he had been able to cling to for the past two days. Yet, there was still one lingering doubt. "Where's the mare?" he whispered.

"She's down there in the timber somewhere."

"You sure it's the right bunch of mustangs? I don't see her, or the Steel Dust Gray."

"There!" Jubal said in a whisper. "Comin' out of the trees."

Jay Blue caught sight of the motion, and the Thoroughbred mare trotted into view. His heart thumped as if he were walking into Flora's Saloon to attempt a flirtation with the lovely Jane. Then, from the same opening in the creek-side undergrowth, the Steel Dust Gray stepped into view with his neck bowed and his head high, the morning sun painting a sheen on the ripples of his musculature. His tail switched with every step of his strut. He came sniffing up behind the mare, but she squealed and kicked at him, dodging toward the water, where she paused to take a good long drink.

"He still hasn't had time to have his way with her," Jubal whispered.

"Hey," Jay Blue said, almost too excited to keep his voice down, "are y'all thinkin' what I'm thinkin'?"

The dark lenses of Jubal's glasses turned on him. "Son, I wouldn't bet that you and me have *ever* had the same thought in our heads at the same time."

"Since when did you start thinkin'?" Skeeter added.

Undaunted, Jay Blue motioned for his two trail mates to follow him back down the slope a way where they could talk out loud.

"Mr. Hayes, she's filling up on water right now." Jay Blue grabbed the coiled lasso lashed to the right fork of his saddle. "I can catch her easy when she's full of water. I can ride around downwind, come through that draw, sneak through the cover, and get within fifty yards of her before she ever sees me."

"Are you as good with a rope as you are with a banjo?"

"Music is just an avocation, Mr. Hayes. Cowboyin' is what I do for a *livin'*! I can swing a rope a whole lot better than I can play a banjo."

"Now, Jay Blue," Skeeter said, "don't sell yourself short on that banjo. I've seen you rope."

"I'm serious, Skeeter."

"I am, too. He's a damn fine banjo picker, Mr. Hayes, but he can barely hit the ground with a loop."

"Shut up, Skeeter. Mr. Hayes, I can rope that mare out of that herd, and you'll be shed of us."

Jubal nodded his agreement. "Skeeter and I will ride further to the west, and come up the canyon. That's the way Steel Dust will try to escape." He looked at Skeeter. "We'll need to get two ropes on that killer. You ain't scared, are you?"

Skeeter grinned and shook his head. "No, sir. I live for this shit."

"Let's go," Jay Blue said. He turned his mount toward the draw.

He could already feel the tug of the mare on the business end of his rope. He picked his way quickly, but as quietly as possible, across the slope, to the head of the draw he had spotted from the overlook. The wind, the angle of the draw, and the timber all covered his approach toward the herd of wild horses. He built a loop as he eased through the woods.

Coming out of the draw, the trees became more widely spaced. His mount began to get excited, and Jay Blue knew the cow pony could smell the mustangs. He heard the grunts, the snorts, and the nickers of the animals interacting. Then, coming around a cedar bush, Jay Blue caught sight of the Thoroughbred, not sixty yards away.

He did not hesitate. He raked his spurs across a rib or two and his mount shot forward. The mare threw her head up and ran away at half speed, trying to gain an understanding of this new arrival. She seemed to gather the fact that a rider was coming for her, and she appeared to desire capture.

Jay Blue gained on her quickly, but now he sensed the panic that had electrified the entire herd of mustangs. He heard limbs snapping, rocks clattering, and hooves drumming. From the corners of his eyes, he detected all shades of horseflesh scattering every which way, but he kept his gaze focused on his target. The commotion spooked the mare to three-quarter speed, but she continued to run across an open stretch on the creek basin, and the roper closed in, his loop still in waiting at his right side.

Jay Blue squeaked a smooching sound out between his recently busted lips, and his roping pony responded with a burst that pressed his hip pockets hard against the high cantle. He could feel the space closing between him and the mare, who now angled to her right, giving him a sure shot at her head. There had been no need to whirl the loop above his head until now. Instinctively, he could feel that he would circle it twice to build momentum, and release it on the third revolution forward. Gracefully, the way a chef might grasp a serving ladle, his right hand swung forward over his mount's ear, sending the large loop he had built swinging far out in front of his pony's muzzle.

Two revolutions overhead, and he was there. He released the loop the third time around and saw it hit behind the mare's right ear and flip perfectly over her regal nose. He yanked the slack, and had her, just shy of some brush that might have spoiled his throw.

Then the flash of silver appeared. It swooped past with the speed of a diving hawk, glinting briefly in the sun like a huge bass being hauled up from a clear pool. With it came a shriek of equine rage—a shrill whistle, a guttural roar, and a shuddering scream all rolled into one.

Now flashes of steel dust gray seemed to come from everywhere. Feathered fetlocks cut between Jay Blue's black eye and his cow pony's mane. Hard hooves hissed through the air. Teeth ripped at the roping pony's mane, tearing hair and flesh. The muscled chest of the stallion slammed against Jay Blue's mount, staggering him sideways. Only the tightening of the rope attached to the Thoroughbred prevented the cow pony from falling.

There was a whirlwind of mane and tail swapping ends, and the sharp edges of two hind hooves shot toward Jay Blue and his mount as if fired from a cannon. The cow pony was still stumbling to the right from the recent collision, and the Steel Dust Gray just barely connected, missing the saddle pony altogether, but tapping Jay Blue on the left thigh, about as hard as a sledgehammer would hit a railroad spike.

Reeling from the pain of the kick, Jay Blue saw a hell of a wreck coming on, considering that he was still tied to the powerful Thoroughbred, his cow pony was terrified, and the Steel Dust Gray wanted him dead.

Relief came in the form of Skeeter Rodriguez, who appeared out of nowhere to get a loop on the stallion. Steel Dust turned on Skeeter for committing such an outrage, but Jubal was in position with a second lasso just in time to secure the famous wild stud between two stout roping horses.

"The pen's up the canyon!" Jubal cried. "Lead that mare. He'll follow."

Jay Blue understood that logic, and the Thoroughbred was well trained to lead, so he trotted her upstream and soon spotted the high cedar rails of the mustang trap Jubal had built. He led the mare inside through the open gate.

Keeping the lunging mustang stud between them, trying their best not to choke him senseless, the ropers managed to coax Steel Dust to the opening of the pen. Jubal rode in first and, with a final exhaustive effort, dragged the crazed wild thing inside with him.

Skeeter knew to stay outside of the pen and throw his loop over the top of a rail so he could pull Steel Dust to one side of the pen, allowing Jubal to slack his lariat and ride back out through the gate. By the time this was accomplished, Jay Blue had led the mare out of the pen and closed the gate on the Steel Dust Gray.

The stud still had two ropes around his neck, which ran over the top rails to the saddle horns around which they were tied fast.

"Pull him up next to the fence!" Jubal ordered. He and Skeeter muscled the stallion hard against the rails. "Jay Blue! There's a hook hangin' on that tree limb!"

Jay Blue looked and saw a tool that looked like a long fireplace poker. He jumped down from his saddle, trusting his mount and the Kentucky mare to behave themselves at the opposite ends of the same rope. He ran for the hook and grabbed it.

"You gotta snag both nooses at once!" Jubal ordered.

While Jubal and Skeeter kept the wild stud pulled up next to the inside of the fence rails, Jay Blue used the hook to reach between the rails of the pen and snag both nooses around the gray's neck, though it took some fishing to hook both loops with the stallion lunging and screaming and dancing around just on the other side of the rails. At last he pulled both nooses open.

"Slack!" he shouted.

The ropers stepped the ponies forward and the Steel Dust Gray shook his head out of the choking loops, taking some comfort in the freedom from the hemp.

"Back off!" Jubal shouted. "Give him some room in there."

They all withdrew from the corrals with their mounts, the Thoroughbred following calmly at the end of her lasso. They went to a nearby patch of shade under a live oak. The three of them stood panting, wide-eyed, amazed at their own accomplishment. Jubal yanked his protective scarf down. A huge smile enveloped his face. Jay Blue had tears in his eyes, and felt his grin stretching from one ear to the other. Skeeter just seemed dazed.

Jubal clasped both young men by the shoulders. "I told you boys last night that good luck comes in mighty peculiar packages sometimes. You messed up bad when you let that mare run off. But you got her back, and that ain't the half of it. The three of us just cinched the braggin' rights of a lifetime!"

Jay Blue nodded. "We corralled a myth," he said.

"We roped the Steel Dust Gray!" Skeeter blurted. "We caught El Grullo!"

19

THE MUSTANGERS gloated and lunched in the shade of the live oak and made their plans for El Grullo's future.

"After you boys get that mare home, I need you to make a supply run. I ain't lettin' that stallion out of that pen until I've tamed him some, so you'll have to fetch some things for me." He reached into a shirt pocket and pulled out a piece of paper. "Luz and I made a list last night. There's some things on there she needs at the cave, so you can stop off there on your way back here."

Jay Blue took the list. "You sure you'll be okay here alone?"

"Like I told you, the Indians are scared to death of me. I'm a ghost to them. I'll be okay if I don't starve to death, so I need you to get to town and bring me some supplies as soon as you can."

"Don't worry about that," Skeeter said. "We won't let you down, Mr. Hayes."

The cowboys left Jubal in the canyon with the Steel Dust Gray, and led their recovered Thoroughbred back toward the east, and the Broken Arrow Ranch. Once out of the canyon, Jay Blue took the list out of his pocket to look it over.

"Good Lord," he said. "We're gonna need a pack mule to haul all these supplies to the cave. Sugar, flour, coffee, lard, beans, fatback, yards of cloth, five pounds of nails . . . It goes on and on. And look here at the bottom. Licorice sticks and saltwater taffy!"

"Saltwater taffy!" Skeeter blurted. "I love that stuff! Makes me hungry just to think about it. *¡Dios!* I wish I had some fried chicken!"

Jay Blue folded the list and slipped it back into a pocket while scanning the skyline for trouble. "You're not the only hungry one around. Look." He pointed up at the flock of buzzards that had come into view around a bluff.

"I ain't hungry for whatever they're after," Skeeter replied. "Can't be more than a couple of miles away, though. You want to ride over there and see what's dead?"

"Alright, but let's be careful. Daddy says buzzards and crows follow the Indians."

"If there's Indians over there, I'd just as soon sneak up and find them before they find us."

"Let's keep our voices down now, until we find out what those buzzards are circling."

Skeeter nodded, and they angled into the wind.

The trail from Fort Jennings had been difficult to follow, but Hank and his old Indian scout, Tonkawa Jones, had made relatively quick work of pursuing the boys. A track here, a broken twig there, a pile of horse dung, even a ripped spider web between two bushes—the most minuscule disturbances kept them on the right path.

As the trackers studied sign, Policarpo Losoya kept an eye on the horizons for trouble. A subtle mourning dove whistle was the signal agreed upon for the day, so when Hank heard Poli's dove imitation, he looked up from the trail and saw his foreman pointing at the sky. A whirlwind of black wings circled a few miles away to the northwest.

"Funny how vultures lure the living to the dead," he said to Tonk. "Let's go check it out."

He leaned ever so slightly forward, squeezed with his knees, and the good ranch horse under him took off at a canter.

Jay Blue and Skeeter took their time riding up under the sky full of vultures, keeping a constant lookout for Indians. Then they began to spook the big ugly birds out of tree branches, and knew whatever had drawn them earthward was near.

After searching the terrain for some time, Jay Blue finally saw a foot wearing a moccasin, sticking out from some bushes, toes upward. "Skeeter!" he hissed. He pointed. Together they approached, their hands on the grips of their revolvers.

Coming around the bushes, they saw the body of a young warrior lying on the ground. His wound oozed a glistening red. Black blood stains caked the soil all around the body where the warrior had dragged himself, or rolled over.

"It could be a trap," Jay Blue said. "You keep your eyes and ears open. I'll get down and see if he's alive."

Jay Blue dismounted, drew his revolver, cocked it, and approached the body. He eased around until he could see the face of the warrior. The eyes were closed.

"He doesn't look any older than you or me," he said.

"Is he dead?" Skeeter got down from his mount, tying his reins to the same mesquite sprig Jay Blue had used as a hitching post.

"I can't tell."

Skeeter shuffled up beside Jay Blue, both of them covering the Indian with their revolvers. "I think he's breathin'!"

The Indian groaned—a weak, sorrowful lament. The boys scooted a foot back, as if they had heard a rattlesnake.

"Careful," Jay Blue ordered. "He might just be playin' possum."

"Well, if he is, it's a damn fine act. There's possum blood everywhere."

"What should we do?" Jay Blue said, expecting any second to find himself filled with arrows from an ambush.

"I don't know!"

"Well, let's look at the choices. We can put him out of his misery, and he'd never know what hit him. We could just ride off and leave him to the buzzards. Or we could try to help him."

"What would the captain say to do?"

Jay Blue thought about that for a moment. "He'd say to do the honorable thing. Doesn't seem to be much honor in killing a man who's already half dead."

Skeeter nodded.

Jay Blue put his pistol away. "No honor in abandoning a man to die, either."

"So how do we help him?"

"Water," Jay Blue said. He turned to his mount and fetched his canteen from his saddle. "Put your gun away, Skeeter. Prop him up a little, and I'll pour some water in his mouth." He pulled the cork stopper.

The warrior groaned when Skeeter lifted his shoulders, but offered no resistance.

"Tilt his head back a little." Jay Blue poured a few drops of water on the warrior's cracked lips. The Indian's tongue came out to lick up the moisture, so he poured more. Clumsily, the wounded man swallowed the water. His eyelids began to flutter.

"Maybe he ain't so dead after all," Skeeter suggested.

Just then the warrior's eyes flew open wide.

"Oh, shit," Skeeter said.

The warrior glanced at the faces of Jay Blue and Skeeter, then down at the grip of the Colt in Jay Blue's holster. His hand grabbed the revolver, but Jay Blue was quick to drop the canteen and take hold of the warrior's wrist.

"Watch out, Jay Blue!" Skeeter had sprung to his feet and now drew his own pistol.

"Don't shoot him! He's weak. I can handle him."

With these words, the Indian eased his struggle and grimaced in pain, shutting his eyes tight.

"*Somos amigos*," Jay Blue said, knowing the Comanches had learned to speak Spanish long before English-speaking white men moved onto their ranges.

The warrior's eyes opened again. He let his hand fall away from the pistol grip. His voice came out in a gravelly groan: "Water." He looked at the canteen, half its contents having spilled on the ground in the scuffle.

Jay Blue motioned to Skeeter, who put his gun away and lifted the wounded man as before. The Indian drank, paused to catch a few short breaths, then drank some more.

"What's your name?" Jay Blue asked.

"The Wolf."

"Where'd you learn English?" Skeeter asked him.

"Missionaries. School."

"Who shot you?" Jay Blue said.

"Cowboys. Buffalo soldiers. Many people dead. Warriors. Mothers. Dead. Chief dead."

"They say your people killed a white man. I saw him. Lots of arrows stuck in him. Scalped."

The Wolf shook his head. "Not my people. We come to hunt. The arrows Comanche, but not alive Comanche. The chief tell me."

"He told you what?"

"*Ghost* arrows," the Wolf whispered.

"Looked like real arrows to me," Skeeter said.

The Wolf angled his eyes toward Skeeter. "Real arrows. Made by ghost."

"He's delirious," Jay Blue said. "He needs medicine."

The Wolf seemed to be fighting to keep his eyes open. Then his hand reached out and grabbed Jay Blue's wrist with more strength than expected. "Ghost arrows," he insisted. "My people not kill white man." The grip loosened around Jay Blue's wrist, the eyes closed, and the Wolf slipped back into unconsciousness.

"What the hell was that all about?" Skeeter said.

"I don't know. But, whatever it was, he sure as hell meant it." Jay Blue sighed. "One of us has to stay with him. If he lives, he'll need more water. He might even get hungry. I'll stay if you don't want to, Skeeter."

Skeeter shook his head. "I'll stay."

Jay Blue nodded. There was nothing to argue about. It was just as dangerous to ride alone as it was to stay alone. "I'll be back in twenty-four hours. I promise. If he dies, just head home."

They took Jay Blue's bedroll from his saddle and spread his blanket on the ground next to the Wolf. They lifted him onto one side of the blanket and folded the other side over him to keep him warm. Jay Blue rode to the nearest water hole and filled his canteen with clear spring water. He would leave both canteens with Skeeter and the Wolf. They started a fire, just large enough to boil some beans, flavored with bacon, should the patient gain enough strength to eat.

They devised an escape plan. Skeeter's mount was tied securely down in the timber, whence Skeeter could run through the brush should he get attacked while waiting for the wounded Indian to die.

"Don't worry, Skeeter. By the sound of things, the army has run the Indians clean out of the country. Or killed 'em all."

"Right. Nothing to worry about now but that ghost warrior."

"Don't put any stock into that crazy talk. Comanches are superstitious to begin with, and he was probably hallucinating because of all the blood he lost."

Skeeter sniffed aside his concerns and forced a smile. "You better get going."

Jay Blue nodded and gave Skeeter an encouraging slap on the shoulder. He mounted, smiled at his friend, and reined his pony to the east.

But, in spite of his words of encouragement to Skeeter, Jay Blue couldn't help putting some stock into what the Wolf had said. Not that he believed in ghosts. But, *someone* had killed that man he saw shot full of arrows at the fort, and Jay Blue's instincts told him to believe the Wolf when he said his people had had nothing to do with it. The resolve in the Wolf's voice had made him think that the warrior actually believed a ghost was responsible.

So, who *had* killed that stranger? Whoever it was had likely fomented an Indian uprising because a handful of souls from that Comanche band had probably survived the cavalry attack. They would take word of the massacre back into *Comancheria*. Comanches lived by the code of revenge. This wasn't over. Scalps would peel.

20

TRYING TO KEEP UP with Poli and Tonk as they dodged and ducked brush and timber would ordinarily have made great sport, but right now Hank was too anxious about his boys to take much pleasure in the excursion. They rumbled across hills, creeks, and prairies in the direction of the flock of vultures for ten or twelve minutes before Poli pulled up at a vantage point.

"Look!" the foreman said, pointing.

A rider leading a horse had just come out of a tree line a rifle shot away. At a glance Hank knew that it was Jay Blue, trailing the Kentucky mare. He whistled through his teeth, and saw his son react.

"Good job, Poli!" He gripped his foreman's shoulder with gratitude before spurring his winded mount ahead to meet his son. His relief was tempered only by a nagging concern over Skeeter, who was nowhere in sight.

"Son!" he cried, coming within earshot.

"Daddy! Am I ever glad to see y'all!"

"Son, where's Skeeter?"

"He's okay. Not far back."

Hank's relief came out in a weary groan. He got down to loosen the cinch on his still-heaving mount. Poli and Tonk did the same.

Jay Blue stepped down to their level out of respect and gestured with pride toward the Thoroughbred. "We got the mare back! And that ain't all!"

Hank turned away from his saddle and stalked toward his son. "Jay Blue, I don't care about the damn mare." He took the boy in his arms and hugged him roughly, slapping his back as if putting out a fire. "I thought you'd been killed a dozen times by now."

"You're not gonna believe it, Daddy. We caught the Steel Dust Gray, and we found a wounded Indian! That's why I left Skeeter behind!"

"Slow down, son. Tell me what the hell you've gotten yourself and Skeeter into, and give it to me straight."

As he shook the saddle kinks out of his legs, Hank listened to Jay Blue tell what had happened since he skipped guard duty.

"We didn't know what else to do with the Wolf," Jay Blue finally said.

"You did the right thing."

"I think he told me the truth. His camp had nothin' to do with scalpin' that drifter. He said the arrows in the man were *ghost arrows*. What do you think he meant by that?"

"I know exactly what he meant," Hank said. "The killer who murdered and scalped that drifter, Wes James, seems to have come back from the dead."

Jay Blue and Poli looked at each other, puzzled.

"Huh?" Tonk said.

Hank immediately felt foolish for having brought it up. It was the last thing he wanted to talk about. "It's a long story. We'll get into that later if we have to. For now, here's what we're gonna do: Poli, you'll go stay with Skeeter and the wounded warrior overnight. Son, you and I and Tonk will ride to town to get some medicine for that Indian. Tomorrow, Tonk can accompany you back here."

"I need to get supplies for Mr. Hayes, too. Skeeter and I promised we'd deliver the stuff to his cave, and to the corrals where he's breaking that stallion."

Hank frowned. "You boys don't need to be out here ridin' around with Indian trouble brewin'."

"We gave our word. You've got to let us."

Hank started to argue the point, but caught himself before he spiraled into another outburst of hotheadedness. He sighed. "Alright . . . I've been thinkin' about this, son. This ain't easy for me to allow, but I reckon you're old enough to make your own decisions.

Hell, when I was your age, growing up back in Tennessee, I'd spend months at a time in the wilderness, so I guess you're a chip off the old block. You go help that mustanger, like you promised."

Jay Blue beamed. "We'll be careful, I promise. But what about you? You've got something on your mind. I can tell."

Hank nodded. "I may be retired, but I've still got some Rangerin' left in me. I aim to find out what's behind these so-called ghost arrows." He turned to tighten the cinch on his saddle, his mount having recovered from the gallop. "We've got the rest of the day and most of the night to talk about it on the way to town, son. I hope you're ready for some tall ridin'."

Jay Blue smiled. "Yes, sir!"

Hank mounted, then turned to his foreman. "Poli, don't let Skeeter shoot you when you find him. He's liable to be a mite jittery."

The riders arrived at Luck in the night, stabled their horses at Gotch Dunnsworth's livery, and collapsed on hay piles to sleep for a few hours. At daylight, they ate breakfast at Ma Hatchet's Inn and Café. Taking a look at Jay Blue's ripped and trail-soiled clothing, Ma Hatchet insisted on preparing a bath for him.

Hank went down to Sam's store to buy his son a new change of clothes.

"Damn, son," Hank said, looking at the bathwater his son had stepped out of. "You had more Texas on you than a pack of javalinas."

Next, they went to Doc Zuber's office to obtain some medicine for the Wolf. After Jay Blue described the warrior's wound to him, Doc Zuber gave him a piece of an aloe vera plant to use as a topical treatment to fight infection around the entry and exit wounds. Then he reached for a bottle labeled Darby's Carminative.

"You won't tell anybody we're nursing a wounded Indian out there, will you, Doc?" Jay Blue asked.

"Every vord spoken in my examination room is confidential," Zuber said in his thick German accent. "It's my duty to treat all human beings, no matter their race. I vill tell no one of the voonded varrior."

"How much of this stuff should I give him?"

"A shot every day for pain and internal damage. But only one shot a day! This is laudanum. Made from opium. It's highly addictive."

Jay Blue thanked the old doctor. The Tomlinsons then paid the medical bill and stepped out of the office onto Main Street. Hank pulled his watch from his vest.

"It's past noon, son. Let's have a snort of something besides that laudanum."

Jay Blue grinned. "I wouldn't mind an eye-opener."

Walking down the street, Jay Blue began to notice a certain commotion gathering in his wake. Faces peered through windows. Doors shut behind them, as a string of citizens began to follow at a respectable distance behind the Tomlinsons.

"I may have let the news slip about your capture of the Steel Dust Gray," Hank admitted. "They're gonna want to hear the details."

"But noboby knows about the Wolf, right?"

"These folks don't need to know a thing about any of that."

Just then, the door to the hotel opened, and Ma Hatchet stepped out, holding Jay Blue's discarded trousers. "Jay Blue, what do you want done with the trail duds you left behind?"

"Throw 'em away, ma'am!" Jay Blue shouted with a casual wave of his hand.

"But burn 'em first," Hank added. "They ain't hardly fit for a trash heap."

At the hitching rail in front of the saloon, one mount stood—a well-muscled sorrel gelding, quite striking in appearance, wearing a finely tooled saddle.

"Good God," Hank said, pausing to gesture toward the horse. "Would you look at that collection of bad ideas."

Jay Blue followed Hank's thinking, of course, having learned all he knew about horses from his father. "Bald face, one glass eye, four white socks, flaxen mane. Gotta be crazier than hell." Still, aside from the color issues, he had to appreciate the way the horse was put together. "Too bad. Looks like a waste of otherwise good horseflesh."

"True," Hank agreed. "Look at the hindquarters on that rascal—built for speed. Long straight legs, deep chest, round feet, fine head. The neck's weighted just right, and ties in perfectly at the withers. Still . . ."

"Yeah . . . I wonder who this lunatic belongs to."

"Let's go find out."

As they stepped in through the swinging doors of Flora's Saloon, Jay Blue feeling as close to equal in stature to his father as he had ever come, he noticed three men standing at the bar. Two were local entrepreneurs who had walked in from businesses down the street. The third man had to be the owner of that bald-faced thunderbolt tied outside.

This man looked as if he belonged with the horse. Both were mature, and in their prime. The man was a six-footer who looked as if he could handle himself, and there was a bit of flash about him that bespoke a warning. He wore his hair long and straight, tucked behind his ears. It fell out of a rather citified black felt hat. His muscle filled out a dark suit with matching trousers and jacket, the latter left open to reveal a silk vest and gold watch chain, not to mention a tooled gun belt with two Smith & Wesson revolvers. Jay Blue figured him for a slick gambler looking for rustics to fleece. Right now, the man had a large smile on his face and seemed to be enjoying himself. He was getting an eyeful of Flora Barlow, but that certainly wasn't unusual.

Flora put everything aside to greet the two Tomlinson men. Hank ordered them both a beer and a whiskey.

"Whiskey?" Jay Blue asked, shocked.

"You've earned it."

The two locals wanted to know about Jay Blue's adventures, so he began to tell the story. But halfway through, two more townsmen came in and demanded that he start over, which he did. Then another few patrons arrived and, in turn, lobbied for a retelling of the story, from the beginning, and then more customers shuffled in . . . It took Jay Blue an hour and a half, three beers, and two shots of whiskey to tell his tale of the rescue of the Kentucky Thoroughbred and the roping of the Steel Dust Gray.

The timing, he thought, could not have worked out better, because when he finally came to the part about throwing the loop on the mare and the attack of El Grullo, the beautiful Jane Catlett just happened to walk into the bar and started her workday by collecting all the coal oil lamps from the saloon. Certainly this story would impress her, he thought, so he made sure he told it loud enough for everybody in the saloon to hear, especially Jane. The pleasant hum of beer and whiskey in his head made the story sound pretty remarkable to him, and the faces of the men in the bar seemed to reveal the high entertainment value of the account, yet Jane scarcely deigned to grant him so much as a glance as he rhapsodized.

Eventually, the tongue oil got into every man's system, and the talk of wild horses and Indians became a general discussion that included subjects such as the murder of one Wes James, the attack of Crazy Bear's camp on Flat Rock Creek, and the death of Major Ralph Quitman during that fight. Jay Blue, satisfied that he had held sway long enough, withdrew from the nucleus of the gathering with his third beer in his hand.

He found Jane at a table in the corner, polishing the soot out of all the glass globes she had removed from the kerosene lamps that served to illuminate Flora's Saloon at night. Jay Blue could see that she was only halfway through with her task. Finally, he had caught her sitting still so that he didn't have to chase her all over the saloon to get in a flirtatious word or two.

"You need some help?" he said, pulling a chair back and setting his beer on the table. To his alarm, his words came out with a bit of a slur, and some beer sloshed out of his mug from the simple task of setting it down on the table. "Whoa!" he said. "I'm not accustomed to drinkin' quite so many drinks in a row."

Jane glanced up through a strand of stray hair hanging between her eyes and his. "You're a cowboy. You'll get used to it. And I don't need any help, thank you. In fact, I'm almost done if you want to go back and join your admirers."

He sat down anyway. "I take it you're not one of 'em."

"I have no opinion one way or the other."

Disappointment fueled his frustration, and he became suddenly very frank with this barmaid he had tiptoed around for months. "Well, just what does it take to impress you, anyway?"

Unmoved, she went back to polishing lantern globes. "My, you're snippy when you're drunk."

"I'm not drunk! Anyway, you're snippy all the time, so you're not one to talk."

She gasped at the comment, but offered no rebuttal.

Jay Blue saw that she was down to two lantern globes, and she was now cleaning with a fury, so he thought he'd better patch this situation up fast, if he didn't want to leave town with a bad feeling in the pit of his heart.

"Look, Jane, I didn't really come over here to help you. I came to ask you for *your* help."

"A Tomlinson asking someone else for help?" Then she softened a bit. "Help with what?"

Conspiratorially, he looked over both shoulders. "I can't tell you, unless you promise you can keep a secret."

"Are you kidding? I could ruin half the men in town with what I've overheard in this place. Of course I can keep a secret." She was polishing the last globe.

Jay Blue leaned in close. "I've got the Wolf."

Her eyes narrowed. "What?"

"The Wolf. He's a warrior wounded in the fight with the buffalo soldiers. Skeeter and I found him, half dead. I'm taking some medicine back out to him, trying to save his life."

For a moment, her mouth hung open, breathless. "So, how can I help?"

"First of all, don't tell anybody."

"I won't!"

"I need evidence. I have reason to believe that the Wolf's people had nothing to do with killing that drifter, Wes James. I think somebody faked the murder to make it look like Indians did it. If you hear anything that could help me prove the Wolf and his band were wrongfully accused in this whole deal, it could help us head off an Indian war. If it's not already too late."

Jane looked across the saloon to where Hank Tomlinson and Flora were deep in their own discussion. "Does your father know about all this?"

Jay Blue nodded. "He's trying to find out the truth about who killed Wes James."

"I was here when your father got his first look at the dead body with all the arrows in it. I never thought I'd see fear in his eyes, but I don't know what else it could have been."

Jay Blue nodded. "Something strange is going on. He won't even tell me what it is. Something from his past. But, anything you see or hear, you can tell him. I'll be out there trying to nurse the Wolf back to health. Then Skeeter and I have to take some supplies to Jubal Hayes, the mustanger. But Daddy will be around, and you can tell him if you pick up on something out of the ordinary. Anything."

"Let's start with that guy at the bar. He ain't from around here."

"Not much trail dust on those duds," Jay Blue agreed. "Looks like he came here straight from Austin."

"Maybe he's a gambler."

"That was my thought. Anyway, keep your eye out for strangers like him, or anything unusual. Tell my father anything you know, even if it seems inconsequential." He lifted the beer mug, mopped up the little bit he had spilled with his sleeve, then stood.

"Are you leaving?"

"I've got to stock up on some supplies and get back out there to my patient. I just hope he lived through the night."

Jane put her chores aside and stood. "Well, hey . . ." she said. "I'm sorry I snipped at you about your story. It's just . . . I've heard a lot of stories in here, you know?"

"I imagine." Now that he was getting somewhere, he couldn't think of a cotton-picking thing to say. "Well, I've got to make tracks."

"Okay. Hey, not that I care, but . . ."

"What?"

"Watch yourself out there." Her eyes met his briefly, then fell bashfully to the floor. She began gathering up the lantern globes.

He tried not to grin too idiotically. "I'll see you soon, I hope." He turned and walked away, leaving the unfinished beer on a barroom table.

21

I'LL TELL YOU THIS MUCH . . ." Hank paused to take a sip from his shot glass. He had noticed someone coming nearer from the corner of his eye, so he looked sideways to find his own son approaching.

"I'm going to buy my supplies," Jay Blue said.

"Put 'em on the ranch tab, son."

Jay Blue slapped Hank on the shoulder the way a horseman would pat a favored mount. "I've got my own tab." He tipped his hat to Miss Flora and headed for the door.

"Come get me before you leave," Hank ordered. He saw the boy wave an acknowledgment of the order as he strode out.

"Anyway," Hank continued, leaning in close to Flora again. "I'll tell you this much about it. Years ago"—he jutted his thumb toward the doors Jay Blue had just set to swinging—"long before *he* was born, there was a string of murders by a renegade Comanche. There were certain men that he *hunted*."

Flora rolled a tumbler of brandy elegantly between her fingers. Her features looked beautiful as ever, but her brow had just become quite serious. "What men?"

"Rangers. And not just any rangers, but four men from a specific company. My company. This renegade killed three of my best friends."

Flora gasped. "Why, Hank? What did he have against you and your friends?"

"It's a long story. I don't even want to dredge it up if I don't have to."

Flora was curious, but respectful. "This renegade—what was he called?"

"We never knew his real Indian name but we dubbed him Black Cloud, because that's the way he hung over us, waiting to strike like lightning." Hank threw half a shot of whiskey past his teeth, shook off the old memories, and composed himself. "Anyway, Flora, this buck had a certain way of making his arrows. The craftsmanship was the finest I ever saw. The markings in red and black paint were typical Comanche designs, but he always used the exact same patterns. You could tell the same hand had made all the arrows. The dogwood was straight as a guitar string; the feathers trimmed just so, fastened expertly with sinew; the war points were filed from barrel hoops, weighted just right, sharp as razors. He was an artist. He had a flare. A signature."

"Whatever became of him?"

Hank smiled. "I went huntin' for *him*. We had a fight way up on the Concho. He put one of those arrows in me." Hank flinched and rubbed the shoulder where the old wound still galled. "But I shot him up pretty good, and he rode off wounded. I was bleedin' bad enough that I couldn't chase him down. But he was never heard from again after that, and I always figured he'd died of his wounds."

"But you think he's back, don't you? You think the arrows found in Wes James's body were made by Black Cloud."

Hank gritted his teeth. "I'm not sure yet. It was so long ago, Flora. The arrows *could* be the same. I got a hunch the moment I laid eyes on 'em. But . . ."

"What?"

"There's a way to be sure. I kept the arrow he shot into me, but I'll be damned if I can remember where I put the thing after all these years."

"I do that all the time. Last week, I found a hundred dollars I had squirreled away in a snuff jar so that I wouldn't forget it. Well, I forgot it."

"Exactly. Maybe I *wanted* to forget where I put that damned thing.

But if I could find it now, I could compare it to the arrows Sam pulled out of Wes James, and I could be sure of what we're dealing with here. I've been racking my brain trying to remember where I put it."

"I'll help you look."

Hank put his sandpaper palm over Flora's soft knuckles, and smiled at her. No woman had graced his home since the death of his wife. Emilie's portrait was still on the fireplace mantel. "Thank you, Flora, but I need you here. You might see or hear something funny."

She looked a little disappointed, but quickly covered it. "Funny, like that stranger at the bar?"

"He looks a little funny, alright, but not as funny as his horse."

Flora smiled. "Well, you know I'll help you any way I can. And, speaking of overhearing things . . . I hate to tell you this, Hank, but you may be too late to learn anything from Flat Rock Creek."

"What do you mean?"

"I gather from talk in the saloon that a group of yokels rode out there while you were gone and picked up all the souvenirs they could carry away in their saddlebags and spring buggies."

Hank snorted his chagrin. "Doesn't take the buzzards long to smell death, does it? I'll have to put off lookin' for that old arrow Black Cloud stuck in me. I better get out there, sniff around before all the sign gets too cold."

Flora turned her hand and interlaced her fingers with Hank's. "Be careful. If it is Black Cloud . . ."

"I know. If it's him, he's come for me."

By the time Jay Blue finished purchasing his mustanging supplies, Tonk had woken from his nap to help him secure the provender on the pack saddle. Then Jay Blue went to the saloon to tell his father he was ready to ride.

"You and Skeeter have got to stick together, son. I don't want anybody out there ridin' around alone. It's too dangerous right now."

"Yes, sir, I know."

"Now, of an evenin', find a thicket somewhere and make your camp on the south side of it—"

"I know, so if a blue norther should happen to blow in, we'll have a windbreak."

"Right. And, at the end of a day on the trail, if you come to a river, or even a creek—"

"I know, go ahead and cross it, and camp on the other side, in case a flash flood makes the creek rise overnight. You've taught me everything, Daddy. Don't worry."

Hank allowed himself to smile at his son. He gave him a hug, then said, "Now get the hell out of town, you saddle tramp, but take a little Luck with you."

Jay Blue reached down, scooped up a parcel of dirt from the street, and sprinkled it into his shirt pocket. "I always do." He mounted and nodded at Tonk.

Hank watched his boy ride out of town with Tonk, the pack mule following behind, and thought about the day he decided that a town at the confluence of the Pedernales and Colorado would save him a lot of miles riding into Austin for supplies. He had a main street surveyed out of land he owned, staked out lots, dug a well to prove sweet water could be had, and advertised the lots for sale cheap in the Austin newspaper.

"What are you gonna call it?" Jay Blue had asked. "Tomlinson?"

"No, son," Hank replied. "I'm going to name it after a lady."

"My mama?"

"In a way, yes. She was the luckiest thing that ever happened to this ol' Ranger. She was my Lady Luck. I'm gonna call the town Luck, Texas."

They were standing on what would soon become Main Street. "Well, then," Jay Blue said, "looks like we're sure enough in Luck now."

Hank laughed. "Wherever you go, you're either in Luck or out of Luck, son."

Watching his son—now grown up and riding away—he prayed for the former. He wasn't a very religious man; he rarely prayed, thinking it selfish. Yet now—silently but sincerely—he asked for the safety of his only blood son.

Feeling the daylight fast slipping away, Hank stepped into Gotch's livery stable and saddled a fresh mount Gotch provided. Riding out of the livery, he was surprised to see the stranger from the saloon, sitting on the bald-faced sorrel gelding, waiting for him in the street.

Hank squinted curiously. "Can I help you with something, mister?"

"I believe you can," the man said, a touch of arrogance in his voice.

"Well?"

"You can guide me to the place where the dead man was found."

Hank frowned. "What makes you think I'd know where the dead man was found?"

He shrugged. "You're Captain Hank Tomlinson."

"And just who might you be?"

"You may have seen the name Max Cooper in the newspaper. I'm a writer for the Austin *Daily Statesman*."

Hank nodded. "The statewide police beat. I've read your stories with interest." He looked at the gun belt. "Since when do newspaper reporters carry?"

"Just a precaution. I've heard about the Indian trouble. So, would you mind guiding me to the crime scene?"

Hank shrugged. He had to admit he liked seeing his own name in print. "Why not? Just so happens I'm heading that way for a look-see myself."

"So, you *do* know where the man was murdered?"

"Not exactly, but I know from hearsay it was on the top of Shovel Mountain, and the top of Shovel Mountain is not that big. We'll find evidence."

"I'd be obliged."

They rode straight toward Shovel Mountain at a fast trot. Hank had to admire the way that flaxen-maned gelding covered ground.

Still, four white socks? A bald face and a glass eye? Deep down that sorrel had to be loco.

"You find those Smiths reliable?" Hank asked.

Cooper shrugged. "They're light and fast. They load easier and quicker than a Colt."

"Fast, maybe, but they won't stand up to rough use on the frontier like a good ol' hog-leg Colt."

"I'm not much of a frontiersman," Cooper admitted. "I cover crimes in the settlements."

"Have you ever used those things?"

"I was a police officer in San Francisco, California, for six years. I found occasion to use them."

Hank nodded and quickened the pace. They didn't speak again on the ride to Shovel Mountain. Surmounting the flat top of the landmark, Hank pulled rein, glad for his horse's sake that the climb was over.

"We'll crisscross the mountaintop in a grid pattern," he suggested. "It's a standard search technique." He was gratified to see Max Cooper pull a pencil and a notepad out of a pocket. He could already see his own quotes in black and white.

Hank searched the mesa until he found himself looking over the ashes of a burned-out fire. He got down and dropped his reins, knowing the well-trained saddle pony Gotch had provided him with would stay put. He went ahead on foot up to the charred circle of ground. Cooper dismounted, tied his sorrel to a cedar sapling, and followed.

"Stay right behind me, Mr. Cooper. That way, you won't trample any evidence."

"As you wish," Cooper replied.

Hank stood over the site of the small fire. "Here's the question, Mr. Cooper: Why a fire? Why here?"

"You tell me," Cooper suggested.

"My guess: a branding. Wes James claimed he was a mavericker."

"So I've heard," Cooper said, scribbling.

Hank pointed. "Here are Wes's boot prints." He could virtually see Wes rise from his squat by the fire. "He walked to the left. There—

that's where it happened!" The blood had turned black, staining the stalks of grass that were still flattened from where the body weighed them down. Next to the blood-caked ground, he found another area of pressed-down grass too large to have been made by the body of a man. "There was a long yearling thrashing around here, roped and hogtied."

"A long yearling?"

"A year-and-a-half-old calf," Hank explained to the citified writer. "Now look over here, the length of a lariat away. You can see the hoof prints of a big, strong mount. He's well trained at roping, digging in deep to keep the rope taut."

"The claybank," Cooper said.

Hank glanced at him. "You've done your homework."

Cooper shrugged. "I asked around. What are these tracks over here?"

"Wagon wheels. Jack Brennan and his men from the Double Horn Ranch drove a buckboard up here to pick up the body." He walked carefully back to the place where the body of Wes James had been scalped. "There's not much sign left behind by the scalper," he said, "other than the blood of his victim."

"Why is that?" Cooper asked, taking out a pocket knife to whittle on his pencil point.

"There are still men on the frontier who know how and where to step in order to create little or no footprint." Now he concentrated on the last boot prints that Wes James left on this earth. One had stood on grass, and didn't tell much. But the other—the right foot—had pivoted in some dirt. "He turned to his right," Hank said, thinking aloud. Hank put his own sole on Wes's boot print, and turned, the way Wes had. He heard the thump of the bow string, felt the tingle in his chest where Wes had taken the first arrow. He experienced part of what Wes had felt at this moment, and the feeling was not a good one.

"You alright?" Cooper asked.

"Yeah. Why?"

"You grabbed your chest. Are you having pains?"

Hank frowned at the reporter. "Hell, no. I'm as healthy as your bald-faced pony." He pointed toward the nearest trees in front of him. "The first arrow came from right there. An easy shot for an expert archer."

He bade Cooper to follow him to the place where the slope began to drop away from the flat top of the hill, and the line of trees began. The ground there was strewn with large slabs of rimrock between which the trees had taken root. "The murderer left no footprints," he lamented. "He might as well have been a ghost."

Hank walked back to the place where Wes had died, noticing that Cooper had stayed behind, looking for evidence, as if he'd find something. Again, Hank stood in the last tracks of the dying man, feeling that he had overlooked something. Looking around his feet, he saw that some of the grass beside his right boot had briefly caught fire. He squatted and probed his fingers around the charred grass, and felt something. Cold iron. He lifted the short rod from the grass where it had lain hidden. A running iron.

"Paid the fiddler, didn't you?" He was speaking to Wes.

"What was that, Captain Tomlinson?" Cooper shouted from the slope.

"Nothin'."

Like any cowman, Hank knew a running iron when he saw one. Men had been lynched all up and down the frontier simply for possessing one. Sure, they'd claim that they were maverickers, and didn't like carrying around a bulky branding iron when a sleek running iron fit so much more handily into their saddle pockets. But that was always a pretty sorry excuse, and even more pitiful as a last statement choked out past the tightening grip of a hastily tied hangman's noose. A drifter carrying a running iron was probably a brand doctor. Everybody in cow country knew that.

So, Hank had to wonder: If he reported this running iron, would any investigator come to look into this crime at all? The death of a murdered cow thief? So what? Who would care? Would the newspaper even print the story? He looked up and saw Max Cooper stalking back toward him, so Hank slipped the running iron up his sleeve, unsure as to whether or not he wanted the reporter to know about this little bit of evidence at this particular moment.

"So . . ." Cooper said, the wind whipping his long brown hair over his shoulder as he tucked his notepad into his vest pocket. And then, as if he had been reading Hank's mind, he asked the obvious question: "What do you think became of the long yearling poor ol' Wes James was branding when he suddenly began looking like a human pincushion?"

22

"THAT'S A GOOD QUESTION," Hank said. "Can't say that I know the answer."

"Well, I've seen enough. I'd better get back to the city and pen my story."

"You'll have to go alone. I'm not quite finished here."

"I can find my way, Captain. I paid close attention on the ride out here."

Hank shrugged at the unexpected haste of his riding companion. "Very well, sir. I look forward to reading the article."

Cooper smiled as he mounted the bald-faced sorrel. "I think you'll find that you'll be featured in it quite prominently. You've been a great help." He turned and rode away, his mount switching its flaxen tail.

In reality, Hank was relieved that Cooper had left. He slipped the running iron from his left shirt sleeve, put it in his saddlebag, and turned back to the evidence at the murder site. Cooper's question had been on his mind, too. What had become of the branded yearling?

The animal had left some tracks hightailing it off the flat summit of Shovel Mountain. The critter had not been killed and butchered—at least not at the scene of the murder. The remains of a carcass in the area would have attracted buzzards galore by now. Hank didn't bother to trail the beef far. Those tracks were almost two days old by now. A scared yearling would find some other bovines to herd up with, and its tracks would just get mixed in with theirs until it became impossible to find.

The tracks of Wes James's claybank horse seemed of greater importance, but Jack Brennan's cow-hunting crew had trampled the area so thoroughly while loading the corpse in their buckboard that the claybank's hoofprints were going to be very difficult to differentiate from the general traffic, particularly after forty-some-odd hours.

Right now, daylight was slipping away, and evidence was getting colder over on Flat Rock Creek where Major Quitman's party had attacked the Comanches led by old Crazy Bear. Hank decided to ride straight over and have a look around, even though he knew the souvenir hunters had beaten him to the site of the skirmish.

Once he got down the rough slopes of Shovel Mountain, the way leveled off and he did some pretty tall galloping over the four miles to Flat Rock Creek. He already knew exactly where the Comanches had camped because Tonk had been keeping an eye on them before the corpse of Wes James turned up and created all the fuss.

When he got to the site of the battle, he quickly saw that artifact seekers had robbed the camp of any souvenirs that might have been left. Still, there were some pieces of evidence that collectors cared nothing for. One such exhibit, should Hank happen to discover it, could strengthen the case against the Indians when it came to the murder of Wes James. That would be the skeletal remains of a freshly butchered long yearling.

The fact that the claybank gelding had been found among the Indians was damning enough. But the remains of a dead yearling that could be back-trailed in the direction of Shovel Mountain would prove much harder to explain away.

So, Hank rode over the blood-stained and cartridge-strewn ground, looking for beef bones, a piece of cowhide, a hoof, a horn, or anything else that could help him place the yearling here—the long yearling that Wes James had been branding just before the first of several razor-sharp arrow points ruined his evening. Hank circled out some distance and looked in hidden places, in case the Indians had tried to get away with the butchering in secret. He didn't find so much as a spare rib.

He did find a possum tail, a jackrabbit's ear, and a roasted turtle shell. The turtle especially was way down the list of palatable fare in

Comanche culture, while possums and jackrabbits were not exactly delicacies to a people who prayed to the spirits to bring buffalo, deer, antelope, and black bear to their meat poles. It seemed to Hank that this hunting trip of Crazy Bear's had not been a very successful one, and that the Indians had been reduced to near-starvation conditions.

If they had caught a white man branding a steer, and killed him, they would have killed the steer, too, and eaten it.

There was enough daylight left to trot over to Fort Jennings, so Hank took advantage of it. After checking in with the perimeter guard, he rode past the sutler's store, which doubled as a saloon. Hank recognized First Sergeant July Polk relaxing in a chair outside of the store. He angled toward the store and stepped down.

"Evenin', First Sergeant," he said politely.

"Captain Tomlinson." Polk rose from his chair, which had been leaning against the log wall, and stepped away from some other soldiers to shake the former Ranger's hand. "Did you find your boys?"

"Alive and well. Thanks for your concern. Has the army sent you an officer yet?"

"No, sir. I'm still the ranking soldier for now. Can you believe that? An enlisted man, the commander of an army post?"

Hank looked around. "No wonder things are running so smoothly."

Polk chuckled. "What brings you back here?"

"Just a hunch. What became of the claybank horse and the saddle found at Flat Rock Creek?"

"They're in the stables."

"Would you mind if I had a look?"

Polk smiled. "Not unless you ride off with 'em. That's a fine hoss, and a pretty saddle."

Hank turned away and mounted. "Obliged. Keep up the good work." He trotted to the stables, dismounted, and took Wes James's running iron out of his saddlebag. He slipped the iron rod up his sleeve so it wouldn't look like a gun barrel jutting from his fist, and entered the stables on foot. He found two privates mucking out stalls under the glare of a corporal. The privates were probably being punished for fighting, for one of them had a busted lip and the other had one eye swollen shut.

"What do you want?" the corporal said as he stepped into Hank's path.

"Captain Hank Tomlinson, Texas Rangers," he replied, offering his hand as he almost unintelligibly coughed out the word "retired!"

The corporal refused the handshake and stood fast. "I ain't got no orders to let nobody in here."

Hank pulled a cheap cigar from the pocket of his jacket and almost put it to his lips, then offered it to the corporal instead. "I just need a quick look at the murder evidence—the claybank horse and the saddle. First Sergeant Polk said it was okay."

The corporal accepted the cigar, shrugged, and stepped aside. He pocketed the stogie to smoke later and said, "The hoss is in that third stall on the right. The saddle is in the tack room past that."

"Thanks."

Hank looked over the stall door at the claybank first. A fine mount, indeed—tall and stout, with plenty of muscle in his hindquarters. He patted the claybank on the neck and went next door to the tack room.

The tooled cowman's saddle was easy to pick out among the uniform McClellans of the cavalry service. It was well made, with plenty of artistic leatherwork. The saddle maker was out of Omaha, Nebraska, but that didn't necessarily mean anything. Wes could have bought this rig secondhand from any odd saddle tramp.

The buckles to the flaps of the saddlebags were undone, and both pockets were empty. He assumed the Indians or the soldiers had rifled through the pockets, taking whatever they wanted. These were not store-bought saddlebags. They were custom jobs not made by whomever had crafted the saddle, for the scrolled tooling on the bags was different from that of the saddle. There was no maker's stamp on the saddlebags. They were slightly oversized, and Hank could just bet that he knew why.

He took the running iron from his sleeve and dropped it into the nearside saddle pocket. Sure enough, it fit perfectly. However, he didn't see or feel any indentions that the iron rod should have made in either saddle pocket had it ridden there mile after jolting mile as its weight settled it into a low spot to which it would naturally gravitate. But this didn't necessarily mean that the running iron and the rig didn't go together. He lifted the saddle pocket nearest to him and inspected the stitching along the back leather panel. There was a spot where the saddle maker seemed to have missed a stitch or two. Prodding at the spot with the running iron, he found that the rustler's branding tool slipped right into a secret sleeve formed between two layers of leather.

Now Hank knew that if he wanted to prove that Wes James was a cattle rustler, he could point to that hiding place for the running iron and convince anybody in the great state of Texas. He wasn't sure that meant a whole lot to his investigation. But he was starting to get a clearer picture of what had happened three evenings ago up on Shovel Mountain, and it didn't involve poor old Crazy Bear, or any of his warriors.

One thing was becoming obvious: Jack Brennan had flown way off the handle when he launched the attack on Crazy Bear's camp. The survivors of the attack would remember him. Hank mused that he wouldn't want to be in Jack Brennan's boots should the Comanches recruit a revenge party and raid the Double Horn Ranch.

23

JUST AFTER SUNDOWN, Jay Blue and Tonk came within earshot of the camp where the Wolf lay wounded. Jay Blue made the bobwhite quail whistle known to all Broken Arrow ranch hands. Hearing the whistle answered, Jay Blue and Tonk rode into the open. Jay Blue saw Poli stand from a clump of bushes and wave the two new arrivals over.

"How did my bobwhite sound?" he asked Tonk.

"Like a white man."

They found Skeeter cooking the last of the beans. Jay Blue tossed him a can of peaches that made him as happy as a kid on Christmas morning. The Wolf was still lying on the ground, covered to his chin, exactly where Jay Blue had last seen him.

"Well, he ain't dead yet," Jay Blue said.

Skeeter shook his head as he used a rock to hammer his knife blade through the top of the peach can. "He groaned in pain all last night. Then he started sweatin' like a whore in church. He won't wake up to eat anything, but we got him to swallow a little water."

Jay Blue took the bottle of laudanum out of his saddlebag. "The doc said to give him some of this stuff. Help me prop him up."

Skeeter pried open half the top of the peach can, but only had time to spear and eat one of the peach quarters from within before he put the can down on the ground to help Jay Blue. "Jesus Cristo, that's good! I'm gonna sit down and eat that whole can this very night, and ain't nobody gonna stop me."

The four men gathered around the Wolf, elevated his torso, cradled his head, opened his mouth, and poured the medicine in. He spit some of it out, so Jay Blue poured in more until they were sure he had swallowed at least some of it.

"That ought to kill the pain or kill the patient."

Suddenly the warrior coughed. His eyes fluttered and opened.

"I brought you medicine," Jay Blue said, speaking slowly, holding the bottle in front of him. "And a horse." He pointed at the extra mount.

The Wolf's eyes followed his finger to the horse, but he only frowned, and groaned, and closed his eyes again.

"You're welcome," Jay Blue said sarcastically. He shoved the stopper back into the bottle neck, and the men let the Wolf lie back down.

The four men held a quick council, and decided there was no reason for Tonk and Poli to stick around when there was work to do back on the ranch. The two older men gathered their few things, wished the boys good luck, and left for the long night ride to the Broken Arrow Ranch.

"Let's get that pack saddle off that mule and cook us up something better than beans," Jay Blue suggested.

Skeeter looked longingly back at the can of peaches he had left on the ground, but decided they could wait a little longer to slide into his stomach.

The cowhands tied the horses at a picket line and led the mule closer to the small fire so they could see to unpack and sort through the provender Jay Blue had brought from the store. He presented Skeeter with some new clothes so he could get out of the grimy duds he wore, and they commenced to discuss the ghost arrows and the murder of Wes James, and Captain Tomlinson's promise to find out who had really killed the drifter.

"Hey, guess who's helping me?" Jay Blue asked.

"That's easy. Me."

"No, I mean back in town."

"I don't know."

"Guess."

"Hell, I don't know. Mr. Collins?"

Jay Blue looked puzzled. "How could he help?"

"He's the undertaker, ain't he? He could be buildin' us coffins."

"No! Jane."

Skeeter seemed disgusted. "How's she gonna help?"

"People talk in a saloon. She listens."

"You should have got one of the ugly girls to help. That pretty one ain't got a brain in her head."

"What makes you say that?"

"She's helpin' you, ain't she?"

"What does that say about you?"

"Shut up."

Distracted by their talk and their camp chores, they were suddenly alarmed to hear hoofbeats. They reached for weapons as they located the source of the noise. The Wolf, more dead than alive, had slipped out of his blankets, crawled onto the spare horse brought for him, and was already fading into the dark, so weak that he could ride only by lying facedown along the horse's neck.

"Shit!" Jay Blue shouted.

"I guess that medicine kicked in. Should we go after him?"

Jay Blue slipped his Colt back into the holster. "Chase a chestnut horse in the dark?"

"Should we fire our pistols and get Poli and Tonk to come back?"

"You want to look like that much of an idiot? We'd never hear the end of it. Anyway, he's already gone."

"At least he didn't steal *our* horses."

"Only because he was too weak to lead 'em, more than likely." Jay Blue shook his head and couldn't help but chuckle. "I thought I was a pretty tough hombre, Skeeter. But that rascal—the Wolf—brother, he takes the prize."

Skeeter seemed strangely distracted. "Wait a minute. Oh, wait just a *pinche minuto*!"

"What?"

Skeeter stormed across camp to pick up the empty tin can. "The son of a bitch ate my peaches!"

Jay Blue started chuckling.

"He ate every doggone one!"

Jay Blue laughed out loud.

"He drank all the juice!"

Jay Blue slapped his thigh and guffawed.

"It ain't funny!"

Hank had left Fort Jennings about sundown and had ridden back to the east. The going was slow until the moon rose, then he quickened his pace to a trot. He was entertaining visions of sleeping in his own bed, but he still had one more call to make before heading home.

He approached Jack Brennan's Double Horn Ranch headquarters with caution. The gang of cowboys who worked for Jack were a trigger-happy lot, and he didn't intend to provide them with any target practice if he could help it. So he held back in the brush for a good while, looking over the rattletrap buildings and sagging corrals. The bunkhouse was dark, and all seemed quiet. A lantern light glowed from a cracked window in Brennan's adobe house.

Brennan had bought this place years ago from a Mexican rancher who some said had been bullied into selling cheap. That old ranchero had built the adobe walls thick for protection against Indian and outlaw raids. Brennan had let the place run down, but the thick adobe walls would still stop a bullet. At length Hank noticed an orange speck glowing on the front porch of the adobe, and knew that Brennan was having a smoke in the fresh night air.

"Hello, Jack!" he shouted.

A mean dog scrambled off the porch and started barking and growling all the way out to Hank's position in the brush.

"Who's that?" Brennan demanded.

"Hank Tomlinson."

"What do you want?"

"Just a visit." The dog was now nipping at the hooves of Hank's mount, making the horse dance.

"Shut up, dog!" Brennan shouted. The cur backed off, its complaints tapering off to a low growl. There was a pause, then Brennan shouted, "Well, ride on in, I guess."

Hank rode to the porch, but stayed on his horse as the dog was still growling and Jack didn't see fit to call it off. By the glow of moonlight, the retired Ranger's alert eyes noticed a Colt revolver lying across Brennan's thigh. The weapon was already cocked.

"Expecting trouble?" Hank said.

"Always. You're too late for supper, or I'd invite you to git down." Brennan picked up a jug of whiskey and took a long pull from it.

"I'm not hungry," Hank said.

"Drink?"

"No, thanks. Where are all your hands?"

"In town gettin' drunk, most likely. What did you come here for, Hank? It ain't like you to visit."

"I wanted to talk to you about Wes James."

"Who?"

"The dead man you found."

"Oh. Is he still dead?" He took a draw on the cigar, the ember briefly illuminating a dangerous glare in his eyes.

"What do you reckon he was doin' up there on Shovel Mountain?"

"He was lookin' at the inside of a buzzard's beak when I found him."

"Did you notice the fire?"

Brennan looked to his right, then his left, as if he might see a flame somewhere. "I thought we were talkin' about Wes James."

"I found a burnt-out fire near the spot where his body fell. A brandin' fire."

Jack shrugged. "I didn't notice. I guess I was just a little distracted by the maggots crawlin' around the part in his hair."

"Yeah, that was some part, alright," Hank had to agree.

"What's your point, Hank? And why the hell do you even give a shit?"

"Wes James was a mavericker, at best. Most likely a rustler. The sign showed that he was branding a long yearling when the murderer killed him."

"Then the son of a bitch deserved to die."

"Whoever killed Wes didn't kill the yearling he was brandin'."

"So what?"

"Those Comanches on Flat Rock Creek were starvin'. They would have killed and butchered the beef. They didn't kill Wes James. Somebody else did."

Jack laughed and picked up the whiskey jug again. "You've taken some loco notions in your time, Hank, but that one beats all."

Hank mulled that last statement over a moment. "What kind of loco notions have I taken, Jack?"

"Spendin' all your money buyin' up land on a free-range frontier. That's crazy. How 'bout adoptin' that half-breed boy, when you already had your hands full raisin' your own? Or sleepin' alone in that big rock house, when you know you could have that fine piece of woman flesh in your bed."

"Go easy there," Hank warned.

Brennan laughed. "Now, don't Ranger-up on me. My point is you have a funny way of lookin' at the obvious, that's all."

"What is the obvious, from your point of view?"

"That's simple. The convenient murder of good ol' Wes James gives us all the reason we need to kill every goddamn Comanche between here and Indian Territory. Those Indians had the dead man's horse! They killed him, and they got what they deserved in return on Flat Rock Creek."

"Did Major Quitman get what he deserved?"

"Quitman was an idiot."

"Word is you started the killin' at Flat Rock Creek by shooting an unarmed Indian boy."

Brennan eased his hand along his thigh until his finger touched the grip of his cocked pistol. "That's a goddamned lie." His voice sounded cold as a spade digging a grave. "I shot in self-defense."

"The Comanches won't see it that way. They're liable to be coming back for you, Jack."

"Any flea-bit Comanches come for me, I'll give 'em some of their own medicine."

Hank had listened to all he needed to hear for right now. "The next light moon's liable to tell the tale, Jack. You take care."

Brennan only grunted, but as Hank reined away, he said, "Hey,

Ranger. I hear your boy and that half-breed kid, Skeeter, went out huntin' the mare you lost. You sure they're not scalped by now?"

"I found 'em. They're alright."

Jack shook his head. "You shouldn't ought to let a couple of runts like that go stumblin' around in the wilderness."

"I taught them well. They'll be fine."

"You hope."

Hank ignored the belligerent tone. He urged his pony to a trot and got the hell out of there, with the dog snarling at his mount's heels.

Hank arrived at the Broken Arrow before midnight and whistled the descending notes of the screech owl to signal the night guard, Long Tom Merrick, who answered the quavering call. Hank met Long Tom at the corner of the smokehouse. He knew Tom liked to sit there on guard because of the view of the grounds the spot afforded. The moon, three nights past full now, was still plenty big enough to illuminate the grin on Tom's face.

"You got company," he said. "She's up at the big house, waitin' for you in the parlor."

"Flora?"

Tom nodded.

"Must be news from town," Hank said in a businesslike tone.

"She looks like good news to me."

"Quit grinnin' like a possum, and see to my horse for me, will you?"

"Yes, sir."

When Hank opened the door, he smelled the flowery scent that always gave him a hint of thrills to come. But, this time, the aroma made him uneasy. Flora had never visited the Broken Arrow Ranch. No woman, in fact, had set foot in this house since the death of his wife eighteen years ago. When he stepped into the parlor, he saw the lamplight illuminating the shapely curves of Flora Barlow as she stood to greet him. She could take a man's breath away. But, with the next blink, he saw the portrait of his departed Emilie hanging on the parlor wall, and suddenly felt very uncomfortable having both women in the same room.

Flora read his eyes. "She was an extraordinarily beautiful woman, Hank."

Hank's eyes darted from the portrait, to Flora. "Thanks. I mean, not that I deserve the credit." He tried to regain his composure. Rationally, he knew there was nothing wrong with Flora's being here. In fact, he should have invited her out here long ago. That made this meeting doubly awkward. He felt as if he were failing both women somehow.

"She was from Germany?"

Hank nodded. "She was a countess over there, but she renounced her title when she immigrated here. She chose democracy over royalty."

"I'm sure you miss her."

Hank pulled his hat from his head. "It was a long time ago."

"I've heard that you rescued her."

Hank shrugged. "She was married. Her husband was killed, and she was carried off by some renegade Wacos and Kickapoos. I tracked 'em down, killed 'em all, and rescued Emilie. We were married not long after that. Her maiden name was Blumenthal, so we named our first born Jason Blumenthal Tomlinson."

"Jay Blue."

Hank nodded. "She died in childbirth with our second. The baby didn't make it, either."

"I'm sorry."

"Like I said, it was a long time ago."

Flora picked up a crystal tumbler of whiskey and glided across the parlor to place it in Hank's hand. "I found the bourbon," she said, almost apologetically. "I know this is a surprise, Hank, but I felt I had to come here."

"What's happened?"

"The ranch hands from the Double Horn came into town. They had one of your beeves with them."

"One of mine?"

"Yes. The brand had been altered. Your Broken Arrow had been changed to a W J."

Hank's eyes shifted. "As in Wes James."

She nodded. "That newspaperman was in the saloon asking questions when the Double Horn crew drove the steer in."

A sickening realization told Hank that he had all but tightened a noose around his own neck. He had led the reporter right to the scene of the murder and told him details of the crime that, in the mind of the typical citizen, only the murderer would know. Now he had a motive to kill Wes. "Let me guess. I'm his prime suspect now."

Flora grimaced, as if in apology. "I poured him a few drinks and acted friendly. I got him to talk a little. He's taken it into his head that you killed Wes James for rustling your stock, and made it look as if the Indians did it to put the blame on them."

Hank rolled his eyes. "Not an altogether ridiculous scenario—I mean, for a greenhorn newspaper hack."

"I'm afraid it gets worse, Hank. You better have a drink."

Hank took an ample draught of the whiskey. "You might as well tell me."

"He asked me to deliver a message to you. He says he knows all about your past, and has known for a long time. His newspaper career is just a sideline, Hank. Max Cooper is only a pen name. He's a lieutenant in the State Police. His real name is Matt Kenyon."

Hank's heart quavered. "Kenyon?"

"He said the name would mean something to you."

"That it does. It surely does."

"He intends to arrest you, believe it or not."

"Now, *that's* a ridiculous scenario."

"He says he's going back to Austin to gather his evidence and get a warrant. We've got some time. Maybe a couple of weeks."

With his past rushing up from behind to bite him in the ass, Hank was suddenly grateful for at least one thing: this beautiful woman who had come to warn him. His hand reached out to embrace Flora's arm, and, to his surprise, he felt no scathing disapproval from the portrait of Emilie. "You did the right thing, Flora—coming here."

Her smile did more to light up the room than the lantern. "I thought while I was here, I could help you look for that old arrow you've lost. It's evidence that could help you clear yourself, right?"

"I need to find that arrow for my own purposes, but it can't clear me. In fact, Kenyon might use it against me. There's a lot you don't know about this deal, Flora. All that arrow can do is tell me whether or not Black Cloud is back."

"Tell me what's going on, Hank. What's this all about?"

"It's complicated, but I'll tell you the short version for now. There were those who thought, all those years ago, that *I* was Black Cloud."

Flora let the thought sink in. "But why would you kill your fellow Rangers?"

"I wouldn't, and I didn't. Like I said, it's complicated."

"What about that policeman's name? Kenyon. What does that mean to you?"

"I rode with his father, Jim Kenyon. He was one of the Rangers Black Cloud killed."

Flora gasped in realization. "Matt Kenyon thinks you killed his father."

"It's a long story and I'd rather not dredge up the past if we can just solve this business without it."

"Let's start in the morning, Hank. I'll help you turn this place upside down until we find that old arrow."

He nodded, then gulped the rest of his whiskey. The lantern light was dying, but he saw no reason to adjust the wick. "Yes, first thing in the morning. Right now, it's past my bedtime."

Flora took the whiskey glass and put it on a shelf. She grabbed his hand and led him out of the parlor and toward the staircase as the light faded on Emilie's beautiful smile.

"Come on," Flora said. "I'll tuck you in."

24

WHATEVER THAT MEDICINE was that the cowboy gave him certainly worked well enough at first. The pain went away, as if by magic, until about the time the moon came out. By then, the Wolf knew that he had made a clean escape, but the pain came back worse than ever, and he felt as if he had torn something apart inside that bullet wound given to him by the leader of the cowboys. The wound was bleeding again, too. He was lucky to have stolen that can of sweet fruit, though, for it had given him enough strength to stay mounted.

But the medicine had made other things happen. Strange things. Visions of ghosts. Dreams of horrible storms. He was having trouble differentiating between what had happened in the real world and what he had seen in his dream world. He had always been told that the two were not completely separate anyway.

Now dawn was approaching, and he found himself riding down into the valley of the big river the Spaniards had long ago named the Colorado. He spent most of his time lying across the neck of the horse, gripping the mane to keep from falling off. He would look up every now and then, wincing through pain that racked him with every jolting step of the pony, to make sure that he was heading in the right direction. Now that the sky had begun to brighten, he could see that he was getting close to the place where the smaller river, called the Llano, joined the larger Colorado. A high bluff overlooked that confluence and served as an easily recognizable landmark that could be seen miles away, even in the moonlight.

He was pretty sure he could make it to that place without falling off. But would he find his band of beleaguered travelers camped there? Had any of them even survived the battle? He knew he was a dead man if he failed to find friends on this morning. He rode closer to the big bluff and saw smoke rising—from the fires of his friends, he hoped. The Colorado turned to the north here, and the Llano came in from the west. The smaller Llano would be easy to cross. He wouldn't even have to swim his pony.

When he got to the near bank of the Llano, he heard the keening songs of the mourners and knew he had found the survivors of his band. They were probably mourning him, he mused. His vision began to blur, but as he rode his horse into the shallow river, he noticed the tops of tepees ahead and saw much more smoke than his small band of refugees should have made. All his people's lodges had been left behind in the attack, so he could only assume that they had met up with some other Comanche people here. Perhaps they would even have a healer in this camp.

As he rode into the broad, level plain above the opposite bank, several warriors and boys spotted him. People rushed to him. He did not know the people of this band, but they knew to help him, taking the halter rope of the pony, holding him up on the back of the horse.

"I am the Wolf," he said. It was all he could manage.

He was led into the camp, where his cousin, Crooked Nose, came running up to him, an astonished smile contrasting against his sad eyes. "Cousin! You live! I could not find you!"

"The others . . ." said the Wolf.

Crooked Nose's smile melted away. "Our chief—your grandfather—was killed. And the other warriors. All killed. Some women were shot by the white men, but they are all alive."

"And the children?"

"Safe." Crooked Nose looked down with shame. "I could not carry the bodies of our brother warriors away when they were shot dead. I left them. I left you. I had to fight on the run, along with some of the women. I should have fought harder, Cousin. I should have died in battle."

The Wolf was lowered from his horse by the hands of numerous warriors and women, and he was aware that he was being placed on a blanket, which was then lifted to carry him away—probably to the lodge of some old man or woman who knew the spirit secrets of healing. Crooked Nose trotted along beside him. The Wolf was lowered to the ground under a large pecan tree, its branches laden with nuts.

A woman brought water, and some pemmican made from tallow, dried meat, and some of those nuts that this band of True Humans had come here to harvest. With help from the woman, the Wolf drank, and ate some pemmican, though the small act of chewing the food almost exhausted him.

"The big white man who started the killing—who did he shoot?" he asked his cousin.

"I cannot speak his name, for he is dead." They both knew the danger of speaking the names of the dead. "He was the one who played the eagle-bone flute."

"Was he carrying a gun? The big white man said he saw a gun, just before he started shooting."

"Maybe he was carrying that flute, but he did not have a gun. As I retreated, I saw his body lying dead. There was no gun."

The Wolf's scowl deepened. "It is well you did not die," he said. "We have both been shamed by those white cowboys, and it is true that we deserve to die, but we have been spared for a reason. We have a chance to avenge what has happened."

A spark of hope glinted in his cousin's eyes. "What will we do?"

"Pray that I live, Cousin. For if I do, I am going to seek spirit medicine and raise a war party. We will take many horses and eat all the cattle we want. Some warriors may claim scalps. I want only one. The one from the head of that big white man who started the killing at our camp. I will not rest until he is dead. I have seen this as my duty in my visions. And anyone who tries to stop me will die."

Crooked Nose was looking over him, smiling. "Yes, Cousin. That talk sounds good to my ears. Rest now. There is an old man in this band who can heal the worst wounds. He is coming to make medicine for you. I am going to make weapons."

The Wolf wanted to stay awake long enough to get a look at this old medicine man, but he was so completely exhausted that he drifted off with the morning sun glinting through the branches, the autumn breeze cooling his brow, and the excruciating ache of his wound burning his insides like stones in a sweat lodge.

25

HANK AND FLORA all but turned the house upside down looking for the old Black Cloud arrow Hank had collected decades before. In the search process, Hank took all the books off the bookshelves, dusted them, and replaced them. Flora unfolded and refolded all the blankets, quilts, and sheets. Hank ransacked cabinets and desk drawers, and rifled through armoires and cedar chests while Flora opened all the guitar, banjo, mandolin, and fiddle cases in the parlor, finding only instruments inside.

"Well, it just ain't here," Hank finally admitted, stomping into the parlor from his most recent foray through the china cabinet in the dining room.

"Do you play all these instruments?" Flora asked.

"I play *at* 'em all."

"Where'd you learn?"

"I learned the guitar from a freedman down the road from the family farm in Tennessee when I was a boy. I'm a pretty fair hand with a guitar after all these years. Those other instruments are for the boys, and anybody who visits and knows how to play one."

"You've got three fiddles," she declared.

"Have I only got three? It's a wonder I don't have half a dozen. I've bought many an instrument from broke Rangers and cowboys. Got a weakness for 'em I guess."

"The instruments, or the men?"

"Both, I reckon. Anyway, that arrow isn't here, Flora, and we've wasted half a day lookin' for it."

"I wouldn't say it was wasted. We just got some spring cleaning done a few months early, that's all. Let's go outside and see if your men did any better."

"Well, they'd have come runnin' if they'd have found it," he groused, "but I guess we can go see what they did find."

Hank had put all the ranch hands to work at first light, searching the barn, the bunkhouse, the cook shack, and all the other outbuildings. When he and Flora went outside to check on them, they found that the men had straightened up a lot of clutter but had failed to find the grisly old souvenir.

"No luck, Poli?" Hank asked his foreman.

"A little."

"What do you mean, a little?"

"We found a jug of whiskey in the hay loft that nobody will own up to."

Long Tom Merrick and Beto Canales came sauntering up about then, mainly to get a closer look at Flora.

"You wouldn't happen to have a false wall in one of these buildings, would you?" Flora asked, knowing that almost every Southerner who kept arms had built such a contrivance after the war, when wild rumors held that the conquered Confederacy would be completely disarmed.

"Did you check all the hidey holes?" Poli asked Long Tom Merrick.

"Yep," Tom said, taking a tally book from his shirt pocket. "I inventoried fourteen Winchesters, a dozen Colts, nine Hawken rifles, seven shotguns, three cavalry sabers, and a six-pounder cannon. But nothin' with a feathered caboose."

"A cannon?" Flora said.

"I guess I've got a weakness for things that go *bang*, too," Hank admitted.

"It's just a little cannon," Long Tom added.

Hank pulled his watch from his pocket. "Damn," he said, his frustration in the wasted time clear in his voice. "We'd better get to town. I have some telegrams to send."

Hank didn't travel much by three-spring buggy, but he had to credit Flora's rig for handling a lot better than any buckboard or freight wagon he had ever driven. He hardly felt the bumps at all. She sat on the seat beside him as they trundled toward Luck. Hank held the reins, driving the horse that drew the light buggy. His own saddle horse trailed along behind.

"I like this buggy," he admitted. "I wish things were different right now. We could just be out for a picnic down by the river."

"When we get beyond this little bit of trouble, you can take me for a picnic anytime, Hank. Just make sure it's in a private spot. Picnics make me frisky."

"Flora, honey, I could make a list of things that make you frisky."

"You don't have enough paper and ink." She snuggled against him as they drove at a trot around a sharp curve. "Do you mind my asking about the telegrams you intend to send?"

"Course not. I aim to wire all the brand inspectors I know between Nebraska and Mexico. I need to find out everything I can about this WJ brand—like when it was registered, where, how many head of WJ beeves have been sold . . ."

"What exactly are you looking for?"

Hank shook the reins and tapped the flagging buggy horse with the whip. "I don't know yet. But sometimes when you go looking for an old arrow, you turn up a jug of whiskey, if you know what I mean."

"A lucky find."

"Precisely, Miss Barlow."

When they arrived in Luck, Hank dropped Flora off at her saloon. She sent Harry out to put the horse and buggy away, and Hank walked next door to the livery barn. Flora had told him that the heifer with the WJ brand had been ordered kept there as evidence by Lieutenant Matt Kenyon of the State Police, also known as Max Cooper, crime journalist for the Austin *Daily Statesman*. Hank found the heifer standing in the corral, eating hay, and walked around to her left side to view the brand. Now that he was beyond the reach of the haystacks and the kindling-dry barn wood, Hank took a cigar from his pocket, struck a match on a cedar corral post, and lit the stogie.

Gotch Dunnsworth had been forking hay in the stables when he spotted Hank at the corral out back. He came to join the visitor.

"Howdy, Captain."

"Gotch," Hank said without diverting his eyes from the heifer.

"That State Policeman said the government would pay the feed bill for that brindle."

"Good luck."

"Yeah. That rustler had some nerve, doctoring your brand."

"Yep. Those scabs look about three days old to you?"

"'Fraid so," Gotch mumbled.

"He had a touch. I've seen amateurs make a mess of a poor brute's hide. Some don't even have sense enough to burn the original part of the brand over again to disguise the doctorin'. This Wes James was a professional."

"Professional scoundrel," Gotch growled.

"Now, Gotch," Hank chided, "no need to speak ill of the dead."

"You talk about him like an old friend," Gotch said.

He put his hand on Gotch's shoulder. "Wes and I are gettin' acquainted. He's gonna help me get to the bottom of all this."

Gotch shook his head and scowled. "If you say so, Captain."

"Did you ever see him around town?"

"He stabled that claybank of his in the livery once't or twice't. Bought me a whiskey over to the saloon. Claimed he was headed west to maverick."

Hank pointed the stub of his cigar at the brindle heifer. "Apparently, he liked to maverick already-branded stuff."

Gotch shrugged. "Easier to find than slicks."

"*Easy* can get a man into trouble."

"Yeah, but even an honest mavericker would have made good target practice for them Indians up on Shovel Mountain."

"Those Indians didn't kill Wes, Gotch."

"Damn, Captain! If you pin this on the Indians, you're home free! Otherwise, you're making yourself the prime suspect. The State Police have got it out for your Ranger ass."

"Gotch, I never pinned anything on a man in my life, red or white, black or brown."

Gotch sighed and stalked back toward the stables, shaking his head.

"Come around to Flora's place when your chores are done, Gotch. I'll stand you to a whiskey."

"Now you're talking sense again," he said as he disappeared into the barn.

Hank smoked his stogie and watched that brindle heifer eat her hay for a while, then walked through the alley and up the side street to Main. He finished his cigar while strolling down to Sam Collins's general store, which also served as the telegraph office. Along with everything else he did for the town of Luck, Sam had learned Morse code to become an agent of the Western Union Telegraph Company.

Sam's twelve-year-old son, Sam Junior, was sweeping the floor when Hank walked in.

"You missed a spot, Junior," Hank said, smiling and nudging the boy in the ribs.

"Thanks, Captain Tomlinson." Sam Junior grinned at the local hero.

"How are your lessons goin' at school?"

"I get all A's."

"Good. That way you won't have to push a broom for a livin' your whole life." He looked up at the store owner. "Howdy, Sam. Is the wire up today?"

"Up and workin' fine, Hank."

"Put on your Western Union hat for me, will you? I've got several telegrams I need sent."

"Sure thing, Hank."

26

WHEN **JAY BLUE** rode with Skeeter and the pack mule to Jubal's canyon corral, he found Jubal Hayes inside the large cedar pen with the Steel Dust Gray, making him walk around in circles.

"You're a brave man, climbing in there with that killer," Jay Blue said.

Jubal climbed out over the rails. "I ain't brave, but I ain't foolish, either. We had a good, long talk before I ever set foot in his house."

"Talk?" Skeeter said, as he began unloading Jubal's supplies. "You talk horse?"

"Yeah, I talk horse, coyote, and hoot owl. I talk wolf, mountain lion, and red-tailed hawk. I can even talk javalina, chachalaca, black bear, and leopard cat. And I don't *speak* no rattlesnake, but I *do* understand what they say."

"I just speak Spanish and Texan," Skeeter admitted.

Jubal lent a hand unpacking the supplies. "Did you boys deliver the things Luz wanted?"

"We left the rest of the supplies at your cave and got here as quick as we could," Jay Blue reported.

"And Luz is okay?"

"Yes, sir," both boys said.

"No Indian trouble?"

"Not exactly," Jay Blue replied. He then began telling Jubal the long story about finding the Wolf wounded.

"You know what the Wolf said about those arrows in the dead

man we saw at Fort Jennings?" Skeeter added. "He said those were *ghost arrows*."

Jubal caught both boys gawking at him. "Well, don't look at me. I may be a ghost to them Indians, but the only bow I ever held is the one that goes with my fiddle."

"Who do you think killed that man?"

"I don't know, but here's what I do know. That brave, the Wolf, is gonna survive his wound—them Comanches are tougher than a damn rawhide boot. The Wolf will be horseback again by the time the next light moon rises. You know what that means?"

The two cowboys looked at each other.

Jubal shook his head at the greenhorns. "Comanches believe in revenge. The Wolf is gonna raise a war party, and he'll come back to get even with anybody he thinks wronged him. Maybe against any fool who ain't Comanche enough to suit him. So, we've got about three weeks to get this stud broke to ride—or at least to lead home—before the Wolf and his warriors come back here lookin' for scalps."

"Well, then let's get after it," Jay Blue said. "What do you want me and Skeeter to do?"

"You ever bust a bronc?"

"Plenty."

"Well, you ain't bustin' this one. You dang cowboys are always in a rush to get things done. We'll do this the slow way. My way. We start by walkin' him down in there. There's three of us, so we can take turns and tire him out. He'll learn that we don't mean to hurt him, but that we don't aim to let him hurt us, either. You boys sit here and watch what I do. If you don't watch and learn, you're gonna get hurt."

"Yes, sir," Jay Blue said.

Jubal climbed back into the corral with El Grullo and began teaching horse and horsemen alike.

Visions of a rumbling black cloud tormented him in the agony of what passed for sleep. Not just a gray cloud. Not just dark, like a cloud of the natural world. But *black*. Evil. It shot lightning that became arrows. When he woke, it was the thing he remembered first.

Compared to the frightful miseries of his dreams and visions, however, the world of humans seemed much better now than when he had drifted away. The feverish pain of his wound was gone. He heard chanting, and opened his eyes to find the pleasant drone of the magical noise coming from an old man. A pretty young woman knelt to his other side, washing him with a piece of shaggy buffalo hide that soaked up water. This, too, was pleasant.

The girl noticed that the Wolf's eyes had opened, and she smiled. "Grandfather!" she said.

The wrinkled old conjurer ceased to sing, and looked down at the Wolf. The misery and infirmity of the wound seemed to have been drawn up into the old man, and he looked terribly exhausted. This made the Wolf feel deeply ashamed.

"You have cured me," he said to the old man. "Now you can rest." He fought through his weakness and the lingering soreness in his torso to rise and prop himself up on his elbows. "I am through lying around here like a little baby girl. I am ashamed of myself. Woman, is there food? I am very hungry."

The girl beamed, but the old man only rose and turned to trudge away.

"Great shaman," the Wolf said, "you will have many horses. And robes and lodge poles. Whatever you wish, I will pay it."

The grizzled healer did not reply, or even turn around to look. He vanished into his nearby lodge.

The girl helped the Wolf sit up, and put a back rest behind him so he could lean against it in comfort. His stomach felt like a cavern full of hungry bats. She handed him a length of pemmican stuffed into a cleaned buffalo gut. He bit off a huge chunk and chewed it voraciously. It tasted of rich tallow, dried grapes, pecans, acorns, seeds, and jerked buffalo meat pounded thin. She handed him water with which to wash it all down.

It was strange. He was practically dying of starvation, yet the sight of this girl was more interesting to him than the food. A more beautiful face he could not imagine. Her cheeks were so large and full that she looked like a pretty little chipmunk who had been busy gathering a cache for the winter. Her mouth was straight and strong. Her black hair hung in a combed mane to her shoulders, and shone like her eyes, which danced with cleverness. A golden deerskin dress covered her tastefully, yet revealed the curves of her bosom and hips. Her arms emerged from the fringed and beaded sleeves, well-formed and muscular, yet feminine.

"Tabe Nanika," she said, as if reading his mind.

So, this was her name. It meant "voice of the sunrise," but he knew it referred to the song of the birds heard at dawn. He would think of her as Birdsong. His mouth was full of food, and he could not respond.

"I know you are called the Original Wolf," she said. "Your cousin told me."

He gulped some water. "Where is that cousin?" He tore off another bite of pemmican.

She turned to some other girls working nearby. "Find Crooked Nose!" she ordered in a good, strong voice.

"I will!" said one, leaping up to the task as the other girls laughed at her.

Birdsong smiled. "That one likes your cousin."

The Wolf, feeling more and more original with each heartbeat, studied her as he bolted another bite of the much appreciated delicacy. "Your people are Kotsoteka?"

"No. We are Quahadi."

"Ah, the fierce ones."

"No more fierce than you, from the stories told by your cousin and the mothers you protected."

"I have not been fierce enough. I will ask my spirit protectors for more courage."

"Your cousin is telling everyone that you will lead a great raid with the next moon. He has already won warriors for your cause. Some have sent riders to other bands. You must heal quickly if you do not wish your cousin's talk to make a fool of you."

"My cousin has always been very cautious. He has not even begun to talk about the raid I will lead. And you must watch your own talk about how quickly I heal, or I will pick up a stick and chase you through this camp with it."

Her pretty cheeks blushed and her mouth formed a true smile. It was plain that she liked his bold talk. "You will heal, fierce one."

Crooked Nose came running up, holding on to a new bow he had been shaping. "Cousin!" he blurted. "Are you truly well?" The girl that had gone to fetch him came running up behind him.

"Better than well." The Wolf was finishing the last of his pemmican, and gestured to Birdsong for more.

"No," she said. "You must walk first. You need to visit the bushes."

"I must eat, woman! I have spoken!"

"My grandfather has spoken! He healed you, and he is your elder! When you return from your walk, you will have more food."

The Wolf scowled, but reached up for Crooked Nose's help in rising to his feet. It hurt to move, but not as badly as he had expected. The old shaman had worked wonders with his medicine.

"This girl thinks that because she is pretty, she can speak to me with disrespect," the Wolf grumbled.

"That is true," Crooked Nose agreed. He glanced at the girl who had gone to fetch him. "But there are other pretty girls in this camp, so she should not act so proud. Come, Cousin, I will help you to the bushes."

The Wolf shook off his cousin's hand. "If I fall, pick me up. But do not help me any more than that. I am tired of being a disgrace to the True Humans. Very soon, I will be ready to fight."

He stepped gingerly away from the place where he had sweated out all the evil, and looked over his shoulder to see those two pretty Quahadi girls standing there, smiling, watching him and his cousin walk away. "I always thought I would take a Penateka girl for my first wife," he said. "But these Quahadi girls . . ."

"They are bad about being mouthy," Crooked Nose observed. "We must make them good with Penateka seed."

The Wolf smiled. "I like that idea. First, we will bring them scalps to see how well they dance. Then we will make them good with our seed."

27

THEY CAME FROM roving bands of Penateka and Quahadi, Kotsoteka and Yamparika. Some brought allies of Kiowa and Cheyenne. Even a few of the northern Noomah people had ridden all the way from the snowy ranges, for the news had spread far across the plains and mountains of a young Comanche leader and the promise of a raid on the Tejanos like the elders remembered.

Some were veteran warriors who preferred death in battle to life on a reservation. Some were youths who had yet to steal a horse, count a coup, or take a scalp. But all had heard of the bravery of one called the Original Wolf, who had vowed vengeance for the murders of a great chief and many of his followers.

The Wolf had spent long days on the mountain that looked over the confluence of the two rivers. There, he could watch for enemies, chant to the spirits, send his prayers up to the Shadow Land on the smoke from his pipe, and renew his strength with fresh meat and pemmican brought up to him from below by the shaman's granddaughter, Birdsong. He could also see the new recruits ride into the camp between the rivers. Every day more arrived, in ones, twos, and threes. His wound was still sore, but he would be ready.

He knew it was time to speak in council, so he came down from the bluff and sent his cousin through the camp to spread the word. All the warriors who had come to fight filed into the biggest lodge in camp, entering by rank behind the Wolf, spiraling inward until the lodge was like a hollow tree full of bees. The lower hides of the tepee were rolled up so still others could gather around the sacred council lodge and listen outside.

Tobacco was stuffed into a pipe, prayers were sent up the smoke hole to the guardian spirits of the Noomah warriors. The drum ceased, and the Wolf stood. He paused for a long moment, feeling the excitement in the middle of this circle of brave souls. Finally, he spoke:

"While I was wounded, I fell into a sleep from which I could not wake, and I rose from the earth and drifted on the border of the Shadow Land. The spirits spoke to me, telling me what I must do. Those who wish to follow must do as I say, or the spirit powers guiding us on our raid will blow away in the wind like the leaves that are falling from the trees in this camp.

"I followed a peace chief to this country. You have heard about the big white man who started the attack on our party. You have heard about the return of the ghost arrows. Many of you know of a ghost who lives in a canyon not far from here. You must know that, in addition to our enemies, there is evil looking for us here, and you should not ride with me on this raid unless you ride with your own spirit guardians."

The Wolf paused to look into the eyes of the warriors, for doubt, for cowardice, for suspicion. He saw none. These were the bravest of the brave. Each had sought his own medicine, chanted to his own spirit protectors, and prepared his own weapons. No man in this lodge intended to die with white hair.

"Our raid will strike like a swarm of wasps, then like a pack of wolves. The target is the rancho of the big white man—the coward who killed an unarmed flute player and started the massacre at a peaceful hunting camp. There, at that rancho, my spirit guides have told me that we must kill and scalp every man, for they have all murdered our warriors, and some have wounded our women and children.

"But . . . we have enough enemies, my brothers. Do not let greed for coups and scalps carry this raid any farther than our one target." He paused to judge the frowns and grumbles he knew this warning would elicit. "Unless some of you want to sneak around and steal some horses in the night, yes?"

A hum of approval followed this remark, and the frowns turned to smiles.

"Now, listen to one more thing. Evil lives in a canyon to the south of this camp. Sometimes it comes out in the form of the most hideous cannibal ghost you have ever seen in your worst dreams. It has snakes for hair, embers for eyes, and pale flesh with veins of blue blood. The elders have told us about it for many seasons. Many of them have seen it. If this thing appears to us, the spirit powers of our raid have left us, and we must scatter to safe places and purify ourselves in sweat lodges.

"I believe this thing is the spirit of a dead warrior who turned evil. It shoots lightning bolts that turn into arrows, and those arrows have brought all the trouble upon us here. Some who look upon those arrows turn evil and take the dark trail—the soldier chief and the big Tejano. Others look upon those arrows and remain good. Like my cousin, Crooked Nose, and me.

"We cannot kill this thing, for it is already dead. But we must kill the men who have been sickened by its hatred—the big ranchero and his men. It is an old evil. It has been around since the Original Wolf walked like a two-legged. It is part of the battle that began long ago. Who knows when it will end?

"Keep your weapons pure and your hearts good, my brothers, and this evil cannot touch you. Strong hearts resist evil. Brave men receive their rewards in the Shadow Land. You have all been waiting for a proper fight. It comes with the next moon. I am the Original Wolf." He placed his fist over his heart. "I have spoken."

28

POLICARPO LOSOYA slipped into the cook shack after his chores for the day were done, and gave the *cocinero*, Beto Canales, a whistle to get his attention, distracting the cook from the chicken carcass he was butchering.

"Hey, Beto. *Voy cazando para un gran vena'o.*"

"*¿Sí? ¿Donde?*" Beto inquired.

But Poli only grinned and shook his head, wagging his finger at Beto. Everything was a competition among the men on the Broken Arrow, and Poli was not about to let on where he had spotted signs of the big whitetail buck he meant to hunt down this evening. "Mañana, we eat venison," was all he would say.

He went to the corrals, chose a horse, and quickly saddled his mount. He slipped his favorite Winchester rifle into his saddle scabbard. Time was running short if he wanted to get a shot at that deer before dark. He had seen some buck rubs that suggested a real trophy deer would return to them.

Leaving the ranch, he rode up a trail that led to an overlook above the ranch. At the overlook, he glanced back and saw riders moving through the oaks at a long trot. A man wearing a bandito mask rode in front. This had to be the albino mustanger Poli had heard about. Behind him came a fiery gray that could only be El Grullo, with Jay Blue in the saddle! Next came Skeeter, and a woman that had to be the mustanger's señora. Poli was anxious to get a look at that albino man, and maybe trade some mustanging stories with him. Of course, he wanted to see El Grullo up close, too, and congratulate the boys for having saddle-trained the killer. But all that would have to wait until after his hunt.

"That's a damn fine sight," Poli said to his horse. "But wait till they see us carry in that buck!" He reined away from the happy scene back at the ranch and struck a canter toward the place along the Colorado River known as the Narrows, where two bluffs on opposite sides of the river pinched it into a gorge like the wasp waist of an hourglass. The buck rubs he had seen were on top of the near bluff, and something told him that he'd spot that old deer there this very evening.

A few minutes later, arriving at the divide between the Colorado and Pedernales rivers, Poli paused to take in the long, open view to the northwest. He squinted. Good heavens, that looked like a dark line of ink on the skyline! A norther was coming. A true Texas blue norther. The first of the fall. Oh, this was good! A coming norther always stirred the wild animals. They could *feel* it approaching somehow. He could kill that buck and make it home just about the time that norther struck, sometime after dark. This was perfect! He could hang the deer carcass to cool in the freezing-cold blast that he knew was coming. Venison always tasted better and chewed easier if you could hang it a few days.

The boys would be safe and warm at the ranch. El Grullo had come to the Broken Arrow. And Poli was going to bag a trophy buck. This was going to be a damn fine night.

"Where's Daddy?" Jay Blue asked after taking the saddle from Steel Dust in the corral.

"He's been in town for days," Long Tom replied. He and the rest of the Broken Arrow ranch hands had gathered around the corrals to get a look at the legendary stallion.

"We can still get to town before dark and give him the good news. Mr. Hayes has offered to breed Steel Dust to some of our mares in exchange for us helping to break him."

"Took y'all long enough," Long Tom replied. "But he sure seems to handle good."

"Mr. Hayes doesn't believe in rushin' a horse," Jay Blue said.

"Hey, Beto, what's for supper?" Skeeter asked, noticing that the cook already had his apron tied on.

"Fried chicken," Beto growled back.

"Fried chicken! This is the best day of my life!"

"Skeeter, we don't have time for supper!" Jay Blue scolded. "We've got to get to town and tell Daddy."

"I'm hungry!"

"You can get fried chicken in town."

"Not like Beto makes it."

Beto stood a little taller and stuck his chest out.

"You can piddle around here if you want," Jay Blue said. "I'm goin' to town to tell Daddy I rode the Steel Dust Gray home to the Broken Arrow."

"Hey, some of the credit's mine," Skeeter argued.

"If you want to voice your braggin' rights, you'd better ride to town with me." He turned to the mustanger and his woman. "Mr. Hayes, you and Luz ought to come along. My daddy wants to meet you."

"I don't know . . ." Jubal answered.

"Come on, I'll introduce you to some good folks in town."

Jubal looked at Luz and found her waiting hopefully for his decision. He knew she wanted to go. Still, he shook his head. "We left a lot of mares at home that need to be fed tomorrow."

"Daddy keeps a guitar in the saloon. Mr. Collins has a banjo I can use, and there are two or three fiddles in town."

"Do tell?"

Luz started clapping her hands. She hadn't been to a town in a long time.

Jay Blue grabbed his saddle from the top corral rail, still hot from having been cinched onto the back of Steel Dust. "Let's put these old hulls on some fresh mounts and light a shuck for Luck!"

Beto turned back into the cook shack as Skeeter sighed and slid down from his saddle. He stalled as much as he could, but soon the four riders were mounted on fresh horses and ready to move out. Skeeter's stomach growled. He looked hopefully toward the cook shack and saw Beto coming with something wrapped in a cloth napkin, which he handed up to Skeeter. The warmth and aroma pleased Skeeter as much as a kiss from Jane would have thrilled Jay Blue.

Opening the napkin, he said, "*Muchas gracias*, Beto!" There, still too hot to eat, lay two fried drumsticks, golden brown and steaming. "Oh, my God, I can't wait for these to cool off!"

"I rushed them for you," Beto announced.

"Hey, you've got two," Jay Blue said. "Why don't you share?"

"Oh!" Skeeter said, his tone a clear mockery. "You can get fried chicken in town!"

Jay Blue reined away from the laughter of the ranch hands, who were still leaning on corral rails admiring El Grullo. "Oh, just come on, will you?"

As the party started toward town, Skeeter paused between breaths blown from his lips to cool the fried chicken. "Hey, later—when y'all are strummin' and fiddlin' in town—I can play the drum. I got two drumsticks!" He laughed as if he had just said the funniest thing in Texas history.

29

POLI LOPED to within a mile of the place where he had seen the buck rubs days before. He decided to sneak ahead on foot from there. He loosened his cinch, tied his reins, slid the long octagonal barrel of the Winchester from the saddle scabbard, and slipped through the timber "like a wisp of smoke," as the old-timers would say.

He approached downwind of the line of buck rubs, looking for a vantage point from which he could watch and wait for the heavy-horned trophy to show up and work his rubs. It was the way of the big bucks to leave their scent on the trees their antlers thrashed. The smell would attract does ready for breeding, and Poli understood the lure of a female who wanted to be chased.

Coming up on top of the southern bluff that formed one side of the Narrows, he finally caught sight of one of the buck rubs, an easy rifle shot away. The wind was in his favor here, and there was a deadfall leaning against a live oak where he could sit comfortably, his rifle propped on his knees. He settled in and resolved to wait until shooting light had faded, hoping the buck would show.

His world suddenly got very quiet. Gone were the hoofbeats and the crunch of dried grass under his boots. He heard his own breath, the breeze, the occasional birdsong. This was one reason he loved hunting. It was the antidote to the rigors of cattle work. Oh, he loved the noisy business of chasing and roping a wild brute, turning a stampede, or riding a green-broke pony. But here, sitting quietly, waiting and watching, he could hear his own thoughts clearly, sort things out, get right with the Great Creator.

His brow bunched between his thick, black eyebrows when he thought about the scalped man full of arrows, and all the Indian troubles likely to come with the next full moon. But he felt safe here, alone, sitting quietly. He was the hunter, not the hunted.

He smiled when he thought about those boys saddle-breaking El Grullo. He wished he had had time to wait and congratulate Skeeter. He'd have to make a big deal of that tomorrow. Skeeter needed it more than Jay Blue. The rancher's son knew where he fit into the picture on the Broken Arrow. Skeeter was forever unsure. *Mañana,* he thought, *I'll get Izquierdo to tell me the whole story while Jay Blue is not around to interrupt.*

In his reverie, he suddenly heard the scamper of deer hooves—light compared to that of a horse, but running fast and accompanied by snapping branches and rattling stones. He looked right and saw a doe running full tilt in his direction, and behind her the buck, carrying his crown on his head, pursuing with singular resolve. The hunter's eyes bulged at the great rack of antlers waving atop the running monarch's head.

Poli raised the rifle butt to his shoulder, knowing the deer would not see his movement while they were running so hard. Thoughts shot through his head: *One chance! Here he comes! Too much timber! There's an opening!*

But just as he prepared to fire, the doe dodged away from him and dove off into a draw that branched out from the Narrows. The buck followed her, never having provided Poli with a clear shot.

Damn, damn, damn! Every expletive he knew in two languages went mumbling in whispers past his lips. There was only one chance. Run to the place where the deer had disappeared, and maybe—probably not, but maybe—he'd catch sight of them running up the other side of the draw.

He sprinted across the top of the bluff to where he had seen the buck's waving white tail vanish. He slid to a stop and tried to listen over his own gasps for breath. He saw no sign of his prey in the draw below. As he caught his breath, he heard nothing that sounded like scampering deer. But he did hear a cow bellow.

Poli cocked his head. The sound was coming from down in the draw, toward the Narrows. Now he heard more than one cow, just barely audible, but unmistakable nonetheless. Hearing cattle low in cow country was not unusual, but Poli knew the plaintive sounds of beeves the way a mother knew the voice of a child in distress. Those cattle sounded harassed, as if someone had them bunched or penned or otherwise held at bay. The fall cow work should have been done by now. This bore investigation.

He picked his way silently into the draw toward the sound of the bovine gathering. He stopped every few yards to listen. As he crept closer, he smelled smoke and burnt hides, and knew someone was branding. Now he really got suspicious.

The timber was thick down in the draw. Not the kind of place you'd want to work cattle, unless you were hiding something. Slipping from tree to tree, he inched closer, until he could see the cattle milling around. Someone had built a hidden pen down here, the workmanship of the cedar posts and rails ugly, but functional. Inside the post-and-rail construction, hundreds of slim cedar pickets had been fixed vertically to the rails, more as a visual barrier to discourage escape, rather than a structural addition. The cedar picket fence ambled about in a rough oval, its shape and size determined by what little bit of flat terrain there was down in the bottom of the draw. Beeves were bunched tight inside the pen—at least twenty of them, and maybe more.

Inside the pen, on the other side of the cow herd, a mounted man heel-roped a long yearling and dragged it to a branding fire where men afoot flanked and tailed it down, penning it to the ground with practiced holds. Poli couldn't see the men on the ground clearly through the milling herd. The man on horseback was more visible, but a long way off, and wearing a bandana over his face against the thick, stirred-up dust. He decided it wasn't as important to identify the men, and risk being seen, as it was to see the brand they were using. If he could sneak close enough to read that, he'd slip back out of the draw and ride hell-bent for leather into town to tell Captain Tomlinson.

The men at the branding fire released the big yearling they had roped and thrown. It jumped up, bawling and kicking against the sting of the fresh brand. It ran frantically headlong into the fence, trying to break through, but only cracked some cedar pickets and bounced back in. The agitated yearling continued to work the fence line, looking for a way out, moving around the perimeter of the pen.

Good, Poli thought. He snuck close to the pickets, hiding behind them. He removed his hat so he'd have a lower profile. When the fresh-branded yearling arrived on the opposite side of the fence, he raised up high enough to let his eyeballs peer over the pickets and he got a clear look at the brand. An inverted V over a capital T.

He'd never seen or even heard of that brand in these parts.

He shifted his eyes to the left hip of another nearby brute. Broken Arrow! Now, quickly he saw in his mind how the Broken Arrow could be converted to a "rafter," with the T added below. They were rustling the captain's stock and doctoring brands—and on a fairly large scale. He sank safely back behind the pickets and replaced his hat on his head. He began his retreat, watching over his shoulder for trouble as he shrank back into the timber, carrying his rifle in one hand.

Poli heard the commotion of the cattle fade in the distance as he climbed up the steep slope, out of the draw. Confident he had made his escape unseen, he quickened his pace. He climbed up to the bluff where he had seen the deer. Looking around, he saw no one, so he sprinted across the open bluff top, back to the place where he had waited for a shot at that big buck. A thought occurred to him. Thank God he hadn't shot at that buck! The rustlers would have heard him and come gunning for him.

Winded, he slowed to a walk as he came up on his saddle pony, still waiting tied. The mount grumbled at him and shifted nervously. Poli looked around but saw nothing out of the ordinary. The horse must have smelled a coyote or something. They would both be happy to get out of here.

"Whoa," he said, patting the horse's neck and slipping his Winchester back into the boot. He pulled in on the latigo, tightening the girth. The cow pony's nostrils were flared, his eyes rolling. This horse did not like this place. Then, just as Poli finished wrapping the end of the latigo around the saddle ring, slick as a Windsor knot, the horse snorted and tried to shy away.

A look into the pony's eye told Poli he had seen something. He turned, drawing his revolver. His eyes searched, but his ears collected. A strange thump. All he had time to see was the arrow shaft sticking out of his chest, and he knew the point had gone all the way through him and stuck his horse in the withers, right in front of the saddle, for the animal squealed and jumped aside. Still standing, Poli railed against the painful intrusion of the projectile, and cocked his pistol, but another arrow came in a blur. He had little time to glimpse his murderer before he fell back on the ground. The stabbed pony had broken his reins and run away.

Poli knew he was dying fast. Two things occurred to him. He was grateful that he would be dead before he felt the knife scalp him. And he regretted that he would never get to congratulate young Izquierdo for breaking the Steel Dust Gray.

30

HANK HAD SPENT DAYS in town, expecting the replies to his telegrams to arrive. Waiting tested his patience, but the time was far from wasted. He owned or had financed most of the businesses in town. Times had been lean around here since before the war, but he never had any intention of foreclosing on any entrepreneur truly trying to make an enterprise float. So there was a lot of renegotiating to accomplish around town, and there were a lot of grateful hands to shake.

Poli and the rest of the boys were taking care of things back at the ranch, and the fall cow work had been accomplished weeks ago, so this was as good a time as any to linger in Luck, take care of business, enjoy a few drinks at Flora's, and appreciate her warm body in bed with him.

The problem was that no replies to his telegraphed inquiries had come in. In fact, no wires were coming into Luck at all. Not long after Hank sent his telegrams out, some unknown party had removed a long stretch of telegraph wire from the poles somewhere between Luck and Austin. The stagecoach driver noticed it, and reported it, but repairs had not been forthcoming.

Then, earlier this afternoon, the stagecoach brought the mail to town, and the mail included several copies of the Austin *Daily Statesman*. On page two, Hank found an article by Max Cooper. It started by describing the murder of Wes James, then went on to tell how Captain Hank Tomlinson, a retired Texas Ranger who had once been suspected of killing three fellow Rangers, had guided the reporter straight to the scene of the crime and seemed to know far too much about the way the killing had happened. Furthermore, there was evidence to suggest that Wes James had been rustling cattle by doctoring the Broken Arrow brand, giving Captain Tomlinson a motive for killing him.

In summation, Cooper had suggested that if "someone with Indian skills" had faked the killing and blamed it on innocent Indians, then the killer also bore the responsibility for the deaths of Major Ralph Quitman, two buffalo soldiers, and an unknown number of Comanches as a result of tensions brought about by the murder of Wes James.

Hank had slammed the paper to the floor of Ma Hatchet's Café and stomped it when he read that part. Few who read the article would know that Max Cooper was really Lieutenant Matt Kenyon of the Texas State Police, and that he was far from an impartial journalist. Those readers would include judges who could be called upon to produce arrest warrants. Any government-appointed Reconstruction Republican jurist currently sitting on the bench would leap at a chance to discredit a Texas Ranger.

So, feeling time running short, Hank had decided to ride into Austin where he could find a working telegraph and try to collect some information that would help clear him of suspicion before Matt Kenyon obtained a warrant and attempted to serve it. Of course, he knew that the capital was the State Police stronghold, and that he might be riding right into a trap, but Hank wasn't much good at avoiding confrontation. He saddled a horse and rode.

He had gotten almost halfway to Austin when, riding up onto a hill, he spotted the telegraph crew repairing the line. His frustration flared. A wasted afternoon. He didn't even ride up to talk to the repair crew. He just turned around, having decided to go on back to Luck and collect his telegrams in the relative security of his own town.

Now, he paused on the hill above Luck. The sun had vanished behind a blue haze in the west. The sight of the coming norther set his teeth to grinding. Jay Blue and Skeeter were still out there, for all he knew. He rode on into town, left his horse with Gotch to take care of at the livery, and stuck his head into Sam's general store for the fourth time today. "Well?" he said.

"I'm sorry, Hank. I just tried, and got nothing."

"Well, I rode halfway to Austin, and saw a crew working on the line."

"Then I won't leave the store until I get something. I'll stay here all night if I have to. You need to stay out of Austin, Hank. For all we know, the State Police might have been the ones to cut the line, so's to draw you into the capital where they can arrest you."

"The thought had occurred to me."

"Well, then, you just stay put, and I'll check the telegraph every ten minutes to see if it's been fixed."

"Newfangled contraption," Hank groused, glaring at the silent telegraph ticker. "You think it's handy until you really need it, then your enemies disable the thing with a dang pair of wire nippers."

"Hank, maybe you should get out of town. I'll send riders with the telegrams if you want to go back to your ranch and lay low a while."

"I don't lay low. I ride high."

Sam smiled and nodded, as if he had expected no less. "Well, if there's anything else I can do to help . . ."

Hank scratched his chin, his eyes angling toward the back of the store. "Have you looked in the jail cell lately?"

"Not in a couple of weeks," Sam admitted.

The town of Luck had one cell. It was really nothing more than an iron cage bolted to the floor of a little lean-to extension to the back of Sam's store. As town marshal, Sam occasionally had to lock some drunk or petty thief in there, but it was rarely used.

"If the State Police do come to town to arrest me, I might be the next resident in there. I'm gonna check now for vermin and such. An extra blanket would be fittin', too. I feel a norther comin' on in my old bones."

"Extra blankets are on the shelf, and the only key is in the lock."

"We just have one key?"

Sam shrugged. "That's all we've ever had."

Hank passed through the back of the store as a lady walked in the front door to do some end-of-the-day shopping. *Good*, he thought. The lady would keep Sam busy for a while. He opened the door to the lean-to and found everything pretty much in order. The tin bucket that served as a toilet was clean and empty. The iron shelf that served as a bunk had a thin mattress on it, and a blanket.

The cell door was open, and as Sam had said, the key was in the lock. Hank reached into his pocket and fished out a second jail cell key that Sam had never known about. He tried both keys in the lock and they both worked fine. He returned the original key to the lock and took his other key to the mattress on the bunk. Drawing his bowie knife, he used the razor-sharp tip to cut a few of the stitches along one of the seams. Carefully, he slipped the key into the sparse cotton stuffing of the mattress. He knew that the line between lawman and outlaw sometimes became very thin on the Texas frontier. He couldn't have predicted the current scenario, but he had always had a plan of escape from his own jail cell in case it ever came to that.

When he returned to the store, Sam was just saying good-bye to his customer.

"How did it look?" Sam said.

Hank shrugged. "A little dusty. A few scorpions here and there. Better than many a Ranger camp I've slept in on the hard ground with a blizzard freezin' me nigh to death."

"Let's hope you don't have to actually spend any time in there. Surely, if they do arrest you, it'll will be under your own recognizance."

"I wouldn't count on it, Sam. Kenyon seems hell-bent on making a show of this whole thing. It doesn't hurt to be prepared, if you know what I mean."

"I think I do," Sam said.

Hank nodded at his friend, grabbed the brass knob, and opened the door, stepping outside. Just before he slammed the door behind him, that confounded Western Union machine started tapping away like a redheaded woodpecker.

Sam listened to it with his head cocked aside for a few seconds. "It's fixed!"

"I gathered that," Hank replied, still standing in the open doorway.

Sam tapped something in reply and grabbed a pencil he kept near the ticker. "There's a logjam of replies to copy. Most of 'em for you, Hank. This is gonna take some time to get down on paper."

Hank smiled. "Meet me in my office." He pointed down the street toward Flora's place.

Leaving Sam to his scribblings, he angled across the dirt thoroughfare. *Liable to be hock-deep in mud by this time tomorrow*, he thought. That blue norther looked like a bad one, and his knee joints *were* aching. He thought about Jay Blue and Skeeter again, and hoped they'd find shelter, wherever they were. He was almost across the street, and was already tasting some of the good stuff Flora kept hidden behind the bar just for him, when he caught sight of motion to his left, way down the street. In the twilight glow he saw four riders coming in at a trot.

Within seconds, he recognized Jay Blue. After that it was a simple enough task to pick out Skeeter. He didn't know the other two riders, but guessed whom they might be. He took in a breath of sweet, pure relief, and exhaled a world of worry. He could handle whatever might happen to himself with this Black Cloud mess, but if any tragedy ever befell that boy—those boys—he'd go crazy as a rabid wolf.

He stepped into the livery barn. "Gotch! You got business comin'!"

Gotch Dunnsworth stepped out to greet the late arrivals. "I'll be damned," he said, recognizing the boys.

The party trotted up, grins painted on their faces. Jay Blue told of their successes with Steel Dust before they even stepped down from their saddles. They introduced Jubal Hayes and Luz, and Hank thanked the mustanger for helping the boys recover the Kentucky mare.

"This is Gotch Dunnsworth. He'll take care of your stock and your tack." Hank turned to the one-eyed war veteran. "Oats all around, Gotch, and put it on my tab."

"Sure thing, Captain." Gotch began gathering reins.

"I reckon it's time to celebrate now," Hank announced.

"Yes, sir," Jay Blue sang. "We're gonna get something to eat, and then Mr. Hayes wants to show everybody in Luck how to saw on a fiddle, if we can find one."

"He can use mine!" Gotch said.

Hank turned and studied the livery owner. "You own a fiddle, Gotch?"

Gotch started laughing. "Don't you remember? You give it to me back before the war. I never learned to play it much."

"I gave you a fiddle?" Hank had absolutely no recollection of the event.

"There was whiskey involved," Gotch admitted. "It was back in those days . . . You know . . . Well, you've cut back, even if I haven't."

"I'll borrow Mr. Collins's banjo," Jay Blue said. "You've got a guitar in the saloon, don't you, Daddy?"

"Huh?" Hank said, still dumbfounded and embarrassed that he had given away a fiddle in a drunken stupor years ago and forgotten about it. "Oh, yes, son, I'll get my old guitar down from the wall."

"Mr. Hayes can dang near make a fiddle shoot sparks!"

"I'll warn the fainthearted," Hank said with a smile.

"Don't get nobody's hopes up," Jubal said modestly.

"Skeeter, help me with these horses," Gotch said, handing two pairs of reins to Skeeter.

Pride swelled up in Hank as he began to appreciate what his son had accomplished. He extended a hand for Jay Blue, but then just went ahead and gave him an *abrazo.* "I'm proud of you, son."

He realized he hadn't spoken to Skeeter yet, and looked up to congratulate him, too. But Skeeter had already disappeared into the livery barn with Gotch.

31

SKEETER HELPED GOTCH unsaddle the horses and rack the saddles. He rubbed down two of the mounts and stabled them.

"Skeeter, be a hand and throw them hosses some oats," Gotch ordered. "Fork 'em some hay, too. I've got to find that fiddle the captain give me."

Where the hell was Jay Blue while he was taking care of all this?

By the time he got to Ma Hatchet's Café, Jay Blue, Jubal, and Luz were already half-finished with their meals.

"'Bout time you got here," Jay Blue said. "I ordered you a steak." He pointed to a bleeding slab of beef on a plate.

Skeeter didn't care much for steak that rare. "I told you I wanted fried chicken."

"You said not unless it was Beto's fried chicken. You heard him, didn't you, Mr. Hayes?"

Jubal shot a glance at both boys, but just kept chewing.

"I said that so Beto wouldn't get his feelin's hurt. Some folks are like that, you know. They don't want to hurt nobody's feelin's."

Jay Blue threw his knife and fork on his plate and dragged a cloth napkin over his mouth. "Just eat it, Skeeter. I'm goin' across the street to borrow Mr. Collins's banjo." He scooted his chair back and shot upright. He was on one of those tears where everything revolved around Jay Blue Tomlinson.

"Hold on!" Jubal said, taking one last bite. "You gonna leave a couple lookin' like us to walk into that saloon alone?" He made gestures toward Luz and himself.

"It's a nice town," Jay Blue insisted.

"I've been run out of nice towns and shot at with live ammunition. I don't want to go nowhere in this town without somebody named Tomlinson holdin' my hand." He stood, then grabbed the back of Luz's chair with gentlemanly grandiloquence. "Come, my darlin', we're late for the ball."

"Alright," Jay Blue said, his impatience clearly shining through his attempts at being a gracious host.

The three of them left, and Skeeter was alone again. He cut a sliver off of the edge of the steak where it was actually cooked a little, but it didn't appeal to him much. He satisfied what was left of his appetite with some biscuits and butter, some mashed potatoes, and some green beans.

Trying to catch up to the party, he stormed out of the café and saw a light on in the general store. Stepping in, he found Sam Collins furiously scrawling as the telegraph ticker tapped away like an annoying rattle on a buckboard wagon. Skeeter was always amazed that Sam could make sense of that racket.

Sam glanced up over the lenses of his glasses. "Howdy, Skeeter." His pencil point had worn itself dull, but he didn't seem to have time to whittle it sharp. "You just missed 'em."

"Thanks, Mr. Collins." He started to go, but the ticker paused.

Sam looked up and smiled. "Jay Blue told me about saddle-breaking the Steel Dust Gray."

Skeeter threw his chest out a little. "It was sure somethin', Mr. Collins."

"Sounded like it. Were you there?"

The ticker took off again like a branch against a window pane on a stormy night.

Skeeter's mouth was hanging open and his breath seemed stuck in his throat in a way that made him feel that he was going to vomit up that piece of raw steak. *Was I there? I did half the riding!* "You might say I helped," he answered. He wasn't sure if Sam even heard him, for the blunt pencil stub was back to scratching marks on paper.

He stepped out of the doorway and quietly shut the latch. He trudged across the street, and happened to see lightning in the northwest. A cold night was coming. There'd be rain, maybe sleet.

As he stepped up on the boardwalk, he heard banjo and guitar strings plucking random notes, and a bow testing the tuning of a fiddle. Then Captain Hank Tomlinson's voice rose above the others:

"Ladies and gentlemen, I give you the man who rode the Steel Dust Gray! Jason Blumenthal Tomlinson!"

A great roar of cheering voices and applause seemed apt to blast the swinging doors outward as it burst from the saloon. Skeeter stepped up to the doors and peered in over them. Jay Blue was sitting on a table with a banjo in his lap. His father stood to one side, Jubal Hayes to the other. As the cheer died down, Jay Blue lit into a rollicking breakdown on the banjo, and the other pickers quickly piled in with him. What was left of the applause organized itself into a steady beat as listeners clapped along and stomped their feet.

As Jay Blue played full-tilt on the banjo, he kept his eye on that pretty girl, Jane. She finally looked up at him and smiled, though she also rolled her eyes as if that would discourage him.

Well, danged if it didn't look like a load of fun being a Tomlinson right now! Jay Blue hadn't been in such an all-fired hurry to get to town to meet with his daddy. He wanted to spark with that girl. That was the one thing on his mind. And, in the process, he had stabbed his old buddy, Skeeter, right between the shoulder blades and taken all the credit for breaking El Grullo.

"Where the hell were you?"

The gruff voice startled Skeeter so that he whirled, wild-eyed, and found Jack Brennan looming behind him.

"What do you mean?" His heart was pounding at the start the voice had given him. Brennan must have been standing at the hitching rail all along, watching.

"When your amigo broke that stallion."

"I did half the ridin'. It just so happens Jay Blue was on him when he finally quit buckin'. Hell, I was the one who put the first rope on him a couple of weeks ago."

Brennan grunted. "You don't get a whole lot of credit around here unless your name is Tomlinson, do you?"

Skeeter shrugged.

"Well, let's go in anyway. I'll buy you a beer."

All the men in the band looked up when he walked in with Jack Brennan, but the rest of the eyes in the saloon remained trained on the musicians. The Tomlinsons seemed a little puzzled to see him in company with Brennan, but Skeeter just ignored them and angled to the bar.

"A couple of beers," Brennan said to Harry, the bartender.

Skeeter waited for his mug and took it, nodding his thanks at Brennan. He gulped about a third of it—that was the only way he could stand to drink the stuff. When he turned back around, he saw that the Tomlinsons had already forgotten about him. They were watching Gotch Dunnsworth clog furiously on the pine flooring. Jay Blue was only watching with one eye, because the other one stayed glued to Jane Catlett's ass like a fly on a big, round horse's butt.

Good God, he looks ridiculous. He can play the snot out of the banjo, but that ain't enough, is it?

"To hell with them," Jack Brennan said.

"Huh?"

"All high and mighty. You ought to come work for me, kid."

Skeeter took another gulp of beer. "I've got a good job."

"That's all you'll ever have there is a job. You're a hired hand. You think they'll cut you in on their pie?"

"I ain't worried about it." He downed the rest of the beer and handed the mug to Harry.

"You might be straw boss some day, but that's the best you can hope for. You'll never move out of that bunkhouse."

"I ain't got much choice."

"You ain't listenin'. I'm *givin'* you a choice. I don't offer a job to just anybody, and it's a one-time offer, so you better think about it. You come work for me, and I'll guarantee you more than a wage. All my hands have a stake in the operation."

Skeeter felt bloated with all sorts of pressure. He belched, and that helped a little. He took the refilled mug Harry had slid to him on the bar. "I never worked anywhere else."

"And you never will if you don't take my offer."

"I don't know, Mr. Brennan."

"Listen. Tomorrow, while these Tomlinsons are doing whatever they do—struttin' around pattin' each other on the back most likely—you ride out to my place. I want to talk to you about it. It ain't just the job, either. There's somethin' else."

"What else?"

"Come out mañana and I'll tell you."

Skeeter shook his head. "That's a long way to ride."

"Listen, kid. I know somethin' I should have told you a long time ago."

Now Skeeter looked up at the big man's face. "About what?"

"I know who your daddy is."

"Who?" Skeeter demanded.

"Goddamn it, I can't tell you here. I hate music. I can't stand to listen to these sons of bitches make that racket. Only came for a game of poker. Think I'll ride out to the Mexican whorehouse instead. You want to go?"

Skeeter shook his head. "This is supposed to be my celebration."

Brennan threw a coin on the bar. "They didn't ask you into the middle of it, did they? Suckin' hind tit, as usual, aren't you?" He stepped away from the bar.

"But, Mr. Brennan, I got a right to know."

"Ride out to my ranch tomorrow. We can talk there."

"But . . ."

The big man stomped off toward the swinging doors, leaving Skeeter's head swimming with all sorts of thoughts, good and terrible. Nobody had ever told him anything about who his father was. And Mr. Brennan had said, "I know who your daddy *is*," not *was*, as if his father might still be alive. Nobody had ever offered him a job, either. Not just a job, but a stake in the outfit.

He took another gulp of beer. This second mug didn't taste as bad as the first one. The trio had finished playing whatever that first song was, and Jubal Hayes had lit into a lively rendition of something else—one of those fiddle standards, maybe "Whiskey for Breakfast" or "Hell Among the Yearlings." They all sounded alike to Skeeter.

He stood there, an outcast at his own celebration. Over the rim of the beer mug, Skeeter saw Sam Collins step into the saloon with a handful of Western Union telegram slips in his right hand. The hat and wool coat he wore glistened with raindrops and sleet. The norther had struck. Skeeter thanked God that he wasn't still out there sleeping on the ground tonight. Sam waited at the door until Captain Tomlinson looked his way, then he waved the telegrams. Skeeter saw the captain return the wave with a jut of his bearded chin, but he had never known Hank Tomlinson to quit playing right in the middle of a song. Sam tilted his head toward the bar.

"Beer, Harry," Sam said, stepping up next to Skeeter and giving him a familiar jab with his elbow.

"What have you got there, Mr. Collins?" Skeeter asked.

"Telegrams for the captain."

"What do they say?"

"You know I can't tell you that, Skeeter."

"Oh, yeah."

Sam got his beer about the time the song ended, so he started across the room with his mug in one hand and Hank's telegrams in the other. Skeeter chugged his brew and found Harry already had another waiting for him. He grabbed it and followed Sam, intent on insinuating himself into the middle of the celebration whether they wanted him there or not. Captain Tomlinson was leaning his guitar against the wall.

After two songs, the crowd inside the saloon had deigned to forgive the weird appearance of the fiddler, Jubal Hayes, and someone shouted out, "Bear Creek Hop!" Jubal knew that one, so he began sawing away, with Jay Blue accompanying on the banjo while he cast his lustful eyes on Jane. Sam handed the telegrams to the captain.

"What have we got to work with?" Captain Tomlinson asked, feeling his vest pocket for spectacles that weren't there.

Sam shrugged. "I was writing too fast to take it all in, but I think there are a couple of leads in there."

Skeeter sensed that the captain was torn between looking through the telegrams and picking his guitar back up. He gathered that the telegrams were about the murder of Wes James. In all the excitement about Steel Dust, he had almost forgotten about all that. The recollection of it shook him. He started thinking about the dead man, and the probability that the Wolf was going to lead a revenge raid back to these parts. It looked like recovering that Thoroughbred and breaking Steel Dust had not solved all his problems, and in fact had quite possibly led to new ones. He took a deep pull from his third mug of beer. He guessed life would just always be this way.

"Well," Hank finally said, "it's time to celebrate right now. I don't have my glasses with me anyway. I'll look these over in the morning." He picked up his guitar and somehow, with the magical know-how of musicians, jumped into the exact right part of the song.

Gotch Dunnsworth had caught his breath from his previous jig-dancing episode. He threw a shot of whiskey back and offered his hand to Luz, who had been sitting near Jubal the whole time, clapping her hands, watching her man fiddle. She looked at Jubal for approval, and he nodded. Gotch grabbed her by both hands and started circling, then switched to a hook-in-wing and some other square dance moves he invented on the spot. The whiskey seemed to be kicking in, and Gotch's antics began to whirl out of control as the crowd egged him on. He grabbed Luz's hand and spun her like a pirouetting ballerina, but in the process he lost his own balance and stumbled hard onto a table holding the open fiddle case.

A collective "Oh!" spontaneously burst from the crowd as the table toppled. Gotch and the fiddle case slammed to the floor. The fiddle case splintered, and a dusty old arrow shaft with crumpled feathers rattled out into view at Luz's feet.

32

LUZ SPRANG BACK as if someone had thrown a rattlesnake at her feet. The trio quit playing, and everyone in the crowd leaned forward for a closer look at the artifact on the floor. Seconds passed in silence.

"Gotch," Hank finally said, "are you sure I gave you that fiddle—in that case?"

"I swear, Captain."

"And you never noticed the arrow in there?" He leaned his guitar against the wall, and got up to stand over the arrow.

"I had no idea!"

"It flew out of the compartment in the lid of the case where you stow the bow," Sam Collins said. "I saw it come out of there when it hit the floor."

"It must have been tucked deep down in there," Gotch insisted. "To tell you the truth, I only got that fiddle out once't and tried to play it. Made such a god-awful noise I never tried it again. I didn't know that arrow was in there under the bow."

"No wonder we couldn't find it at home," Hank said, glancing at Flora. He felt a stabbing pain in his left shoulder, and caught himself rubbing it. He bent at the knee to crouch over the arrow. Old memories, terrors, and stomach-turning worries engulfed him. He shoved them all aside, jutted his chin, and picked up the projectile. "Sam, where did you put those arrows you pulled out of Wes James?"

"I stashed them in the store."

"Let's go take a look."

Hank rose and strode for the swinging doors, the painted dogwood shaft in his hand. The crowd parted to let him through. Jay Blue scrambled off the table he had been sitting on, caught Jane's eye, and urged her to follow with a toss of his head. Flora grabbed the telegrams from the table, folded them, tucked them into the front of her low-cut dress, and followed Hank. Sam went behind her. Skeeter put his beer mug down and fell in line, with Jubal right behind, pulling Luz by her hand.

"Come on, honey, let's stick with the Tomlinsons," Jubal said.

Hank stepped outside into the freezing air, oblivious to the sleet that pelted his face under his hat brim on a hard-driving north wind. A rumble of thunder came from some distant hills. Half the crowd in the bar followed the procession outside, but stopped short of stepping into the fresh mud of Main Street. Gotch Dunnsworth grumbled at the cold, the wind, and the freezing rain, but slogged through the deepening mire and angled across to the general store.

The lanterns were still burning in the store. Sam lengthened the wicks, giving more light, and dug around behind some crates under the counter until he produced one of the arrows removed from Wes James.

Hank lay the arrow shaft from Gotch's fiddle case next to the one from under the counter. "Well, that settles that," he said. "That's Black Cloud's signature, alright. He's back."

"What happened to the point that went with the one from the fiddle case?" Gotch asked, studying the evidence with his one eye.

"Oh, I've still got it," Hank said.

"We should compare that, too. Where is it?"

Hank pointed at his left shoulder. "Lodged somewhere between my clavicle and my scapula."

"Oh," Gotch said.

Sam had put on his glasses and was studying the arrow shafts. "No need for it, anyway. Like Hank said, the markings on these arrows are as good as a signature. No two different hands could have possibly created both of these."

"What's goin' on, Daddy?" Jay Blue said. "You never told me you had an arrowhead embedded in your shoulder. And who's Black Cloud?"

"Just a nickname," Hank said. "Never knew his real Comanche name. His white name was John Rafferty."

"White name?" Flora said.

"I didn't tell you that part yet," Hank admitted.

"Daddy, you've got to tell us what this is about. We've got to know what we're up against."

Hank sighed and quieted the gathering with gestures of his hands, as a preacher would bid a congregation to sit for a sermon. "I never thought I'd have to bring this up again." He took off his hat and rubbed his brow.

"I had three friends. Rangers. Good men you could trust. During the days of the Texas Republic, the four of us scouted together as a routine. Their names were Hornsby, Rogers, and Kenyon."

"Kenyon?" Sam said. "Like the State Policeman, Matt Kenyon?"

"It was his father. But slow down, Sam. Don't get ahead of me."

"Sorry. Go ahead."

"The four of us rode a more-or-less regular route among the settlers along our stretch of the frontier. That included a farm settled by a family named Rafferty up on the Lampasas River. There were three boys in the family. The youngest was named John. He was probably twelve or thirteen.

"One summer day, we found four of the five Raffertys dead and scalped, their cabin burned. Comanche sign everywhere. Young John Rafferty was missing, so we knew they had carried him off to make a warrior of him, if he was tough enough to survive.

"We gave chase, and we got close. We even sighted the Indians. They dodged us, but we hounded them for three days of hard ridin'. That boy knew who we were from our visits to his homestead. He knew us all. But the Indians had fresh horses and we didn't. They outran us. Our mounts went lame, and we ended up walking back to the settlements. That Rafferty boy must have thought we gave up."

Hank shook his head and looked at the floor. He gritted his teeth and prepared to tell the rest.

"Four years later I was in camp with my same three Ranger

amigos, way up on the Concho. Rogers went down to the river to fill our canteens one afternoon, and didn't come back. We found him dead and scalped, a couple of these arrows in him.

"We found no sign to follow. The murderer was careful. We buried Rogers on a lonely hill and started back for civilization. The next day, Hornsby was gatherin' firewood, not twenty steps from me and Jim Kenyon. We heard a bow thump and saw Hornsby go down with an arrow in his chest that matched the one that had killed Rogers. Same as these arrows here. Hornsby was dead before he hit the ground.

"I got mad and shouted out, 'Show yourself!' I said, 'Who the hell are you?' The voice that came back from the woods said, 'John Rafferty, you son of a bitch!' I let a couple of bullets go in the area of the voice, and he cussed me up and down in English and Comanche as he ran off. Again, we found no trail to follow, but Jim Kenyon and I knew what was going on now. That Rafferty boy had gone Indian and learned to hate white men. But he especially hated *us* for givin' up on him four years before, and abandoning him to go through hell."

"But you didn't abandon him," Flora said.

"He didn't know that. He was just a kid, caught in the worst of circumstances, and he was takin' it out on us. So Jim Kenyon and I decided to stick together and ride like hell back to the settlements, and we were way up on the Concho at the time, so we had a ways to go. It was Jim Kenyon who dubbed him Black Cloud. Said he was hangin' over us like a thunderstorm, strikin' us down like lightning. But it's hard to see a black cloud comin' in the night. In my sleep, I heard the arrow that got Jim while he stood guard, not ten feet from me. I buried him in a shallow grave, covered with rocks to keep the wolves from diggin' him up.

"I don't mind tellin' y'all I was scared. Scared of an angry kid gone Indian—no more than seventeen years old. But while I was prayin' over Kenyon's shallow grave, I got an idea. It occurred to me that it wasn't the wolves that were gonna dig him up. It was Black Cloud. He'd want the scalp. So I rode away from the gravesite like I was late for supper, but I stopped a mile away, dismounted, and snuck back on foot, Indian-style.

"I almost got the drop on Black Cloud—John Rafferty—whatever you want to call him. I saw him from a distance through the brush, digging up the grave. It was night, but I could make out that he'd sure enough grown into a tall, skinny, white warrior with long dark hair. I ducked down and snuck closer, to get within pistol range. But somehow he heard me, or smelled me, or saw me. When I stepped out of the brush, he had his bow drawn. You can't often duck an arrow, but it was dark and I got far enough aside to take it in the shoulder instead of the heart. I pulled the trigger on my Colt and caught him in the belly. Knocked him down, but he scrambled, caught his horse, and rode away."

"My God," said Sam, "how'd you survive?"

Hank picked up the arrow that had fallen from the fiddle case. "I tried to push this damn thing through, but it was stuck against the inside of my shoulder blade. So I pulled on it as hard as I could until the shaft came free, leaving the point in me. I was bleedin' pretty bad, but I made it to my horse. I thought about following Black Cloud to finish him off, but I was weak, and decided to let him die of his gut wound. I was half dead myself when I made it to the nearest homestead."

"But Black Cloud didn't die," Jay Blue said, gathering the situation. "He's back. Still makin' arrows. Still killin' and scalpin'."

"Looks that way, doesn't it, son? He might even be trying to pin this one on me. And having this old arrow in my possession doesn't really help my case any. It could be considered evidence against me."

"Against you?" Sam said. "But that's the arrow that wounded you."

"When I reported what had happened to Kenyon, Rogers, and Hornsby, the story got out. People started talkin' about the incident after it came out in the newspapers. Some said that I faked the wound, and that I didn't really have an arrow point in me at all."

"Why would you fake it?"

"Some say there was no Black Cloud. They say I made the whole story up. They say I made the arrow myself. In essence, they were saying that *I'm* Black Cloud—that I killed all my Ranger brothers and covered it up with a wild story. After all, I was the only witness to survive."

"Why would you kill your friends?" Flora asked.

"Oh, there was all manner of speculation on that, too. Some say I lost my temper and killed one of 'em over a trivial matter, and then had to kill the witnesses so I wouldn't hang. Some even say we found Jim Bowie's lost silver mine, and I wanted it all to myself, so I killed my partners. It got that ridiculous.

"Anyway, Jim Kenyon's widow, who was left behind with a baby boy to raise—Matt Kenyon—asked for an investigation. She claimed some whiskey-soaked informant had come to her and told her that I had gotten drunk with him in a saloon and confessed to killing all the men. And I don't doubt some fool told her that. She was a good woman, but the loss of her husband and what that damned fool drunkard told her drove her crazy. She was never the same. And she raised her son to believe me a murderer."

"What became of the investigation?"

"Nothin'. The drunk who accused me couldn't be found, and there wasn't enough evidence to warrant an investigation. The bodies were never recovered. Nobody even went to look for 'em, though I offered to lead a party out there. Nobody wanted to ride with me. People would cross the street to avoid me when I was in some town. It didn't set easy—knowin' that half of Texas believed I had killed my three best friends. Took me years to earn my reputation back and put all that behind me. And now, here it is again, starin' me right in the face."

Hank felt that old craving for whiskey. Not just a shot, either, but a brain-numbing bellyful.

"So what do we do now?" Jay Blue asked.

Hank blinked hard. He threw the old arrow shaft, stained with his own blood, onto the counter, and watched it rattle to a standstill. "Some developments have occurred since you left town, son. You can read all about it on page two of the Austin *Daily Statesman*. The upshot is that Matt Kenyon will be coming to arrest me for suspicion of murdering Wes James. Maybe as soon as tomorrow. The best thing we can do is find out who *really* killed him."

"How?"

Hank felt his eyes bulge. "The telegrams. I left 'em on the table."

Flora stopped him before he could take a step. "It's okay, I gathered them up," she said, holding her hand over her heart.

He sighed, relieved to have her help, but annoyed at himself for forgetting about the Western Union slips the moment that old arrow appeared. He was about to force a thank-you out of his mouth when lightning brightened the night outside, revealing the image of a tall man running across the street toward the store.

"Take cover," Hank said, pulling Flora behind him as he reached for his sidearm. The sky flashed again, and Hank saw Black Cloud, in war paint and full Comanche regalia, running at him with a scalping knife, looking straight through the store window into his eyes.

Thunder shook the windowpanes, and the door flew open, but it was Long Tom Merrick who stepped in, his face drawn with more worry than a night ride through a Texas blue norther should produce. "Captain, we got trouble at the ranch."

Hank shook the image of Black Cloud out of his head. "What is it, Tom?"

"It's Poli. He went huntin'. His horse came back without him."

The news hit Hank in the stomach like an anvil. He had never known Poli to lose his mount. He had never seen Poli get bucked off. Poli knew which horse to choose for which chore. He knew how and where to tie a horse to prevent the animal from breaking loose. "Where did he go huntin'?"

"He didn't say. Beto said he was after a big buck and didn't want the rest of us to know where. And, Captain . . ."

"What is it, Tom? Spit it out."

"The horse had a stab wound right in front of the saddle on the left side. It looked like an arrow point could have caused it."

Hank felt that old black cloud loom over him again. He had to draw on every bit of gumption he owned to maintain his bearing in front of people who looked up to him.

"Gotch!" he ordered. "Sober up and saddle our horses."

"Yes, sir!" Gotch said, charging out into the frigid night.

"A pack mule, too!"

"Got it!" The door slammed behind him, shutting out the howl of the wind.

"Sam, put together a pannier with anything we might need—blankets, bandages, medicine, food."

"I'll do it, Hank. And anybody who needs gloves or coats can get them now and we'll settle up later." Sam turned toward the nearest aisle and started gathering provisions.

"Boys," Hank said to the Broken Arrow men, "we need to get back to the ranch. As soon as the wind dies down so a man can hear, we need to be out there, calling Poli's name. Come daybreak, there will be no tracks to follow after all this rain. We'll just have to roust him out like an old mossback steer. I want everybody searching in pairs. Nobody rides alone. That way, if you find him alive, one man can stay with him while the other rides for help. The signal, if you find him, dead or alive, is three rifle shots."

Long Tom Merrick, Jay Blue, and Skeeter all nodded. Tom turned for the door, leaving a trail of raindrops still dripping from his slicker.

Jay Blue tugged Skeeter's sleeve. "Skeeter, grab some of those warm gloves for me and meet me at the livery."

Skeeter didn't answer as Jay Blue motioned for Jane to follow him out the door, offering his coat for her to use in crossing the street.

Hank turned to Jubal. "Mr. Hayes, may I ask a favor of you?"

Jubal stood taller, lifting his chin. "Anything, Captain."

"I know you and Luz have got to get back to your canyon early tomorrow and tend to your stock. But, on the way, can you search as you go?"

"Of course."

"Once again, I'll be obliged to you. Sam, provide Mr. and Mrs. Hayes with some warm clothes and a couple of slickers."

"Sure thing, Hank."

Jubal led Luz toward the winter clothing.

"What about the telegrams?" Flora said.

Hank shook his head. "I don't have time now."

"Let me help," she said. She put her hand over the telegrams tucked into her bodice. "If you say it's okay, I'll read these. Sam and I can use the telegraph to follow up any leads in your absence. You're running out of time, Hank. You know Kenyon is coming for you."

Hank nodded and gave Flora a forced smile. He turned toward Sam. "Sam, you and Flora will act as my agents while I'm gone. Use my name to follow up on the investigation as you see fit. You're detectives now. Get to the bottom of this business of who the hell Wes James was, and who wanted him dead."

Sam beamed at the promotion. "Yes, sir, Captain!"

"That should lead us right to Black Cloud," Flora said.

"That's why you have to be careful. This is very serious business. It wouldn't hurt to arm yourself."

Flora glanced down the store aisles to make sure no one was looking. She put her high-heeled shoe on the edge of a keg of nails and lifted her skirt to reveal a tiny derringer tucked into a garter that held up her silk hosiery.

Hank's eyes flashed, and he grinned briefly. "Those legs are more deadly than that popgun, but that'll do in a pinch."

She dropped her skirts. "You can pinch anything you want when this is all over."

A lightning bolt attracted Hank's eyes to the window again, and he caught a glimpse of Jay Blue and Jane across the street, huddled close together under the awning of the saloon.

Hank leaned close to Flora. "What's that girl's name—the one Jay Blue is sweet on?"

"Jane Catlett."

"Is she a good girl?"

Flora nodded. "She's a nice girl. Just had a hard start on life."

"What happened to her?"

"She doesn't talk about it. All I know is she lost her mother."

"Let her help you with the telegrams. But don't include anybody else."

"Sure, Hank."

He slipped his hand behind her neck and gave her a brief kiss on the lips, then strode for the door, his spurs ringing.

33

BY THE LIGHT OF A LANTERN up in Flora's room, the saloon owner and her employee, Jane Catlett, began to sort through the telegrams that had gushed into Luck once the wire was fixed. Hank had sent dozens of inquiries all over Texas, and as far north as Nebraska, asking stockyard bosses, brand inspectors, and range detectives he knew—and he knew them all—whether they had ever heard of a Wes James, or anyone who matched his description or that of the horse he rode, or if anyone had any recollection of Wes's vertical WJ brand.

"Most of these just say, 'No,'" Jane said, thumbing through the stack of unorganized telegrams.

"Mine, too. Let's deal with them first. We'll arrange them on the floor geographically."

"What do you mean?"

"Imagine a map of Texas and the Southern Plains here on the bedroom floor. Wherever the telegram came from, put it in the right place on the map. Then we'll start to get an idea of where Wes James *hasn't* been seen. That's a start."

"Hey, you're good at this," Jane said, sounding impressed. "I wish we had some thumbtacks. We could put them on the wall."

Flora's eyes brightened. "I've got stick pins galore. That's a better idea."

They took down an oil painting and a mirror between two windows facing Main and began arranging the negative replies geographically.

"Here's Brownsville," Flora said, kneeling to pin a telegram near the baseboard.

"I have a Lincoln, Nebraska," Jane said.

"Pin it as high as you can reach. A little more to the right."

"You really know your geography." Jane stood on her tiptoes and pinned the reply in place.

"I *have* been around, Janie."

"I didn't mean it like—"

"Relax, honey. I know what you meant. Here's a negative from Denver while you're up there. Way over to the left by the window frame."

"Where the heck is Waxahachie?"

"Here, I'll show you." Flora eyeballed the imaginary map. "Dallas will be about here, and . . . Waxahachie!"

"I'll just give them to you," Jane suggested. "You pin them. Here's a big, fat 'No' from San Antonio."

Flora took her time placing the telegram on the wall. "So . . . what were you and Jay Tomlinson talking about on the boardwalk in the freezing cold a while ago?"

Jane blushed. "It's funny. He doesn't like to be called Jay. He likes Jay Blue. And I don't like Janie. I prefer just Jane." She handed over a scrap of paper. "Kansas City."

"I'm sorry, but I'm just used to Janie by now."

"Oh, I don't mind you calling me that, Miss Flora. It's just everybody else."

"You're avoiding my question."

"Here's a place called Ogallala. It's in Nebraska."

"I know Ogallala. So, what's going on between Jay *Blue* and Jane Catlett?"

"Nothing. I swear. I mean, I think he wanted to *kiss* me tonight." She blushed again, and rolled her eyes toward the North Pole.

"It's about time. Did you let him?"

"Fort Worth says, 'No.'" She handed over the telegram.

"So much for Fort Worth. What did *you* say?"

" 'No,' of course!"

"Jane! He's been trying awful hard for weeks. He may not try forever. What are you waiting for?"

"He's nice to me. I like him. But I promised my mama."

"Promised her what? That you'd stay a virgin your whole life?"

"Miss Flora!" Jane hissed, blushing an even deeper shade of red.

"Well! You can make him wait till you get married if you want to, but don't swear it off completely. I don't care what you promised your mama."

"I'm not a virgin. That's just it. When he finds that out . . . You don't know what happened to me, Miss Flora. I had a stepfather. He . . . He's the one who used to call me Janie. That's the reason I don't like it much."

Mortified, Flora grabbed Jane's arm. "Oh, honey, I am so sorry. I will never, ever call you by that name again. I didn't know. But what that man did to you doesn't count, do you hear? You've kept your real virginity, and nobody can take it until you want to give it up."

"But when Jay Blue—or whoever—when he finds out . . ."

"Jay Blue doesn't even have to know about any of that if you don't want to tell him. You're a sweet, young girl. You're perfect, just the way you are."

Jane smiled uncertainly and handed over another sample of Sam Collins's chicken scratchings. "I like Jay Blue. He's a gentleman and all. But I promised my mama."

Flora turned to pin Waco on the wall. "What's this promise all about?"

"She told me to wait for a rich man—somebody who could take care of me. She said he might not be young or handsome, but as long as he was real nice and had money . . . She said I should wait for that kind of man."

"A rich man? What do you think Jay Blue Tomlinson is? A dirt farmer?"

Jane employed that pretty smirk of hers. "Worse. He's a cowboy."

Flora put her hands on her hips. "Jane, sit down." She pointed at the edge of the bed and waited for the girl to sit there. Flora sat nearby. "His name is Tomlinson. He's Captain Hank Tomlinson's son. Doesn't that mean anything to you?"

Jane shrugged. "I listen to the talk in the saloon. They say Captain Tomlinson never puts any money in the bank. He spends it all on land. He's got good horses and a lot of land, but he doesn't have much money. He never dresses up. He doesn't wear silk hats or diamond tie pins. He doesn't even own a tie, probably. They have no money, Miss Flora."

Though it was cool in the room, due to the roaring norther outside, Flora pretended to dab sweat from her brow with her sleeve. "Dear, dear, dear. Oh, my goodness, Jane. Did your mother make you promise that your future husband *had* to be old, bald, and ugly?"

"Well, no, ma'am, but . . ."

"There are all kinds of wealth, honey. Those Tomlinsons have the greatest kind—they live well and enjoy their time on earth. But, okay, I know you promised your mama you'd find a man who'd take care of you, so let's think about commodities."

"About what?" Jane said, her face a beautiful question mark.

"Commodities. *Riches.* There are a lot of different kinds of riches. I've seen most of them come and go. The gold market fluctuates. They keep digging more of the stuff out of the ground! The treasury will print more currency and mint more coins until they're almost worthless. I've gone broke several times because of it. Stocks and bonds, booms and busts! I've survived more panics than a flock of chickens with a fox in the coop. But there's one commodity that God is not going to make any more of. Do you know what that is?"

"I guess I don't."

"We're pinning it to the wall! Geography! They ain't making no more land, honey! And only a couple of men in Texas own more of it than Captain Hank Tomlinson, which by blood and default includes Jay Blue Tomlinson."

Jane was still not convinced. "But there are miles and miles of free range. Anybody can use it. Why is it valuable?"

Flora sighed bigger than the wind outside. "Don't you read the newspapers? The economy in Texas revolves around cattle since the war ended, and it's booming. They're rounding up longhorns here for a few dollars a head and selling them on the hoof at the railheads up north for twenty dollars a head and up. The profits are huge!"

"I know all that. But the Tomlinsons are just spending it on more land."

"That's what the smartest ranchers in Texas are doing right now. Even some foreign syndicates. The free-range days are coming to an end, Jane. Texas is selling land faster than a two-dollar whore sells *her* real estate. The day will soon come when the richest man in Texas is the man who owns the most land. He who owns the most land can run the most cattle. He who owns the most cattle will sell them, year in and year out, for more money than Jefferson paid for Louisiana."

The look of enlightenment on Jane's face went far beyond any desire for money. "I think I'm beginning to see what you mean."

"What I mean is that Jay Blue Tomlinson—that handsome young gentleman you've been giving the cold shoulder to—is already one of the wealthiest men in Texas on paper land deeds, and will someday in fact be a millionaire. On top of that, he's so head-over-heels in love with you that he can't look at anything but you when you're in the room. But . . . If you think your mama wanted you to wait for an ugly, old, bald man who doesn't anymore know his way around a herd of cattle than he knows his way around a feather bed, that's your decision!"

"Miss Flora!"

"And if Jay Blue is anything like his daddy, he'll *know* his way around a—"

"Miss Flora! I get it!"

"I hope you do get it, honey."

"Miss Flora!"

Flora laughed. "Anyway, if you were to marry that young man, you couldn't possibly make your mama any prouder. That's all I'm going to say. Now, come on, let's finish our map of cattle country."

Jane Catlett seemed a little dazed for the rest of the night and wasn't of much help to Flora. It wasn't surprising. Flora had just given her permission to fall in love with Jay Blue Tomlinson, and she was falling like a drunk from a bar stool. But because Jane was there, Flora could talk the investigation through out loud, using Jane as a sounding board.

When they had completed pinning negative responses to the wall, the lady detectives got down to analyzing the few replies that held useful information.

"These are our red-hot leads," Flora said, "so we'll mark them with a little rouge." She laughed. "I can just feel Hank cringing now."

When they were finished, they stepped back to look at their map. There were four red telegrams dating Wes James's movements, or sightings of his brand, the WJ. The first was from the courthouse clerk in Jack County, and it was brief.

WJ brand registered here last March to John Wesley James.

The next lead came from the elected stock inspector of Brown County, about one hundred miles northwest of Luck.

Saw a line rider and horse matching description of Wes James here last May. Called himself John Wesley James. Herding cattle branded Rafter T in far western part of county. Claimed cattle belonged to his employer.

"What kind of brand is a 'Rafter'?" Flora asked.

"Huh?" Jane answered.

"Never mind. We'll have to ask Hank."

The third red telegram had come from a Texas Ranger assigned to check and record brands on the Chisholm Trail herds heading north during the summer where the trail crossed the Brazos River. Flora knew that trail crossing was well north of Luck, Texas.

One Wes James, mavericker, sold 13 head branded WJ to a Chisholm Trail outfit on the Brazos River, Aug. 1. Received four dollars per head. Rode stout claybank.

The fourth telegram, from the stockyards in Dodge City, Kansas, simply acknowledged that the WJ cattle had arrived there with the trail herd in early September.

Sept. 3, 13 WJ cattle received and shipped.

"Okay," Flora said, talking out the evidence. "It looks like Wes James entered Texas back in March. He registered his brand at the first courthouse he came to after crossing the Red River, in Jack County. That would be in the town of Jacksboro on the fringe of the frontier. I ran a saloon there awhile. Rough place."

"Right," Jane said, trying to stay with the investigation.

"We know from our own observations that Wes showed up here in my saloon in about mid-April, wouldn't you say?"

Jane seemed to snap back to the moment. "It was a slow night because it was the night before Easter Sunday. Only the Double Horn boys, Gotch, and that Wes James were here. And, later, Wes James made Dottie mad because he told her she was too fat to sit on his lap."

Flora giggled, remembering the way Dottie had twisted off. "You've got a good memory. I've been doing this so long that one night just runs into another." She turned back to the map on the wall. "So, Jacksboro in March; here in April. Then he's in Brown County in May, tending cattle branded with a 'Rafter T.' "

"Whatever that is."

"Yeah. Then we saw him a couple of times here during the summer. Always alone, right?"

"Always," Jane agreed.

"Then in August he turns up on the Brazos River north of here, selling cattle branded WJ to a Chisholm Trail outfit for only four dollars a head. If he had thrown in with one of the trail outfits, he could have gotten twenty to twenty-five dollars a head up in Kansas for the same thirteen beeves, plus the wages he would have earned as a trail hand. Looks like he just wanted to turn a quick dollar."

"He never struck me as ambitious," Jane agreed.

"The fourth telegram, from Dodge City, only says that the thirteen WJ beeves were received at the stockyards there."

"There's just one thing that doesn't fit," Jane said.

"The Rafter T," Flora said.

Jane nodded.

"Here's what we'll do. First thing in the morning, we'll get Sam to send telegrams to the same places Hank sent the first batch."

"But this time, we'll be inquiring about the Rafter T instead of the WJ."

Flora smiled. "Hey, you're getting good at this detective work."

"It's kind of fun."

"Yeah. Until Black Cloud starts shooting arrows at us. That's the reason this information doesn't leave this room, agreed?"

Jane's eyes had grown wide. She nodded.

"Good. Now, you'd better use the cot in the spare room tonight. No need for you to walk home in this weather."

"Yes, ma'am," Jane said. She turned to leave.

"Oh, Jane," Flora added. "If you ever want to talk about anything—anything at all—I'm always here. I may be a sorry substitute for your mother. I'm sure she was a much finer lady than me. But I take care of my girls, and I'll do anything I can to help."

Jane smiled. "I think you're a mighty fine lady, Miss Flora."

34

THE WIND CEASED TO HOWL at daybreak, but the rain and sleet continued to fall in waves. Though the temperature remained below freezing, the warmth of the earth melted the precipitation to pools of slush that oozed everywhere and clung to boots and the hooves of horses, freezing to clumps of ice on feathered pasterns of the Spanish cow ponies. The very clouds of breath exhaled by the riders froze on their whiskers.

Skeeter had approached Captain Tomlinson early that morning and asked if he could search for Poli out toward Double Horn Creek, claiming he knew those ranges well, and thought he knew where Poli might have gone hunting. The captain agreed, but insisted that Jay Blue and Skeeter ride together.

Now they were riding and yelling their lungs out for their lost foreman, worried over whether or not Poli was even alive, and if so how he had fared through the cold night. As they came to the head of a rough arroyo that carved its way through the hills, Skeeter saw his chance to make his break to the Double Horn Ranch alone.

"These gloves you got me are too damn small," Jay Blue was just grumbling.

"You should've gotten your own damn gloves, then," Skeeter said. "Maybe if you could get your head out of that barmaid's ass."

"Hey, watch your mouth. Anyway, that's none of your business."

"It is if you're gonna complain about the gloves."

"I've about had it with her anyway," he said, as if Skeeter cared. "You know I went to kiss her last night, and she wouldn't let me?"

"Maybe she doesn't want you bossin' her around like you boss me around."

"I don't boss you around."

Skeeter forced a laugh, even though none of this was funny any more. "'Skeeter, get me some gloves.' 'Skeeter, saddle the horses.' 'Skeeter, gather the firewood.' I've about had a bellyful of it."

"Well, somebody's got to make the decisions. I've learned from my daddy how to run an outfit."

"You've learned how to run your mouth. You haven't done a tenth of what your daddy's done in life."

"Yeah, well at least I've got a daddy!" Jay Blue blurted.

Coming from anybody that would have hurt, but from Jay Blue . . . Skeeter saw that Jay Blue regretted saying it immediately, but he didn't wait for an apology. This was his chance. "I'm gonna ride the other side of that draw, and you'd damn sure better stay on this side of it if you don't want me to get off this horse and whip your ass."

"Hey, Skeeter, come on. I'm sorry."

"Kiss my ass, Jay Blue." He reined his horse away.

"Daddy told us to stick together!"

"You mind him! He's your daddy, remember? Not mine!"

"Well, keep hollerin' for Poli where I can hear you across the draw."

Skeeter looked over his shoulder and saw Jay Blue slumped in the saddle, looking as foolish as he must have felt. He remembered what Jack Brennan had said to him the night before. What if he did take a job with the Double Horn Ranch? That would show the damned ol' high-and-mighty Tomlinsons.

"Poli!" he shouted at the top of his lungs, his throat already ragged from shouting all morning. He almost wanted to cry. He was truly worried about Poli and he was tired of feeling like a nobody without a home. He hated being an orphan. No matter how folks tried to treat him like family, they couldn't quite do it. Everyone knew what he was. A charity case. Another mouth to feed. A drain on the resources. There had to be another way, and maybe Jack Brennan had the answer.

He heard Jay Blue's voice across the draw, farther away now as the canyon widened. "Poli . . ."

Spending every waking hour with Jay Blue the last few weeks had worn his patience thin. If he only knew how ridiculous he looked worrying over that barmaid. "I just wish some stupid girl was all I had to worry about," he muttered to himself. He drew in a deep breath of cold air. "Poli!"

He rode on like that—shouting for Poli, listening for Jay Blue, working himself into a pitiable state of mind. Then he caught sight of the Double Horn Ranch buildings a couple of miles away at the foot of the hills below. The freezing rain started falling hard again. His tracks would be obliterated in no time, in case Jay Blue rode around the canyon to look for him. He didn't care what Jay Blue thought anymore. Not even Captain Tomlinson. He just wanted to be somebody. Jack Brennan had said he knew who his daddy was. *Is*. He reined his horse down the slope and rode through the timber toward the Double Horn Ranch.

A feeling had come over Hank. He felt a strong pull toward an area up the Colorado River. He couldn't say why, or how the urge came to him, but he knew his course before he had even put a foot in a stirrup. Having sent most of the boys out in pairs, he had given Tonk his orders: "Swing around to the Gridiron Branch. I'll ride past Eagle Bluffs, then meet you at the Narrows."

"The Narrows?" Tonk said.

"You know the place?"

Tonk nodded. His frown had darkened as he turned to mount. It was as if he had felt the same pull to that place.

Now Hank had Eagle Bluffs behind him, having found no trace of Poli. Not even a buzzard would be flying on a day like this, he thought. Perhaps that was just as well. He cursed his own thoughts, the cold, and that damned competitive streak all the Broken Arrow hands kept constantly alive.

"Poli!" he called.

His head ached, and his throat was raw from yelling. So much so that he had taken to alternating the yells with shrill whistles he sent through his teeth. His bones ached from this numbing cold, especially the old shoulder wound. He was approaching the Narrows when the rain turned to a hard, driving sleet.

He reined his horse to a stop, and could not even say why he had done it. Whatever it was that had drawn him here was behind him. He could feel it. He didn't want to look. He had passed a clump of bushes on his left, but had not looked at the other side of the brush as he rode past, his eyes busy elsewhere. But he knew he had to look now. Maybe it was nothing. He had gotten false signals from these strange urges before. He set his jaw. His neck was stiff today, so instead of wrenching it around, he reined his horse to the left.

The sight dragged his heart down into the deepest of dark pits, and tears burst from his eyes. He roared in anger and sorrow. He leapt down from the saddle, his boots splashing frigid mud that oozed through the stitching and soaked his socks. He trudged toward the arrow-riddled body, feeling as if he would vomit up the little bit of breakfast he had managed to choke down this morning. He only glanced at the arrows to check for the markings of Black Cloud.

Hank had seen scalped corpses plenty of times before. It was something a man never got used to, but learned to stomach. You just trained your eye away from the grisly abomination intended to break your morale and got on with the sad business at hand. But this was Poli. His head of thick black hair was gone, cut and torn from his bloody skull. Hank knew this scalping was meant for him and that Poli had somehow gotten in the way.

He fell to his knees beside the body of his friend, sobs escaping from his lungs in spite of the heart this frontier had hardened. He could literally feel the pain of the arrow shafts protruding unnaturally from Poli's chest. He tried to shut Poli's dark eyes, but the body was frozen, the face encased in a glaze of ice that seemed to have preserved Poli's last dying visage of fear and pain for all eternity.

"Poli!" he screamed, as he had been screaming all morning. "God-damn it, no!" He choked on his own words and felt his anger and grief turn to guilt. "What did I bring here?" he asked himself. The remorse shifted to fear as he thought of his boys being out there now.

There was only one way to torment him worse than this. And Black Cloud was hanging over them all.

He heard a hoof stamp in a puddle and turned, wild-eyed, to see the rider there, looking down at him. Tonk was pulling his Winchester from the saddle scabbard, his face looking even sadder than usual. The old scout cocked it, fired, pumped the lever, pulled the trigger again, flipped another smoking shell into the mud, and sent a third bullet speeding skyward behind the others.

35

MATT KENYON arrived in Luck, chilled to the marrow, but relatively dry under his black oilcloth slicker. He rode first to the Dunnsworth livery barn to have his horse stabled on the state nickel. He had also allocated the funds to pay for boarding the evidence—that brindle heifer with the WJ brand. The payment seemed to shock the one-eyed man who owned the place, but Kenyon believed in doing things by the book, and standing by his word.

"Where might I find Captain Tomlinson today?" Kenyon asked the stable keeper.

"You *might* not find him at all," was the only answer Dunnsworth would offer.

Undaunted, Kenyon stepped out of the livery and looked up and down the cold, muddy thoroughfare of Main Street. Folded in his breast pocket, protected from the weather under his slicker and a wool coat, he carried a warrant for the arrest of Captain Hank Tomlinson on suspicion of murder, signed by a judge appointed by the radical Republican Reconstruction government—the same administration that had disbanded the Texas Rangers and replaced them with the Texas State Police. The judge had read Max Cooper's article in the *Daily Statesman*. Kenyon had been working toward this day his whole adult life—and even before.

Matt Kenyon had no memory of his father; no portrait or tintype picture. All he possessed were the descriptions his mother had shared with him. He had grown up listening to his mother's stories of his father as a kind, brave man; honest, handsome, and honorable. His mother had also told him that one Hank Tomlinson—a Ranger she had never met—had killed her beloved Jim and deserved nothing less than a hangman's noose.

For reasons he never quite understood or questioned, young Matt grew up fascinated with police work and, by the time he was eighteen, had decided upon a career in law enforcement. Not even the Civil War would stand in the way of his ambitions. Matt had grown up with strong Union sympathies, and instinctively opposed secession, so he left Texas and went to California during the war, finding work as a policeman in the city of San Francisco. It was there that he proved himself as a cop in one of the toughest and wildest towns in the West. In three separate gunfights, Matt Kenyon shot in self-defense, killing lawless men who would have happily added him as a notch to their pistol grips.

It was also in San Francisco that he began earning an extra buck or two as a crime reporter, writing under a pen name. City councilmen and judges read the newspapers, and Matt found that he could sway their attitudes and opinions with his pen. He realized that criminals read the newspapers, too, and that he could often flush suspects out of hiding by planting certain bits of information—or misinformation—in his articles.

He returned to Texas to bury his mother after the war. The way he saw it, she died of a broken heart, and the man responsible for her grief—Hank Tomlinson—still roamed free on the frontier as a respected rancher and town builder. It was at this time that the radical Republican government was forming the Texas State Police, and Matt's credentials impressed them. He won a commission as a lieutenant, with responsibilities ranging statewide. The *Daily Statesman* also liked his style—writing as Max Cooper.

When news of the murder of Wes James found its way to Lieutenant Kenyon's desk, he finally saw the opportunity he had sought since boyhood to avenge his father's murder and lay his mother's soul to rest once and for all. The fact that details of the crime came to him in the form of an anonymous letter served only to reveal that Tomlinson had other enemies out there who wanted him brought down for his outrages as the legendary Black Cloud.

Now, standing in the muddy street of Tomlinson's own town, Kenyon's excitement was slowly building, like steam pressure in a boiler. Today would be the day. He had the confidence of his experience and the weight of the state government behind him. This was one crime story he would not have to write himself. Every newspaper in Texas would carry the news of the Ranger gone wrong, finally brought to justice by the son of one of his victims.

The warrant gave Lieutenant Matt Kenyon the authority to bring Tomlinson in dead or alive, as he saw fit.

At Flora's Saloon, Kenyon found the swinging doors latched back and the glazed glass doors shut because of the cold. But there was a horse shivering at the hitching rail, indicating that at least one patron might be drinking in the saloon.

What kind of man would leave a saddle horse to stand in this kind of weather? Then he saw the Double Horn brand in the animal's wet coat on the left hip, and knew it probably belonged to the owner of that ranch, Jack Brennan. He had questioned this man, a neighbor to Tomlinson, and found him less than helpful. He opened a glazed glass door and entered. Inside, he found only Brennan and the barkeep, Harry.

As the two men stared at him, Kenyon said, "I'm looking for Captain Hank Tomlinson. Police business."

"Tomlinson ain't here," Brennan answered, then went on to explain that one of Tomlinson's men was missing, having failed to return from a hunt.

The news took an edge off of the resolve Kenyon had honed preparing for the moment of confrontation. He decided to have a snort to warm his belly after the long, cold ride.

"Whiskey," he said to the bartender, who snarled, but grabbed a glass.

"So, you're it?" Brennan asked.

"I am *what*, sir?"

"You think you can take Hank Tomlinson alone?" He began laughing, whiskey sloshing out of his shot glass.

"I'm sure he'll give up his guns in an orderly fashion."

Brennan almost choked on the shot he had thrown back. He

coughed a few times, then said, "Well, let's figure the odds. I'd say you have a ninety percent chance of dyin', and ten percent chance of surviving a bullet wound or two."

Kenyon was unmoved at the rants of the big rancher. "I'm just here to do my duty. I don't bet odds. I'm not a gambling man."

"Oh, you're gamblin', alright. With your life." He filled his empty glass from a bottle on the bar. "I guess you already know about the arrow," he added.

"What arrow?" Kenyon said, picking up his glass of bourbon.

Brennan looked at the bartender, who had forced a cough. "Well, he's gonna find out sooner or later, Harry," the big man said, having sensed the disapproval of the barkeep. He turned back to Kenyon. "An old arrow matching those found in the carcass of Wes James was discovered in the possession of Captain Tomlinson. It fell out of a fiddle case he owned, last night, right here in the saloon, in front of three dozen witnesses."

The news further brightened Kenyon's spirits. "Where's the arrow now?"

"They took it over to the general store to compare it to the others. Then news of Hank's lost foreman got to town, and the whole Broken Arrow crew left to find him."

Kenyon threw the whiskey past his teeth, his mind whirling to analyze how the new evidence might bolster his case. He charged out of the saloon, sloshed across the street, and swung open the sweaty glass door to find Sam Collins talking to two pretty women whom he remembered as barmaids. One, in fact, was the bar owner, and Tomlinson's gal.

"Oh," Sam Collins said, as if caught doing something wrong. "Officer Kenyon. What can I do for you?"

Kenyon's eyes caught sight of the two arrow shafts that Collins was attempting to move from view.

"Stop right there," he warned. "Obstruction of justice is a serious charge."

The store owner slid the two arrows back onto the counter, becoming instantly defensive. "Sir, you're addressing an elected officer of the court!"

Kenyon remembered that the shopkeeper was a justice of the peace, but ignored the statement all the same. "Excuse me, ladies," he said, stepping between them to gather up the two arrows. The palpable enmity of the three citizens failed to concern him much as he got a close look at the arrow shafts.

One artifact appeared much older than the other. Here was the link between Black Cloud from the old days and Black Cloud of here and now. This new exhibit—because it was found in Tomlinson's possession—could help cinch the case against the old Ranger in the murder of Wes James. And—though he might not ever come to trial for the killing of Jim Kenyon—Texas would know he was hanging for that crime, too, and the murders of two other Rangers, to boot.

Smiling, Lieutenant Matt Kenyon looked up at the bar owner, Flora. Expecting to see a sneer of hatred on her pretty face, he instead found her eyes peering outside through the moisture-fogged store window, a look of surprise quickly shifting to one of outright horror.

Kenyon put his hand on the grip of a Smith & Wesson revolver and turned. The distortions in the glass windows coupled with the condensation on the panes provided a surreal view of a buckboard rolling down the muddy street. The feathered ends of three arrows pointed skyward from the chest of a dead man who could be seen over the sideboards of the wagon. A grim lot of cowboys dragged along with the buckboard. Directly behind the wagon box, staring at the dead body, rode Captain Hank Tomlinson himself.

Kenyon stepped out into the cold, followed by the women and the store owner.

"Oh, Hank!" Flora said. Then she began to cry—apparently in sincere sobs of grief. She stepped right out into the street, dragging her skirts through the mud.

Kenyon looked at Tomlinson, the old Ranger's face a gathering storm of anger. For the first time, Kenyon began to fear his inevitable clash. He thought for a moment that he would have to draw his firearm here and now when Tomlinson reached into the pocket of his heavy coat. But the old Ranger only pulled out a flask from which he took a long pull, turning the container upside down. Then he got down from his horse.

Still holding the arrows in one hand, Kenyon stepped into the street to get a closer look at the body. The Broken Arrow men—seven of them besides Captain Tomlinson—were quietly getting down from their horses, preparing to remove the body from the wagon.

"Wait," Kenyon said, before they could lay hands upon the corpse. He compared the arrows in his hand to the ones sticking out of the body, and found a match. "Is this your foreman?" he said, looking at Tomlinson.

"He was my *friend*," Tomlinson growled. "You still think I'm Black Cloud?"

Kenyon rolled the stiff corpse to one side and found the back of the dead man's coat dry. "Looks like he fell back on dry ground. This man was killed before the norther hit yesterday. Where were you yesterday, Captain Tomlinson?"

"He was here in town," Flora said. "He's been here two days."

Tomlinson took her gently by the arm, silencing her. "I rode halfway to Austin yesterday. When I saw the repair crew fixin' the telegraph line, I came back here."

"Can anyone verify that?"

"No," Tomlinson said. His eyes looked like those of a killer right now.

Kenyon was beginning to think this arrest might not go as easily as he had hoped, with seven of Tomlinson's men standing at his side. He decided to try a change in the plan. "I need to speak with you alone, Captain. Right now, in the store."

"Kiss my ass," Tomlinson said. "Somebody killed my friend, Poli, the same way they got that rustler, Wes James. If you think it was me, then I guess you'll have to do your duty. I'll be over here in the saloon." He looked at the store owner. "Sam, take care of Poli. All the finest, you hear?"

"I hear you, Hank."

When Tomlinson turned for the saloon, a young cowhand followed. Kenyon saw a clear family resemblance in the build and walk of the two, and figured this young man for Jay Blue Tomlinson. The young cowboy grabbed a friend by the sleeve, also a youngster, with a Mexican look to him, though he had blue eyes.

"Come on, Skeeter," the first cowhand said.

The one he had called Skeeter paused for a while, but eventually spat in the mud and followed the other two Broken Arrow men to the saloon. The rest of the cowboys busied themselves with the body of their dead friend. It was truly a sad scene, especially as it was reflected in the faces of those ranch hands. But Kenyon had other business to attend to. He saw his chance to arrest Tomlinson in the saloon now. The odds would be better there. Tomlinson had only the two youngsters to back him up, and probably wouldn't risk injury to his own son.

Kenyon looked at Sam Collins and handed him the two arrows. "As an officer of the court, I expect you to properly catalog and store *all* evidence," he warned.

"Have you absolutely no sense of decorum?" Collins hissed, grabbing the arrows. "This is a close-knit community. This man was one of us."

"This is also a murder investigation. Act accordingly."

With that directive, Kenyon walked in front of the wagon team, crossed the street, and strode long to enter the saloon not far behind Tomlinson and his two young hands. Inside the saloon, the former Ranger went straight for the left end of the bar. Kenyon angled to the right. Though his mind was absorbed with his plans to disarm and arrest Tomlinson, he nonetheless noticed an odd, unexpected exchange among the men in the bar.

Jay Blue Tomlinson followed his father, as one might expect. But the one called Skeeter lagged behind. Then, the big rancher, Jack Brennan, donned a smile and spoke to the young cowhand.

"Hey, Skeeter!" he said. "Come here and have a whiskey."

And Skeeter joined Jack Brennan at the bar instead of the Tomlinson duo. Not only did this strike Kenyon as odd, but he noted that Jay Blue Tomlinson apparently disapproved, too.

That aside, Kenyon had work to do, and the sooner the better. So, he sized up the situation. To the far left, Hank Tomlinson stood, waiting for a drink. His son stood beside him. Next to them was Brennan, then Skeeter. Taking a moment to gather his gall, Kenyon stepped up beside Skeeter, and he happened to hear words pass between the kid and the big rancher.

"Did you tell 'em yet?" Brennan asked.

"No, sir. Not yet."

Jay Blue pushed back from the bar. "I heard that, Skeeter. Tell who what?"

"We weren't talkin' to you, Jay Blue," Skeeter replied.

With this distraction working in his favor, Kenyon swung away from the bar, toward the middle of the room. His heart was pounding with excitement. "Captain Tomlinson!" he said, his voice suddenly booming in the room. Everyone turned to look at him *except* Tomlinson. The retired Ranger was half turned away from him. "I have a warrant for your arrest!"

A moment of silence passed as Tomlinson took a shot glass and drained it in one fluid motion. "You want to serve it in hell?" he said.

Suddenly, he was itching for Tomlinson to pull that hog leg from his holster. "Put your hands up and we'll have no trouble."

Tomlinson's neck turned, his cool blue eyes drilling the State Policeman. "We *already* have trouble. You picked the worst day of the year to mess with me, Kenyon."

Kenyon's eyes widened to take it all in. He knew his Smith & Wesson was ready, and so was he. Now he was really hoping Tomlinson would try something. It would make his police career to take down an old Ranger gone bad. "Put your hands in the air!" he ordered. He was awaiting Tomlinson's next move, but it was Jack Brennan who spoke up.

"Now wait just a goddamn minute!" As he spoke, he pushed Skeeter farther away and passed in front of Jay Blue to stand at Tomlinson's side. "Who the hell do you think you are to storm into our town and boss our citizens around like this? Goddamn Republican State Police."

"I don't need your help, Jack!" Tomlinson growled, squaring off next to the big rancher.

The two stood there for a split second, side by side. Then, like a sledgehammer, Jack Brennan's fist flew up from his hip, where his thumb had been tucked into his gun belt, and smashed into Hank Tomlinson's nose quicker than a quail could burst from cover.

By reflex, Kenyon drew his revolver, but stopped short of firing.

Remarkably, the old Ranger stood for a moment, his head thrown back from the impact of the knuckles, blood gushing from his nose, until his knees buckled. By the time the elder Tomlinson hit the floor, Brennan had locked his two bearlike arms around Jay Blue Tomlinson's shoulders, preventing him from reaching the sidearm he was groping for.

"Skeeter!" Brennan said. "Get his gun!"

Even in the chaos of the moment, Kenyon noticed the look of abject astonishment on Jay Blue Tomlinson's face as Skeeter rushed forward to yank the Colt from his holster. He carried it aside, butt-forward, and placed it out of reach on a poker table.

"Skeeter!" Jay Blue gushed, locked in the crushing embrace of the much larger man. "What . . . ?"

Skeeter looked at Kenyon. "He carries a knife on his belt and one in his boot top, too."

"Skeeter!" Jay Blue repeated. "What the hell are you doin'?"

"I'm done takin' orders from Tomlinsons," Skeeter said. "I work for the Double Horn Ranch now."

Stunned and disappointed at the interference of Brennan, Matt Kenyon approached the younger Tomlinson, covering him with his Smith & Wesson. As Brennan continued to hold Jay Blue, Kenyon found the knives where Skeeter had indicated. He searched the unconscious Captain Tomlinson for weapons, unbuckling the gun belt and tossing aside a couple of knives.

Now he looked back at Brennan. "Turn him loose and step back, Mr. Brennan! Nobody asked you for your help anyway."

Brennan released Jay Blue and stepped aside. "I wouldn't show you the shithouse door," he insisted. "I did what I did because Hank Tomlinson doesn't deserve to die at the gallows for killin' a shit-ass State Policeman, which he was about to do."

Kenyon had no intention of arguing this point with the half-drunken rancher. "You can be of service now by picking up the captain and carrying him to the jail cell in the back of the store."

The whole time, Jay Blue Tomlinson had been staring in disbelief at the cowboy called Skeeter, who was standing in the middle of the room, looking detached and confused, as if he were about to break down and cry. Kenyon had no idea what was going on there, and didn't really care. His concern was getting the two Tomlinsons behind bars.

"I'm going to have to lock you up, too," he said to the younger man. "You shouldn't have gone for your gun."

Jay Blue stood tall and glared at Skeeter. "I'd rather go with my daddy anyway. Looks like I'm out of friends here."

Brennan reached down with one hand, grabbed a handful of the material of Captain Tomlinson's coat, took hold of a wrist with his other hand, and in one powerful motion hoisted Tomlinson across his shoulder. He proceeded out the door and across the street with Kenyon right behind, his muzzle trained on Jay Blue's back. As they stepped into the store, he saw all the cowhands from the Broken Arrow look up from the corpse they had been hovering over, the shock and outrage quickly registering on every face. Sam Collins and the two ladies from the saloon also gathered the situation and gasped.

"Hank!" Flora screamed.

"Stand back!" Kenyon shouted, moving his Smith & Wesson up to the back of Jay Blue's head for all to see. "These men are going to jail."

"Why, you sorry son of a bitch!" said the tallest of the men, who stepped forward, trying to pull the tail of his buttoned-up coat over the grip of his revolver. At the same time, the Indian, Tonk, eased to one side to spread the field of fire, and Kenyon thought he might not accomplish this arrest without gunplay after all.

"No!" Flora screamed, grabbing the arm of the lanky cowhand. "He's got Jay Blue!"

She seemed to jolt some sense into the men, though the anger in the room remained as thick as the mud in the street.

Kenyon's voice rose to a shout: "I want everybody but Mr. Collins out of here *now*!" He waited as the cowboys and the ladies shuffled out of the store in unwilling obedience, then he ushered Jay Blue into the adjoining room added on behind the store.

"Put the captain on the floor inside the cell," he said.

When Brennan had carried out his order and exited the cell, Kenyon said, "Jay Blue, you sit down on the floor beside your father."

The boy obeyed, pulling the captain's shoulders up to lean against him, so the blood would drain out of his nose instead of running back into his throat, choking him.

"You're dismissed," Kenyon said to Jack Brennan.

Brennan only sneered and left the room. Kenyon heard him stomping all the way out through the front door of the store. Now he holstered his Smith & Wesson. He shook the cage to make sure it was still firmly bolted to the floor. He felt along the tops of the flat iron bars that created the upper part of the cell.

"What are you doing?" Sam Collins said, having stepped into the lean-to room.

"Searching the cell."

"For what?"

Kenyon shrugged. "A file, a hacksaw, a knife." He looked under the iron shelf that served as a bunk. Finally, he took the thin cotton-stuffed mattress from the hard bunk and groped along its entire length. At one end, he suddenly felt something hard. Tearing the cover open at a weak spot in the stitching, he produced a key that looked remarkably like the one stuck in the lock of the cell door.

"Perhaps a key," he said, conscious of the fact that he was gloating. He tossed the mattress out of the cell. Grinning now, Kenyon stepped out of the cage. He slammed the door and locked it, pocketing both keys. A rare sense of accomplishment flooded over him. This was his life's work, all but completed. He felt the approval of his dead mother, vindication for his murdered father.

"Mr. Collins, I'll be needing you to send some telegrams of my success here on this day." He looked into the cell at Jay Blue. "I'll be right here in the store, so don't try anything."

The younger Tomlinson looked at him with exasperated hatred. "What am I gonna try?"

Kenyon just shrugged, grinned, and walked out of the crude little jail.

36

JAY BLUE was sure the temperature was near freezing in the little lean-to jail room. The heat from the woodstove in the store didn't seem to reach the cell at all. He had sat shivering for hours with his unconscious father, shifting his rear end on the iron straps bolted in several places to the wood floor. He was worried about his father. He should have come to by now, but Kenyon had refused his request for a visit by Doc Zuber.

A worse day in his life Jay Blue could not remember. Poli was dead. Jane had rejected him. His father was out cold and accused of multiple murders. He was shivering in a cold jail cell. And then there was Skeeter. Sitting there for hours, Jay Blue had tried to figure out what had driven Skeeter to take a job with Jack Brennan at the Double Horn Ranch.

Stripped now of his weapons, his swagger, and his bold talk, Jay Blue began to hear the things he had said to Skeeter over the past days and weeks. Hell—months and years! He asked himself if he would have let someone talk to him that way all this time. Hell, no. Then there was that one particularly mean thing he had said out there in the hills this morning while they were searching for Poli.

Jay Blue knew Skeeter fretted over nothing more than the fact that he was an orphan, and he had cruelly attacked that vulnerable spot in his friend's heart. He realized now that when Skeeter had ridden to the other side of that canyon this morning—staying gone for hours, making Jay Blue furious—that he had actually trotted over to the Double Horn Ranch. Wasn't Skeeter standing with Jack Brennan at the bar last night while Jay Blue picked the banjo and flirted with the girl who wanted nothing to do with him? He should have seen it then, but it was hard to recognize the obvious with one's head up one's ass. He felt almost sick to his stomach with shame as he listened to the memories in his head, over and over, of the things he had said to his best friend. His *former* best friend, that is. He disgusted himself. He deserved to shiver in jail.

The worst memory was that of Skeeter taking his gun from his holster in the bar. There was a hurt look on Skeeter's face when he did it, but also the determined look of someone who had taken a bellyful of being pushed around. And Jay Blue knew that he was the one who had done the pushing.

The whole afternoon, Kenyon had been conducting interviews with townsfolk in the store, sending Sam Collins out into the cold to drag in witnesses who could testify that they had seen the old arrow fall out of the fiddle case and heard Gotch Dunnsworth declare that the fiddle and case had been given to him years ago by Captain Tomlinson.

Right now Gotch Dunnsworth himself was in the early stages of his interrogation by that relentless State Policeman. Jay Blue could not tell exactly what all was being said, but the tone of the discussion indicated that Gotch was not being as cooperative as Kenyon would have liked.

Suddenly, his father groaned. Jay Blue shifted to see his eyes fluttering open. He scooted to a crouch, and held his father in an upright sitting position. The captain blinked, then reached for his nose. Touching the swollen protuberance in the middle of his face, he winced, looked around at the cell, then focused on his son.

"Thank God you're alive," he said.

Jay Blue put a finger to his lips and pointed into the store.

His father nodded. "Is anybody else dead?" he whispered.

Jay Blue shook his head.

"Then what the hell happened?"

Jay Blue told the story as briefly as he could, keeping his voice below the sound of rain on the leaky cedar shake roof and the whistle of icy wind through the board-and-batten walls.

When he was finished, his father shook his head. "I don't think I heard you right, son. *Skeeter* took your gun?"

Jay Blue nodded in shame. "He says he's taken a job with Jack Brennan."

Hank reached up for his son's shoulder. "Help me up on that bunk." Sitting upright under his own power, the Ranger continued his questions. "Why the hell would Skeeter do a thing like that?"

Jay Blue hung his head. "I said something stupid to Skeeter, Daddy. I said something really bad."

Hank shrugged. "Well, then you'll have to fix it. Apologize to him."

He gestured to the cell around him. "It's too late."

"It's never too late to save a friendship," he hissed. He was blinking his eyes hard and trying to shake the cobwebs out of his head.

"Even if we could get out of here, I don't know if he'd listen to me anymore."

"Bullshit. Fix it. You got that Thoroughbred mare back, didn't you? You fixed that."

"I don't think this is gonna be that easy, Daddy. I can't just throw a loop on Skeeter and drag him back. I haven't been treatin' him like a member of the family lately."

Hank sighed. "Well, maybe neither of us have."

Now Jay Blue watched in astonishment as his father stood up, jutted his jaw, took his broken nose between the fingertips of both hands, and shifted it back into place. He could hear the bone and cartilage grinding, and saw a new trickle of blood run down into his father's mustache. He had always known his old man was tough. But *damn*.

"Oh . . ." Hank groaned under his breath as he rubbed his belly. "That always makes me a little queasy. Now, listen. One thing's for sure. We're not gonna pull Skeeter back into the fold shiverin' our sorry asses off in this cell like a couple of town curs."

"I forgot to tell you. Kenyon found the hidden key."

"In the mattress?"

Jay Blue nodded.

"Good."

"Why is that good?"

"I *wanted* him to find *that* key. Now he thinks he's outsmarted me, and that puts me one step ahead of him. It's a chess match, son."

"Well, he's captured two knights, so I hope you have another hideout key somewhere."

"The match is quite often won with the early moves of the pawns."

"Are you all here, Daddy?"

Jay Blue's father began to look around the room beyond the iron cage. "Do you remember when you were just a little kid, and we realized this town needed a jail? You helped me build this lean-to on the back of Sam's store."

"Yeah, I remember."

He looked up at the ceiling. "We cut these cedar beams down along the Pedernales. You and me, a couple of pawns chopping wood."

"Right . . ."

"I searched a long time for this one particular tree." He pointed to the beam directly over the cell. "Hard to find a cedar with a hollow in it at just the right place." Putting his boots into the squares formed by the crossed iron bars, he climbed two feet up the cell wall as if it were a ladder, reached up through the grate above, and probed with his fingertips into a hidden indention in the natural growth of the cedar beam. It was the only place where he could have reached the beam, there where the slant of the lean-to roof was closest to the top of the cage. When his fingers came back into view, they pulled from the hollow a dusty key, along with a good supply of cobwebs.

Jay Blue grinned and looked through the door, into the general store. "How are we gonna get by Kenyon?"

Hank was slipping the key into the lock. "Like knights on a chessboard. Two steps forward and one step aside." Reaching through the bars, he slowly turned the key, wincing at every little metallic clank. The bolt slid open, and he carefully swung the door ajar.

Over the heated conversation between Gotch and Kenyon in the store, Jay Blue heard the telegraph ticker start to tap.

Stepping out of the cell, Jay Blue tiptoed after his fellow escapee. His father headed straight for the back wall of the room, two steps away. He watched the captain crouch and push at the bottoms of two of the planks that helped form the wall. To his surprise, the boards swung open as if they were hinged at the top, which he figured they probably were, providing an escape route through which the erstwhile captives could crawl.

When he rolled out into the bitter cold of the winterlike evening, Jay Blue found his father urging him to follow through the alley behind the store and the other businesses on that stretch of Main Street. They ran a block, turned on a side street, crossed Main, and ducked into the alley behind Flora's Saloon. Making no attempt to stay quiet now, Hank flung open the side door to Flora's carriage house, revealing two Broken Arrow horses, already fitted with the Tomlinsons' saddles.

Flora and Jane were sitting on the back of the three-spring buggy, wrapped in blankets. They both slid off as the pale cold light and the frigid wind burst in.

"It's about time!" Flora said. "Hurry! The boys are waiting at the ford on the Pedernales." She turned to open the carriage doors.

To Jay Blue's astonishment, Jane came straight to him, catching his sleeve before he mounted. In her eyes he saw a new kind of twinkle. He'd have thought she almost liked him all of a sudden. She slipped an envelope into his grasp, her own palms feeling like furnaces as they wrapped around his cold knuckles and his wrist.

"This is what we know so far about the brands," she said. "We're still investigating." Then, lo and behold, she kissed his cheek. "Go! Hurry!" she said.

Jay Blue saw that his father was already mounted, so he swung into his own saddle without bothering to put a foot in his stirrup. He was riding on air as he left the carriage house.

Hank waited for him to catch up as they turned away from Main to take the back streets. "What's the most powerful piece on the chessboard?" he asked.

"The queen," Jay Blue replied.

"And don't you ever forget it."

They trotted to the edge of town, looking over their shoulders for trouble. When they hit the Fredericksburg Road, they struck a lope for the ford. Just before they dropped off the bluff into the Pedernales Valley, something spectacular caught Jay Blue's eye. The sun had appeared in a narrow swath of clear sky between the horizon below and the clouds above—a glowing orange ball of distant fire announcing a coming end to the sleet and freezing rain.

"The sun will shine tomorrow," Hank said.

"And the light moon will rise tomorrow night," Jay Blue observed.

Hank nodded. "The Moon of the Wolf. Those Comanches are likely to raid the Double Horn."

"If they do, Skeeter will be right in the middle of it."

Hank gritted his teeth. "We've got a lot of fixin' to do in a day's time." Now, for some reason, the captain started chuckling.

"What's funny?"

"I've got half a mind to ride back to the jail room and peek in through a knothole, just to see the look on Kenyon's face when he finds us gone."

Ahead, on the near side of the ford, Jay Blue saw the Broken Arrow ranch hands waiting at the banks of the Pedernales. It was a welcome sight, but still it broke his heart to see no sign of Poli or Skeeter among the men.

The Original Wolf strolled along the river with Birdsong at his side, the warm sun and the cool breeze invigorating his flesh in a most pleasant way.

"The spirits are with me," he said. "The pain of my wound is nothing now. It is less than nothing. The rains have made the earth soft, so our ponies can run far on sound feet. Farther than far. My raiding party has grown to almost ten times ten. Our revenge will be swift and sure. I have smoked and prayed. I have rested and feasted on good food. And . . ."

"Yes?" she said.

"I have loved a beautiful girl, and it was good."

"Better than good," she said.

"Better than any good thing I have ever known." He strolled a while, glanced around for onlookers, then pulled Birdsong behind the trunk of a big cottonwood and penned her between his body and the tree. "How many horses must I bring to be sure your grandfather will give you up to be my bride?"

She smiled and pulled him close. "How many am I worth?"

"All the horses in the world. I had better capture many on this raid."

"You had better come back well. That is all."

He scoffed. "It is up to the spirits. You know that."

Just then some children ran by, spotted them in their hidden embrace, and made loud noises about their lewd conduct.

Birdsong threw a rock at them and giggled. "Come," she said to the Wolf. "We have a great war dance to prepare."

37

REST A SPELL, SON," Hank said. He reached down into the hole, some five feet deep now, and helped Jay Blue climb out.

"My turn," said a solemn George Powers. He dropped down into what would soon serve as Policarpo Losoya's grave, and began chipping away at a slab of limestone with a pickax.

The men had arrived at the ranch last night and posted guards. Hank had ordered everyone besides the guards to get some rest. "Unless he's a complete fool, Kenyon won't try to take me here," he reasoned. "He'll ride back to Austin and gather up a posse. We'll be safe here for a few days."

At dawn, they had risen, eaten Beto's breakfast, and rotated between the gravesite and guard duty. Beto Canales and Americo Limón had wept while digging. Knowing how sensitive Skeeter was, Hank figured he'd be blubbering right now, too, if he were here. It didn't seem right that he wasn't.

The rains had softened the earth, which facilitated the digging of soil with a spade or a shovel. But this bluff over the Pedernales harbored much rock beneath the surface, and there was no easy way through that. Accordingly, the deepening of the grave had progressed by inches.

Jay Blue dusted his hands as he caught his breath. He had gone at the task of digging the grave like he did everything else—all out. With dirty fingers, he reached into his pocket and produced the report from Jane that he had begun studying last night.

Hank had been too distracted to pore over the letter as of yet.

He knew he had bought himself some time. Flora would send word once Kenyon had left town, and then he could collect Poli's coffin and have him buried here. After that he could concentrate on the hunt for Black Cloud. Besides, Jay Blue was working on the case as if his life depended on it, which it might well have. Hank had come to trust his son's hunches on this case and figured his fresh look at the evidence might be just what was needed.

He looked away from Poli's grave, only to see Emilie's headstone. He sank deeper into grief, remembering the sad day he had put her to rest. He wished he had some fresh flowers to place on her grave right now.

"Daddy," Jay Blue said.

"Yeah?"

"The ladies mention a brand. A 'Rafter T' brand."

He looked at his son. "And?" He could tell that Jay Blue was uneasy.

"Well, what *is* it? The rafter, I mean."

Hank smirked. "Son, there's no shame in askin' a simple question. Nobody expects you to know everything at birth. The rafter is like an upside-down V. It usually goes over a letter, like a rocker goes under a W on a Rockin' W brand. The rafter always goes over something else, like the rafter in a barn."

Jay Blue's eyes lit up. "Oh, it goes *over* the T." He smoothed some fresh dirt with his boot and began making marks in it with the blade of a shovel.

Hank let the words sink in. "Did you say 'Rafter T'?"

"Yes, sir," Jay Blue muttered as he continued to draw brands in the mud.

"*Rafter T* sounds a lot like *Rafferty*. That was Black Cloud's white name. John Rafferty."

Briefly, Jay Blue looked up from his mud scrawlings, then went back to work. About that time, Hank noticed Americo Limón trudging from his guard post to the ranch's cemetery plot for his turn at digging.

"It's your shift on guard duty, son," Hank ordered.

Jay Blue threw the shovel down. "Yes, sir."

"Jay Blue, let me see that letter."

"Yes, sir. I've got it memorized anyway." He handed his father the folded paper.

As Jay Blue took Americo's rifle and walked away, Hank tried to read the letter. He found concentration hard to come by. He looked at the moist dirt where his son had been making shapes with the shovel blade. For some reason, the boy had drawn Wes James's brand in the mud.

W
J

Beto had cleared the table and lit another lantern in the cook shack. All the boys save Long Tom Merrick, who was on guard duty, were gathered around the long dining table, having feasted on beef, beans, pickled okra, corn tortillas, and peach cobbler. Now they were slurping black coffee and listening to the Tomlinsons trying to solve the mystery of Wes James's murder.

"Go over that again, son. I don't follow," Hank picked his teeth with a splinter he had pulled from the rough-sawn tabletop.

"Look," Jay Blue said. He pulled a knife from a belt scabbard. "You start with our brand, the Broken Arrow." He used the sharp point of his blade to carve the brand in the pine plank upon which he had just dined.

/\

"It's a good brand," Hank boasted. "If you don't have a Broken Arrow branding iron with you, you can burn it into the hide with two touches of a simple bar brand. Hell, you can even use a runnin' iron or a hot saddle buckle held between two green tree branches if you have to."

"Yes, sir, it's a fine brand," Jay Blue agreed, having heard the merits of the Broken Arrow many times before. "But here's my theory. John Rafferty . . . Black Cloud—whoever he is—starts rustlin' your stock. You've said yourself for years that you suspected somebody was thinnin' your herd. If Rafferty is the owner of the Rafter T brand, he could easily change the Broken Arrow to a Rafter T using a bar brand, a runnin' iron, or a buckle, like you just said."

With his knife tip, Jay Blue joined the upper tips of the Broken Arrow, creating a rafter. Then he added a T below.

^
T

"The son of a bitch!" Hank said. One thing he could not abide was a stock thief.

"So, let's assume that Rafferty's been doctorin' our brand to a Rafter T, holdin' the rustled cattle on the free range up around Brown County, and then trailin' 'em north to sell at the railheads in Kansas."

"The bastard!"

"Wait," Jay Blue said. "You'll like this part even better. John Rafferty hires some saddle bum to help him with the rustlin'. But this saddle bum is thinking way ahead of Rafferty. Before he moves onto our ranges, he assumes an alias—Wes James. There's a good reason for the alias. Before he even comes to work for Rafferty, he registers his own brand way up in Jack County—the WJ."

"This is where you lost me last time," Hank said. "But I think I follow so far."

"I'll go slow. After workin' for Rafferty for a while, doctorin' our brand to a Rafter T, this so-called Wes James decides it's time for him to have a bigger slice of the pie. So, he starts doctorin' the Rafter T to his WJ."

Again, Jay Blue illustrated with cold steel on soft pine, changing the rafter to a W, and the T to a J.

W
J

"I'll be damned," Hank said. "He's doctorin' a doctored brand."

"Rustlin' from the rustlers," said Tonk.

"No wonder he wound up dead," Americo Limón observed.

Jay Blue was getting excited about the acceptance of his breakthrough. "With his WJ brand, Wes can rustle Broken Arrow *and* Rafter T beeves. But now Rafferty sees his profits drop off and gets suspicious. He trails Wes, catches him in the act, and shoots him full of Black Cloud arrows. Maybe as a warning to you that you're next, Daddy. Or maybe to pin it on you if folks still believe you were Black Cloud all along. Or maybe to pin it on the Indians so the army will run them clean out of Texas."

"Maybe all three. But where do you reckon Policarpo figured into it?"

"Maybe Poli saw something he wasn't supposed to see. Maybe Black Cloud just wanted to make you hurt, and knew killin' Poli would do it. Hell, maybe I'm his next target. Or Skeeter! Or any of us."

Hank nodded grimly and tapped the brand on the table with his trigger finger. "That's good work, son. It all makes sense. Except for one thing. Just who the hell *is* John Rafferty? Where is he? Do we even know him?"

"I think it's Jack Brennan."

Hank shook his head. "No, son, it can't be him."

"But everything points to him, Daddy. He conveniently found Wes's body. He started the trouble with the Comanches at Flat Rock Creek. He busted your nose so Kenyon could arrest you. And, worst of all, he's got Skeeter workin' for him and against us now. Why can't you see he's the prime suspect?"

"Simple. He's been our neighbor for almost twenty years. I can't say he's been the best neighbor, but he hasn't killed me, has he? If he came here for revenge on me, he's had plenty of opportunities. Why would he wait till now?"

"It's because of me."

The voice had come from the only door to the cook shack. Every man at the table flinched at the intrusion, and every eye swept up from the brand carved into the tabletop to the armed cowboy standing in the doorway, pointing two cocked Colt revolvers at the whole Broken Arrow crew.

"Skeeter!" Jay Blue said. "What are you doin' now?"

"Just shut up, Jay Blue. For once in your life, just shut up and listen."

"Easy, Skeeter," said Hank. "Why would any of this be because of you?"

Skeeter stepped inside the doorway, and a second armed man emerged from the dark. It was Matt Kenyon, and he had a sawed-off double-barrel shotgun covering the table, with both hammers pinned back like the ears of an angry horse. "Nobody move," he said. "Just listen to young Mr. Rodriguez here."

"How the hell did you get past my guard?" Hank demanded. "Where's Long Tom?"

"Don't fly off the handle, Captain." Long Tom Merrick followed his own drawl into the cook shack. "I've got a surprise for you." He stepped out of the doorway to allow Flora and Jane to follow him in.

"Hank, you've got to listen," Flora said.

Jay Blue could not contain himself. "Skeeter, what the hell is this? First you join the Double Horn bunch, now you bring *him* here?" He pointed a damning finger at the State Policeman.

"I didn't join the Double Horn bunch," Skeeter said, a knowing sneer on his face. "It's called *infiltrating* the outlaw gang. Ain't that right, Mr. Kenyon?"

"That's precisely what it's called, Skeeter." Now Kenyon pointed the muzzles of the scatter gun at the ceiling to ease the tension in the shack. "Everybody just stay calm and listen to Mr. Skeeter Rodriguez and you'll all understand."

Skeeter let his pistols point at the floor as if they were the heaviest things he had ever held in his life. "It's because of me that Jack Brennan hasn't killed you yet, Captain Tomlinson."

"What are you sayin', Skeeter?"

"He offered me a job. He told me to meet him at his ranch, and said he knew who my daddy was. I got mad at Jay Blue, so I went to talk to Brennan. He told me *he* was my father. He *is* my father. That's why he's waited to kill you. He wanted you to raise me first, Captain. He knew you'd do a better job than he would. Now that I'm grown, he's ready to get his revenge on you."

"He told you all that?"

"No! I figured it out myself! He only told me that he was my daddy. He said he had taken up with a Mexican woman, and they had me. But she died, along with the rest of my family—I guess they took sick. He didn't say what happened, only said he didn't know how I survived when no one else did. I guess he didn't want to raise me, so he left me with an old man he knew to raise—the man I thought was my grandfather. Then my *abuelo* died, and you took me in, Captain. Now Brennan says he wants me back."

Jay Blue shook his head. "Skeeter, Jack Brennan is likely to tell you all kinds of bunk."

"Can't you see, *hermano*? All these years, you told me he's always asking, 'How's that kid, Skinner?' or 'How's Skipper doin'?' or 'Where the hell is Scooter?' You thought it was funny because he never got my name right. Don't you get it? Where do you think I got these blue eyes!"

"Skeeter," Jay Blue implored. "Have you joined his outfit or not?"

"I thought about it. I thought—I could be a rancher's son, just like you, Jay Blue. I could be somebody. But then I noticed some things."

"What things?" Hank said.

"Go ahead, tell 'em." Matt Kenyon put his hand on Skeeter's shoulder, urging him to continue.

"He was showing me around the Double Horn Ranch headquarters, telling me it could all be mine someday. But, in the barn, I saw a big roll of wire. It looked like that wire they use on the telegraph poles. So, I got a hunch. I didn't say nothin', but I thought maybe he was the one who tore the wire down so you couldn't investigate the Wes James murder, *Capitán*."

"That's shapin' up to be a pretty good hunch," Hank said.

"There's more," Kenyon said. "Go ahead, Skeeter."

"After I saw the wire, I started paying real close attention. In the old adobe house, Brennan showed me his deed to the Double Horn Ranch. Then he showed me his will. He's got me down as the one to inherit the ranch when he's gone. It was signed by witnesses and notarized, and everything. He was really trying to smooth-talk me into joining his outfit."

"Well, did he succeed, or not?" Jay Blue demanded.

"Patience, *hermano*."

"Just tell me you're still one of us, Skeeter. Please tell me you're back."

"Just listen." He uncocked his weapons, put one Colt revolver in his holster, and shoved the spare under his gun belt. "While I was pretending to look over the deed and the will, I was really looking at all the other papers scattered around on his desk. He doesn't have a nice, neat desk like you, *Capitán*. It's a mess. But I was looking for anything I might see, like that wire in the barn. I saw a bill of sale for some cattle, handwritten from a Dodge City buyer. I couldn't see the whole piece of paper because it was sticking out from under some other junk, but I saw the brand drawn on the bill of sale. It was a little peak over a T. That seemed funny to me, because that ain't the Double Horn brand. So, I remembered the brand. I told Brennan that I would accept his offer, but I had to go tell Captain Tomlinson and Jay Blue first that I wasn't going to work at the Broken Arrow no more."

"Were you going to tell us?" Hank asked. "Can't say that I'd blame you for making that decision, the way we've treated you around here."

"I didn't know *what* to do. But all day yesterday, after we found Poli, I thought about that brand in my head. I figured out it was halfway between a Broken Arrow brand and Wes James's WJ. I didn't know what that meant yet, but then all hell broke loose in the saloon, and I had to make a decision. I didn't really want to join the Double Horn outfit, but I decided I'd . . . Well, Mr. Kenyon says I *infiltrated* the outlaw gang. There was no way to tell you what I was doin', Jay Blue. I just had to do it."

"You were a step ahead of us all along," Jay Blue admitted.

"I went back to the Double Horn and spent the night with those thugs. That's a sorry bunch of bastards out there. Anyway, this morning, when Brennan—my long-lost daddy—went to the outhouse to take a crap, I got a look at that bill of sale with the funny brand on it and I saw that it was made out to a John Rafferty. That name shocked the hell out of me, because the captain told us that was Black Cloud's name before he went Indian. So I stole that bill of sale with the Rafter T brand on it."

"He secured the evidence," Kenyon said, rather editorially.

"I secured the hell out of it," Skeeter agreed. "I didn't even know it was called a rafter at the time. I thought it was a tepee. Anyway, I told Brennan I wanted to start working some of the green-broke colts, since I was taking over the ranch, so I roped one out of the corral, saddled him up, and went for a ride."

Matt Kenyon eased the hammers to the safety position on the double-barrel. "Skeeter rode straight to Luck and caught me before I left for Austin to gather my posse. He showed me the bill of sale. By that time, the ladies had received some telegrams describing the owner of the Rafter T brand as John Rafferty, six-foot-six, two-twenty, with a prominent scar on his left cheek. We put it all together and rode out here to set the record straight. All charges against you have been dropped, Captain Tomlinson. I, personally, along with some help from Max Cooper down at the Austin *Daily Statesman*, will see to it that your name will forever be cleared of any suspicion of past killings attributed to Black Cloud. Including the killing of my father, Jim Kenyon."

Hank let out a huge sigh. "I guess that means you owe me an apology, Officer Kenyon."

Kenyon paused, searching the room with his eyes. But then he jutted his chin. "Apologize for doing my duty? No, sir. You have to admit, you *were* the prime suspect."

Hank stepped away from the table and drilled the officer with an unwavering glare. He approached Kenyon slowly until he stood a foot away. "You've got a point, Matt. It's a point that could have got you shot, but it's a good point. Just promise me one thing."

"Anything, Captain."

"When this Reconstruction government gives us our state back, and the Texas Rangers ride again, promise me you'll wear the *cinco peso*. The Rangers could use a hardheaded bulldog like you. You're just like your ol' daddy." He stuck his hand out.

Kenyon shook the captain's hand, but had no words to speak just then.

Hank turned to Skeeter and gave him a hug a father would give an only son. "Thank God you're back, Skeeter. That was a gutsy thing you did. You got some *cajones, mí hijo*. But, you know what we have to do now, don't you?"

"Yes, sir."

"We've got to ride over to the Double Horn Ranch and take your long-lost daddy down for murdering Policarpo, Wes James, Jim Kenyon, and two other Rangers. Not to mention all the rustlin'."

"I know."

"Are you with me, or against me?"

"I'm with you, *Capitán*. He ain't no father of mine. You've been more of a daddy to me than he ever could have been." He turned to look at the younger Tomlinson. "As for you, Jay Blue . . . You're a pain in the ass, but you're the only brother I've got. I'm sorry I took your gun. I didn't have a choice."

"And I'm sorry for the stupid things I said, Skeeter." Jay Blue stuck his hand out. When Skeeter took it, he pulled his brother's right shoulder against his own and clamped him there with his left arm. "I'm just glad you're back."

"Alright!" Hank announced. "Here's what we're gonna do. We'll post guards in shifts tonight, and try to get some shut-eye. Tomorrow at dawn we'll have a big breakfast. Then Officer Kenyon will deputize us all and we'll ride over to the Double Horn and bring John Rafferty in alive or dead—along with every one of his outlaw cattle rustlers."

Matt Kenyon nodded. "Sounds like it's gonna be a good day for law and order in Texas."

"Hey, Beto," Skeeter said. "I know it ain't normal . . . but can we have fried chicken for breakfast?"

38

ALL NIGHT LONG the drums had sounded as the moon, having risen full and round, shone down on the camp. It passed over the war dancers, adding its steady white glow to the flickers of a hundred blazing campfires in the village of tepees. The night was cold, but the dancing and the heat of the fires kept all the Noomah people charged with warmth.

The warriors had donned headdresses made from the horns of bison, the heads of wolves or lions, the antlers of deer. Most wove eagle feathers into their black braids. The feathers, like those affixed to their shields, would flutter with the speed of their horses, spoiling the aim of their enemies' weapons. They had painted their faces with sacred designs and paraded through camp for all to see. After the parade, they had commenced dancing.

Now the full moon was nearing the western horizon, and the time came for the Original Wolf to silence the drums. The drummers had been watching him, waiting for his signal. He raised his hand, and all the drummers ended the beat together. Warm air burst from the nostrils and mouths of the dancers, the moonlight illuminating the breath clouds that drifted away to the Spirit Land. The warriors and their women, the children and elders who had managed to stay awake, the nearly grown boys who wished they could join the war party—all turned their eyes toward the Original Wolf.

"All night, the moon and the path of stars in the sky have showered us with blessings. We are strong, we are brave, and we are right to defend our country and seek vengeance on enemies who fight like cowards. Take up your lances and shields, your quivers and your guns, and fight today as our elders taught us: with courage, with brotherhood, with the medicine of our spirit guides. On this day, do not ask the spirits for glory. Ask them to lead us to a place where we can *take* some glory! To your warhorses, my brothers. I have spoken!"

War cries cut through the dry, predawn air and echoed off the bluff over the big river. The Wolf watched as the warriors turned away from the ground packed hard by the moccasins of all-night dancers, but his eyes were searching for Birdsong. He spotted her, standing near her grandfather's lodge. The old man was there, too. The scowl never left that old shaman's face, but he nodded once at the raid leader, then ducked into his tepee, leaving his granddaughter outside.

The Wolf walked to her. "It is time to ride. Time to fight."

Her eyes looked as big as moons. "It is my duty to be braver than even you. You leave here to ride and shoot. I must wait. But I am able to do it, and I will reward you with many pleasures when you come home."

The Wolf smiled. He kissed her, but not tenderly, for his heart was poised for plunder and combat. Then he turned away, and he did not look back.

Jubal sat down to the delicious aroma of eggs, beans, and tortillas that Luz had ready for him. He couldn't wait to get back down to the pens and put the saddle on El Grullo again. He had dreamt of it all last night. The silky strides of that proud steed, the fluid trot, the smooth canter—each gait felt the way a great gray crane looked gliding in for a landing at a favored fishing hole. He was indeed El Grullo—the Gray Crane—not just in his gray coloration but through his gift of flight.

He was fortunate to have met those two young cowboys. They had done most of the rough riding. Now it was up to Jubal to finish the training of the stallion who had once tried to stomp him to death.

He wolfed down his breakfast and kissed his beloved Luz, then marched for the door. "I aim to take that gray for quite a romp across the countryside today," he announced. "Put some miles behind him."

"I know!" she sang, her eyes rolling. "You love him more than me now. All night, in your sleep, you said, 'Whoa! . . . Whoa!'" She turned back to her chores.

He stalked up behind her and grabbed her, making her squeal with surprise and delight. "I don't love him more than I love you. That's loco talk, woman. I just need somebody I can boss. Lord knows *you* won't mind me." He kissed her on the neck, then turned toward the cave opening and the frosty light of dawn.

He walked down to the pens to find Thirsty, the camel, and the Steel Dust Gray standing nose to nose across the cedar rails from each other as if they were having a conversation. Oddly enough, the two had become fast friends.

He took his time saddling the stallion. Steel Dust was still half-wild, after all, and required all Jubal's caution and know-how to handle. As he left the home canyon at a trot, heading for the gap in the hills that led toward Fort Jennings, he looked back and noticed that Thirsty was lumbering along behind him.

He had seen and heard of male animals of different types becoming pals in this way before—elk and buffalo bulls who roamed together between mating seasons, male dogs and tomcats playing in the yard—but this had to be the oddest pairing he knew of: a camel and a killer stud.

"Oh, well, everybody needs a friend, I guess," he had said, watching the gray's ears swivel back his way when he spoke.

His heart sank a little when he thought about what he'd said. Not only for himself, but for Luz. They were the best of friends to each other, but a woman needed the friendship of other women, and Jubal had to admit that he was missing those two blasted idiot cowboys. That night in town was fun, too, with the music in the saloon and all—right up until the discovery of the old arrow and the news of the lost foreman. Jubal hoped the man had been found alive, but he had a bad feeling about the whole mess.

Steel Dust suddenly made a marvelously agile leap sideways, dodging some terror Jubal had failed to identify. He just barely managed to stay seated, and decided he'd better keep his mind on his task if he didn't want to watch the mustang go galloping back to favorite haunts, carrying his best saddle.

He arrived at the gap and guided Steel Dust up the steep trail to the lookout point so he could get a view of the country to the east before he went gallivanting blindly around on a green-broke stallion. Thirsty chose to remain at the bottom of the trail to wait at the gap. At the overlook, Jubal sat in the saddle as Steel Dust caught some wind. He watched the country through his telescope awhile, but it wasn't easy, as Steel Dust was still antsy under the saddle and didn't like just standing. He was about to ride on when he caught a brief look at a large party of riders streaming over a ridge, heading toward Double Horn Creek, and riding fast. There was too much flash among the horses to be anything but Indian pinto ponies on the move.

"Damn," he said. This looked like the revenge raid he had dreaded. A party that size might even take on the settlement of Luck, Texas. But before those warriors got to town, they would pass the headquarters of the two biggest ranches in the area. The Double Horn first, then the Broken Arrow, home of those two young cowhands who had talked him into catching the marvelous beast he straddled now.

The least he could do was to gallop over to Fort Jennings and tell the troops which way he had seen the war party turn. After that . . . well, he would make that decision when he came to it. Right now Steel Dust had plenty of bottom left and needed a good training run anyway. Even Thirsty was still game.

Jubal carefully urged the stallion down the slope. "Like I said earlier, ol' hoss, everybody needs a friend, I reckon. Let's git."

39

HANK TOMLINSON peered through the brush to take in a clear view of the Double Horn Ranch headquarters. Officer Matt Kenyon pulled rein to his right, Skeeter and Jay Blue to his left. The rest of the men waited behind.

"Skeeter," Hank said in a low voice, "when you *infiltrated* the Double Horn gang, how many men did they have there on hand?"

"There were three or four I never saw before in my life," Skeeter recalled. "Then the usual hands: Eddie Milliken, Joe Butts, Ham Franklin, Bill Waterford, and Johnny Webb."

"Nine or ten," Kenyon said. "We have nine."

Hank watched a few more seconds. "There's smoke comin' from the old adobe, but I don't see anybody movin' around. Did they post guards, Skeeter?"

"No, sir. Everybody just pretty much stayed drunk and ornery."

Through the brush, Hank saw a side door to the adobe fly open. "Shh!" he warned.

They watched as Eddie Milliken stepped out with a bottle of whiskey in one hand. With his other hand, he slipped a stack of poker cards into his pocket. He tipped the bottom of the whiskey bottle up, drained what little there was in it, and then commenced to piss on the dirt.

Jack Brennan's voice came from the adobe: "Milliken! You in or out?"

Milliken pulled the cards back out of his pocket and looked at them. "I fold!" he moaned, finished his business, and stepped back into the ranch house.

"That place looks pretty well fortified," Kenyon said.

"The walls are a foot thick," Skeeter assured him.

"And that dog on the porch is gonna raise all kinds of hell when he sees us ride in," Hank added.

"Let me go first and I'll whistle at the dog," Skeeter said. "That dog likes me."

"Alright," Hank agreed.

"Then we'll need to draw them out of there somehow." Kenyon looked at Hank. "You got any ideas?"

Hank nodded. "After Skeeter calls off the dog, you and the boys get the horses into the barn and stay out of sight. Dismount and be ready. I'll talk 'em out of that adobe."

Minutes later, Hank stood alone in the mixed mud, gravel, and dirt between the adobe ranch house and the wooden barn. Through the barn door to his right, he could see his men waiting in reserve, out of sight of the door to the adobe. Skeeter was petting the dog. He turned left, toward the adobe stronghold, and began shouting.

"Jack Brennan! Come out here, Jack! I want a word with you!" He waited. The door creaked open.

"Git your sorry ass out here, Jack!" For once in his life, he didn't have to hold his temper. He *used* it. "I want to talk to you about Skeeter! And about you bustin' my nose, you son of a bitch!"

Now the crack in the doorway widened, and John Rafferty, alias Jack Brennan, stepped out, buckling his gun belt on. He smiled as he eased farther out, seeing no one but Hank in the yard. "I figured you'd break out of your own jail quick enough."

"Jack, what's this nonsense you've been fillin' Skeeter's head with?" He waited and watched as Rafferty moved out into the open, followed by eight armed men, the last one staggering and rubbing his eyes as if he had just woken up.

"Why, Hank, I have no idea what the hell you're talkin' about. But I'll guarantee you one thing. You made a big mistake showin' up here a-hollerin' at my door. No man speaks to me in that tone of voice."

Hank smiled. "Sorry, Jack. I mean, John. It is John Rafferty, isn't it?"

He glanced into the barn just long enough to signal Kenyon with a toss of his head. The men came out of the barn as a group, facing off at fifteen paces with the Double Horn outlaws.

The smile slipped from Rafferty's face. "You sons of bitches ain't got nothin' on me."

"To the contrary," Kenyon said, "we have plenty of evidence to convict you of numerous crimes. Including the murders of Wes James and Policarpo Losoya. And that of Jim Kenyon, my father."

Rafferty scoffed.

"It's true," Hank added. "We can link you with the Rafter T brand. That proves you're John Rafferty, and we all know that John Rafferty has done a mess of killin' over the years." He paused to watch the reality register on Rafferty's face. "Now, if you'll come with us peacefully, and plead guilty to your crimes, I give you my word that I'll ask the judge to sentence you to life instead of the gallows. It wasn't your fault you were captured by Comanches all those years ago."

Rafferty's men kept their eyes darting between their outlaw boss and the posse come to collect him. Rafferty himself hadn't budged. He just glared at Hank Tomlinson.

"You chickenshit," he finally growled. "You could have saved me, and you quit."

Hank shook his head. He knew exactly where Rafferty's mind was: on a sunny summer day, some three decades past. "I never quit, John. None of us did. Our horses just gave out. We couldn't keep up."

Rafferty shook his head. "You left me with the same murderin' savages who killed my whole family in front of my eyes. I had no choice but join 'em, so I did. And I dreamed of killin' you and those other three for givin' up on me. Three out of four ain't bad, but I've been waitin' for years to finish the job."

"Waitin' for me to raise Skeeter?"

Rafferty nodded. "My mistake, I guess. Looks like he abandoned me quicker than you did."

"One thing I don't get," Hank said. "The Comanches adopted you. You *were* a Comanche. What happened? When did you become an Indian hater?"

"It was after that shoot-out that you and me had. I hit you with an arrow, and you gut-shot me. I got back to my Indian camp alive, but it took me a long time to heal. I wasn't right for a year or more. Then, one day, I came down with the smallpox of all the damned things, and those Indians abandoned me. Left me to die of the fever. Some Mexican goat herders found me, and saved my life."

"That's it? That's why you risked stirrin' up an Indian war along the whole frontier?"

"You haven't heard it all. I took up with a Mexican girl from that family that nursed me back to health. She didn't seem to care that I'd lived like a wild, murderin' savage, and I guess I loved that little ol' gal for that. But one day while I was out stalkin' game, the Comanches raided and carried her off. I went hunting for her—and huntin' Indians. I killed some Indians, but I never found her."

"So, you figured you could get even with everybody who wronged you. You figured you could steal my cattle, kill anybody that got in your way, pin the blame on me for the murders, and get the Comanches run out of Texas once and for all in the process."

Rafferty shrugged. "Seemed like a fine plan to me. Except, I didn't want you to hang. I wanted to fill you full of arrows and scalp you myself."

"Well, I've got to hand it to you, John, it almost worked. But it's over now. The best thing for you to do is lay your guns down, and tell your men to do the same. Let's not get any of these boys hurt. No need to shoot it out over a lost cause."

"Oh, we're gonna shoot it out, Hank. That long hair of yours will make a dandy addition to my collection." An expression of bemused surprise—one that seemed to have no explanation—appeared on Rafferty's face. "But, right now, I'm afraid all that is gonna have to wait."

"Wait?" Hank said, almost out of patience. "For what?"

"Look over your shoulder." Rafferty began laughing. "Go ahead, look."

Something had come over Rafferty's men. Their eyes were no longer focused on the posse, but looking beyond. If they were playing along with their boss, they were doing a damn fine job.

Still, Hank wasn't about to take his eyes off of Rafferty. "Matt?" he said.

From the corner of his eye, he saw Kenyon turn.

"Glory be to God," Matt Kenyon said in a tone of voice a man might use but once in a lifetime.

An arrow flew by Hank's ear and stuck in the dirt between the posse and the outlaw gang, followed by the war cries of a hundred Comanches. Still, Hank did not take his eyes from Rafferty's smiling face.

"Get in the barn!" Hank said, backing away, watching Rafferty.

"To the house, boys!" ordered Rafferty, though four men had already run there for cover. He, too, had his eyes glued to his rival. Just before he backed into the door, Rafferty drew his Colt. Hank mirrored the move and splinters leapt into both men from shattered barn wood and door framing. Hank stayed at the door just long enough to look west at the attackers. He almost smiled. A line of horses thundered toward the ranch buildings—horses of all colors, ridden by warriors bedecked in all manner of nature's finery. Lance points jutted skyward, arrows arched with speed almost too fast to follow, white puffs of smoke preceded reports that followed. And all along the line, as if the warriors carried the charm of eagle spirits, feathers fluttered in such a way that they made a man dizzy.

Hank reached out and pulled the big hinged barn door closed as arrows rattled into it and lead slugs split lumber. Jay Blue was at his side, pulling the other barn door closed as the fastest of the warriors galloped between the house and the barn.

Hank began barking orders almost faster than he could think them. "Skeeter, you and Jay Blue get all our horses in those stalls. Tom! Americo! Cover these double doors! Build a barricade out of whatever you can find!" He turned to the opposite side of the barn. "George, you and Beto take the southwest corner. Tonk, you and Matt cover the southeast. Guard every approach. Whatever you do, don't let the Indians set the barn on fire!"

The men took their posts, using rifle butts and boot heels to knock planks from the exterior wall, creating slots through which to aim and shoot.

"What now?" Jay Blue said, having crammed nine mounts into two broken-down stalls with Skeeter's help.

"Gather whatever you can find to build breastworks. And, look out, here comes the second charge!"

Slugs sang weird harmonies to the war whoops that swept by outside.

"Hot damn!" Matt Kenyon yelled.

"You hit?"

"Just a flesh wound," Kenyon growled. "I think it missed the bone."

"Get some cover for these men!" Hank ordered, glaring at Jay Blue and Skeeter.

The two younger cowhands picked up everything they could lift and started constructing crude barricades at the three points of defense Hank had established inside the walls. They stacked up old saddles and barrels, and even tore a trough from the wall with pure adrenaline.

"What's goin' on out there?" Hank demanded.

"They're keeping their distance right now," Kenyon yelled through the pain of his wound. "Looks like their mounts are winded."

"That'll give us a minute or two. Make sure you're reloaded."

"They caught a bunch of hobbled ranch horses that were out grazin'," Tom said, peering out between the big double doors. "They'll be mounted on fresh stock pronto."

"Aw, shit!" said Beto Canales from the southeast corner. "Look!"

George Powers had been reloading his Winchester rifle next to Beto. "Christ Almighty," he said, total exasperation lacing his words.

"What the hell is it now?" Hank blurted.

"Those women. They followed us!"

"*¡Chinga'o!*" Hank cursed. He ran to the corner, looked over Beto's shoulder, and saw the top of Flora's buggy lurching around where the road crossed the rocky creek bed. For the first time, he felt a wave of panic rise up that he had to fight back, but when he turned around to the interior of the barn to grab a horse, he saw Jay Blue already mounted, with the reins of a second horse in his hand.

"No, Jay Blue!" he yelled.

But Jay Blue was already kicking the barn door open beside Long Tom and Americo. "Cover me!"

"Shit!" Hank yelled. "Everybody hold your fire. Maybe they won't see him."

"They already see him," Tonk said. "There they go."

Hank darted to the southwest corner and stepped in a puddle of Matt Kenyon's blood. "Shoot their horses out from under 'em. Don't let them anywhere near Jay Blue or those hardheaded women!"

He heard a scurrying in the rafters and looked up to see Skeeter crawling into what had once been a loft, but could now more correctly be termed a death trap. Skeeter tested rotten lumber underfoot until he reached the slope of the roof. He kicked out a few shingles and peered through the hole he had made.

"You got a good angle?" Hank said.

"Yes, sir! I can see everything up here."

"Catch!" Hank yelled, and tossed a Winchester up to Skeeter. "Make it hot for 'em, son!"

"There they go for the creek!" Kenyon yelled. "Six of 'em!"

Hank scrambled back to the corner and added several rounds to a barrage of lead that flew from the barn. Though beyond effective range, one of the Indian ponies fell dead, the rider limping into the brush. But the other five warriors swarmed through the timber toward the buggy mired at the creek crossing.

"It's up to you now, Skeeter!"

Smoking brass cartridges began to drop from the loft. Hank counted shots as he loaded another Winchester. When he heard Skeeter's hammer click, he hollered, "Catch!" He tossed the new rifle up and caught the one Skeeter dropped. "Give 'em hell!"

"Jay Blue's got the one gal mounted behind him, and Flora on the other horse!" George said. "Here they come!" He punctuated his own words with a rapid succession of pistol rounds.

"The Indians!" Long Tom cried from the barn door, still open from Jay Blue's departure. "They're *all* comin'!"

Hank looked west and saw the main body of the war party gathering speed for an all-out attack on the ranch buildings. He shoved two last rounds into one of his Colts as he strode out of the barn door and waited to cover his son's return when he came around the corner. The Comanches had split into three prongs in order to swarm around and between the adobe house and the rickety old barn. Hank stood his ground as arrows whispered Comanche curses past his ears. He loosed rounds from both fists with such effect that the middle prong of warriors scattered.

The two outer waves of attackers continued, taking fire from the outlaws in the adobe and Skeeter through the barn roof. Finally, Jay Blue appeared, with Jane holding on wide-eyed behind him and Flora riding a step behind, firing a derringer beyond the adobe with one hand and holding both her reins and a leather satchel with her other hand.

"Run for the barn!" Jay Blue said to Jane as he virtually pulled her from the horse. He jumped down beside her and handed her the reins.

"What about you?" she said.

Hank turned to stand guard beside his son.

"Just go!" Jay Blue yelled.

Just as she turned, a warrior appeared around the corner of the adobe, carrying only a lance into battle, leading the left prong of the swarming attack. Hank lifted one revolver, but felt Jay Blue's hand on his wrist.

"That's the Wolf!"

The Original Wolf slid to a halt on his pony, signaling to the riders behind him to stop. He shifted his eyes to the rider of the right-hand prong of the attack, now coming around the barn in spite of the barrage Skeeter had flung. The Wolf shouted something in Comanche and made a whirling motion of his wrist, and the whole wave of warriors that would have swarmed around the barn and in between the two buildings turned instead back to the creek.

Hank backed into the barn behind Jane. Jay Blue came in next, closed the barn door behind him, and turned his back to the door to shout at the loft. "Hold your fire, Skeeter! That's the Wolf with the lance, and he just saved my ass!"

At that moment, an arrow slammed through the planking on the closed barn door, the shaft protruding into the barn just far enough to sink an inch deep into Jay Blue's left hip pocket. He bellowed like a branded calf and sprang forward so hastily that he jumped into Jane's arms, tripping her to the dirt and falling right on top of her. She fell awkwardly on her back, with her legs jutting two different directions. The arrow stayed stuck in the barn door, the point not having sunk quite deep enough into flesh for the barbs to take hold.

Skeeter was almost falling down the loft ladder in a fit of laughter. "Looks like you been shot in the heart by Cupid's arrow!" he cried in guffaws.

"They're regrouping," Matt Kenyon said, watching the movements of the Indians.

Hank turned to Flora. "You promised to stay put at the ranch!"

"No, you *ordered* us to stay put. Don't start, Hank. This was as much our arrest as it was yours. Anyway, we brought medical supplies in case the shooting started. Didn't count on quite this much of it."

Hank bit his lip. "Well, look at Jay Blue's wound, then check on Matt. He's bleedin' pretty bad over there in the corner."

Jane was crawling out from under Jay Blue, who was also trying to regain his footing and his dignity. Flora knelt behind him and ripped open the seat of his britches where the arrow point had poked through.

"This one's gushing, too," she said. She yanked the leather satchel open, pulled out one of the bandages she and Jane had made by tearing up a sheet, and folded it over a couple of times. "Here," she said, placing the folded bandage in Jane's hand. She pressed Jane's hand hard against Jay Blue's wound.

"Grab hard, honey! He won't complain!"

Skeeter started laughing almost too hard to reload as Jay Blue hobbled into position behind the breastworks at the double doors facing the adobe.

"Stay low, Jane," Jay Blue said, his store of dignity almost exhausted.

"I've been reduced to grabbing your butt in front of your father," she replied. "Is that low enough for you?"

Now even Hank had to chuckle a little. "That girl is coming around," he said to Flora as he led her toward her second patient.

"How are we doing on ammunition?" Hank asked as he watched

Flora stuff a wad of cotton into a bloody bullet hole in Matt Kenyon's thigh.

"Low," Tonk replied.

"Me, too."

"Yep."

"How bad is it, Hank?" Flora asked.

"Well, we're almost out of ammunition and we've got ninety-some-odd Comanches out there who all want us dead. Or worse."

She made a knot in the bandage tied tight around Kenyon's leg. "So, what's the good news?" she said.

"I'm not through with the bad news. There are nine outlaws in that adobe house who won't give up without a fight, and you can bet they've been saving their rounds behind those thick mud walls."

"Okay," Flora said. "And the good news is . . ."

"I'm still lookin' for the good news."

"They seem to be poised for another charge," Kenyon observed.

"Hank!" said Long Tom. "The door to the adobe is openin'."

"What the hell?" Hank rushed across the barn to look out through a knothole.

From the darkness of the interior of the ranch house, the form of a man came running, illuminated by an orange flame that came with him. It was Eddie Milliken, Rafferty's top man.

"Stop him!" Hank shouted, but Milliken had already taken two steps outside and flung the torch across the way to the barn. It landed in a pile of old hay and scrap lumber at the dilapidated northwest corner of the barn. Before the arsonist could turn back to the door, Jay Blue sent three bullets into his chest, causing him to shuffle backward and fall. He landed dead in the doorway, blocking it open.

Hank kicked the barn door open in an attempt to rush out and stomp the fire, but a barrage from the ranch house cut his flesh in several places and drove him back.

"Here comes the next charge!" Kenyon warned from the far corner of the barn.

"The bastards have sacrificed us!" Hank fumed. He stepped out again and fired four more rounds into the ranch house doorway before the outlaws could drag Milliken's body inside and shut the door.

"Captain Tomlinson," Skeeter said hopefully. "If that's the Wolf out there . . ."

Hank shook his head. "Don't think you can go out there, son. He can't stop what he's started. He's promised those braves a chance at glory, and he can't yank it out from under them now. He didn't know you and Jay Blue would be here."

"He's already saved us once," Jay Blue argued.

"He got away with it once. He can't give you another chance."

Flames began to crackle, and smoke streamed through the barn.

"What are we gonna do, Captain?" Long Tom Merrick was waiting.

"They're circling four hundred yards out now!" Kenyon called. "Looks like they're going to close in. My God, they're using their horses for shields, riding at a full gallop."

"Hank?" Flora said nervously.

"Take the horses out of those stalls and put them in that big corral upwind," Hank ordered, buying some time to think. "Hold your fire, boys, unless they're right in our laps."

A gust caused the flames to roar louder and sent a whole cloud of smoke barreling through the interior of the barn. Skeeter, Tom, and Beto were taking horses from the smoky stalls and turning them into the corral, in clear view of the Indians.

"Alright," Hank said. "This is bad. But we got one chance."

"We gotta get the girls inside that adobe," Jay Blue said.

"Right, son."

"They're inside two hundred yards and closing the circle!" Kenyon coughed. "I can't see! The smoke, Captain!"

"Come here, Matt! Everybody! Here! Now!" He waited precious seconds as the smoke thickened, the heat rose, and the men gathered at the barn doors facing the adobe. Jay Blue was on his feet now, his arm around Jane, whose jaw was set in fear.

"We've got to storm that house now! I'll kick the door down and go in first."

"Right behind you, Captain," said Kenyon, picking up the double-barrel he had yet to use.

"*Everybody* better be right behind me."

Kenyon cocked both barrels. "We've got to go! The Indians are bound to be in range now."

Flames were crackling up through the rafters and the cedar shakes.

Hank winced at the smoke. He knew he had to go out there. He saw Jay Blue hand a revolver to Jane. Her hand trembled when she took it. He snorted at Skeeter, and Skeeter snorted back, pumping the lever of his freshly loaded Winchester. He winked at Flora. She tried to smile, but a hideous war cry suddenly knifed into the barn, sounding closer than even Matt Kenyon had figured, and more eerily bloodthirsty than even Hank could have imagined.

From a swirl of smoke, Tonk stepped past everyone and walked outside, taking the smoke with him. Hank pursued, and felt the rest of the men surround the ladies, ushering them away from the heat of the burning barn.

The smoke seemed to cover them all halfway to the house, but then it twisted away on a windflaw and lifted like a stage curtain. Hank waved two Colts, anxious for a target. What he saw was too strange to shoot at. Lumbering between him and the adobe stronghold, came a . . . by God, it was a camel!

That hideous war cry screeched against his eardrums again and he glanced up to see what for all the world looked to him, at least for a split second, like a wraith on a ghostly steed. It turned out to be bare-chested Jubal Hayes on the Steel Dust Gray, which was even more of a sight than a soul-reaping spirit. To the west, two companies of blue-coated buffalo soldiers came to the rescue, led by First Sergeant July Polk on a familiar claybank gelding. In every other direction, Comanches left the field, scattering far and wide in fear of the evil ghost.

"The horses!" Hank yelled.

The men scrambled for the corrals to calm their mounts before they pushed through the broken-down fencing in an attempt to flee the burning barn.

• • •

Jubal's green-broke mustang dodged the smoke, so he swung wide around the barn, laughing at the fleeing Indians as he galloped. Polk and the troopers quickly caught up to him, chasing the Indians all the way into the distant timber to make sure they were gone for good.

Feeling the sun on his skin, Jubal yanked at the leather ties on his saddle skirt where he had secured his shirt. He also reached into his saddlebag where he had stuffed his hat. He could feel Steel Dust's heart beating double time to his heaving lungs. He could not have imagined a more challenging training run for the killer stud, but he was still ahorseback after many a mile.

"That wasn't much of a skirmish," First Sergeant Polk admitted. "But that's alright with me."

"I told you they'd run," Jubal said, and he would have carried on in that vein had not the gunfire stopped him.

Polk wheeled as his troopers milled around him, letting their horses blow.

Jubal, too, made his mustang turn. "What in the name of . . ." They had left the ranch house some four or five hundred yards behind. He was sure they had chased off all the Comanches. So, what now? Why the shooting?

"I'll be damned," Polk said. "The fools are killin' *each other*!"

The outlaws had come out of the adobe ranch house like a swarm of hornets, running at the corral. Skeeter figured quickly what it meant. The outlaws had seen the soldiers. They had seen the Indians leave. They knew they were all going to jail or going to hang, so they had to run for the brush or run for the horses.

They didn't do well at capturing the horses. All the Broken Arrow men were there, guarding the stock, and the outlaws came out of one door in the adobe, making easy targets. Skeeter himself saw one of his bullets knock half of Bill Waterford's head off. Then his blood-kin father stepped out and somehow knew right where to fire. Skeeter saw the big man's eye aiming at him, and felt the slug tick his ear as he jumped into the open door of a rundown little smokehouse and ducked low as bullets splintered above him.

He looked out through the door and saw Rafferty running around the far side of the smoking barn, shooting as he retreated. Then he looked up and saw two hairy things hanging inside the smokehouse. He felt his face wrinkle and felt his stomach turn as he realized what they were. One was made of long, curly strands of light brown hair. The other was black hair, thick, but cropped short.

He reached forward and touched Poli's scalp. The gunfire outside suddenly seemed to wake him. He jumped out of the smokehouse and circled the barn in the opposite direction his so-called daddy had run. Before he rounded the corner, he looked back and saw his friends disarming a couple of outlaws who had given up. But there was still shooting going on, and Skeeter knew Jack Brennan would be the last to end it.

Rounding the back side of the burning barn, using smoke for cover, he took to the brush. Passing through mesquites and cedar, he came clear of the smoke and angled back toward the buildings, and there he saw the big man with his back turned, unaware of his presence. He was using the corner of an old rock springhouse for cover, firing at the Broken Arrow men.

Then John Rafferty's revolver hit an empty chamber, and he started to reload.

"Drop it!" Skeeter was startled to hear his own voice. "Drop it or I'll shoot you!" He knew he had the best of the murdering outlaw.

Rafferty turned and looked up at Skeeter, but kept reloading. "You better do it before I get reloaded, son."

"I ain't your son! Drop it!"

He finished reloading and stood with his barrel angling down. "Go on, shoot, Skeeter. Do me the favor. I don't want to hang."

"Well, I don't want to shoot you, so drop it!"

Suddenly, Rafferty's muzzle was pointing at him. "Do it."

"Drop it, I said!"

Rafferty cocked the hammer. He fired between Skeeter's feet, startling him. Still, Skeeter hesitated.

"A man's soul can't get out when he strangles. I won't hang!" He cocked and fired again, and again.

Dust showered Skeeter, then a bullet cut his arm, and he pulled his trigger. The shot caught Rafferty high in the chest. The big man slammed back against the rock wall of the springhouse and slid to a sitting position on the ground, leaving a smear of blood on the rocks.

Skeeter approached him, and noticed he had dropped his revolver at his side.

"Good one," Rafferty said, coughing up a frothy mouthful of blood after he spoke.

"Skeeter!" Jay Blue's voice said from a way off. "Where are you?"

Skeeter stood over the dying outlaw. "What was my mother's name?" he asked.

Rafferty coughed again. "I don't really hate music," he managed to say.

"Tell me my mother's name!" he demanded.

"She was a good woman."

"Tell me, *please*!"

The blood sprayed from his mouth this time, and he seemed to try to form a word that wouldn't come. Then he spit and said, "It means light. Her name . . . Her name . . ." His chin fell down on his chest and his eyes stared at nothing.

"Skeeter!" Jay Blue said. "He's over here, Daddy! He's okay!"

Skeeter glanced up to see the cavalry soldiers and Jubal trotting back. Jay Blue stepped up beside him, then saw the dead man on the ground.

"Daddy! Skeeter got him! Skeeter got Rafferty!"

Captain Tomlinson came around the rock springhouse and grabbed Skeeter by the shoulder. They all stood there and looked at the outlaw's body for a time.

"Skeeter," the captain said. "It's not in the blood, son. He just had a tough life. Don't judge him too harshly."

"Skeeter, we're all the family you'll ever need," Jay Blue added.

But Skeeter was a step ahead of the Tomlinsons again. He had already forgiven everything. And now a beautiful new view of days to come was lifting years of weight from his heart. He remembered his father's last words, finishing them for him: *Her name was Luz.*

Jubal Hayes approached the gathering of men at the rock wall, the Steel Dust Gray dancing sidewise under him a little, but altogether behaving pretty well. Skeeter looked at him, crouching a little to see his eyes under the low curve of his hat brim.

"Mr. Hayes," he said, "how would you feel about being my stepdaddy?"

Jubal must have suspected from the first moment he saw Skeeter and Luz standing side by side. He just sighed, and smiled a little with one side of his mouth. "Well . . . I'm a little white for you . . . but I guess I'll have to do."

40

HIS FINGERS KNEW their way up and down the frets of his banjo like an old saddle horse knew the way to the feed trough. He didn't even have to think about the well-rehearsed tune. His attention was directed more toward the throngs of people who crowded Main Street—people who had come to celebrate Texas Independence Day, March 2. It felt like Saturday in the middle of the week at Luck. The town had never seen such a crowd for the annual Texas Independence Day picnic and social and, of course, the horse race.

He sat in his place with the normal trio—his father on guitar and Jubal Hayes on fiddle—the three of them all crowded into the narrow shade of the awning of Flora's Saloon. The spring weather was perfect for a celebration—blue skies overhead, the thermometer at Sam's store reading seventy-two degrees.

Jubal Hayes had become a familiar sight around town by this time. Right now he was all buttoned up from head to toe, save his beaming face and flashing, fiddle-playing hands. He had hung around enough in company with the Tomlinsons that folks had stopped staring.

Now Jane burst out of the saloon, carrying a beer for her favorite banjo player. Folks hadn't stopped staring at Jane. She was just too beautiful not to notice, especially since she had taken to smiling. Everybody knew she was going to marry Jay Blue Tomlinson. He smiled at her as she came to stand beside him, leaving his brew on the table that the band had dragged outside.

In the bright sunlight that Jubal avoided by habit, Luz kicked up dirt with the son she had thought she had lost long ago, the two of them doing Jubal's dancing in the sun for him. Jubal glanced at both his sidemen and made the flourish that brought the song to an end. A wave of applause greeted Jay Blue's ears as he sipped at the beer and winked at Jane.

"Attention!" Sam Collins shouted. "Attention, everyone!" He stepped up on the boardwalk. "Almost time for the horse race now. The course is the same as every year. Four miles, starting at my store, then across the river at the ford, around the old trading post, and back up Main Street to the finish line, right here in front of Flora's Saloon. We'll start as soon as the riders can line up at the starting line!"

Jay Blue's father leaned close to him. "Put my guitar up, son. I'll go see how the mare looks." Jay Blue nodded. His daddy was pretty excited about this race—the Thoroughbred's first. At this moment, he had Long Tom Merrick walking her in the alley behind Flora's to keep her loose and warm.

He latched the instruments in their cases and grabbed his beer.

"You don't look nervous," Jane said. "This is an important race for the Broken Arrow."

He shrugged. "Darlin', I've been shot at too many times to get nervous over a horse race."

"Oh, *well* . . ." She rolled her eyes in that fetching way of hers.

"You're the only thing that still makes me nervous."

"I plan to keep it that way."

Jubal was latching his fiddle case. "You best be nervous about ol' Steel Dust."

"I'll bet you five dollars our mare comes in ahead of your stud."

"I'll take that bet!" Jubal said, shaking his hand.

Within ten minutes, the horses had gathered on Main Street. Jay Blue's father came to him with last-minute instructions. "Hold her back the first three miles," he insisted.

"I know, Daddy."

"She won't like it, but that's good. Let her warm up gradually, then give her her head when you come back across the river."

"Got it," Jay Blue said. He had lined up at the far right of the field. He looked left to judge the attitudes of the other runners. Next to him was First Sergeant July Polk on the now-famous claybank that had once belonged to Wes James. A good cow horse, but too stout for a course of this length, especially carrying a man the size of Polk.

Polk looked at him and smiled. "My money's on you, Tomlinson, so you better watch that killer gray."

Next to First Sergeant Polk, a couple of cowhands from nearby outfits had entered some pretty good-looking cow ponies, but they had no chance of beating the Thoroughbred or the Steel Dust Gray.

Beyond them, Jay Blue caught the eye of Matt Kenyon, who had ridden to Luck to report that he had put in his resignation with the State Police and was thinking of running for brand inspector in Travis County—unless the legislature reinstated the Texas Rangers between now and election day. He was riding that bald-faced, flaxen-maned, sorrel with four white socks and one glass eye. Jay Blue had to admit that the horse had proven to be highly serviceable, but didn't have a chance in this race.

And finally, at the far end of the line, the notorious, legendary Steel Dust Gray pranced sideways and bit at Kenyon's bald-faced sorrel, causing just enough trouble to delay the start. Jubal was wearing his dark glasses, but Jay Blue knew the old mustanger was eye-balling him. Well, if Steel Dust *were* to win, he mused, at least he and Skeeter still shared the distinction of having helped Jubal catch the wild thing so he could ride it in the first place.

"My *dinero's* on you, *hermano*!"

Jay Blue looked to his right and saw Skeeter standing there with Luz on the boardwalk. "Thanks, brother," he said.

"But my mama's bettin' on El Grullo."

Luz only smiled and shrugged.

Now Jubal, himself a legend for having trained the untrainable gray stud, mumbled something hoarse to El Grullo, and suddenly the racers all had their noses on the starting line. Captain Tomlinson always started the annual Luck, Texas, Independence Day Horse Race. He saw the moment and instantly shouted, "Go, boys!"

The crowd roared, and the mare took off like a cannonball under Jay Blue. He had to pull hard on the reins to keep her from running away from the field right off the line. But he made her slow down and tried to relax in the saddle so she would start slow and finish strong. He even took the time to tip his hat to the spectators and blow a kiss to Jane as he let the entire field of racers stretch the lead in front of him.

Once the runners passed out of sight around the bend in the road at the edge of town, the mare lost interest in the competition and started to feel smooth under him, as if she were just out for a casual lope. Down the slope he cantered, enjoying the feel of the tall, graceful mount.

He crossed the river and gave her some rein to let her build steam up the other side of the gentle slope that led from the ford. As he neared the old trading post that marked the halfway point of the race, and the turnaround, he saw the leaders coming back toward him.

Matt Kenyon rumbled by him first, but Jubal was close behind and Jay Blue knew he would have to do some real catching up after he rounded the ruins of the trading post. His heart finally started to pound at the excitement of the contest, and danged if the mare didn't seem to feel his very pulse. He gave her a little more rein as the rest of the field flew at him, and past him.

Rounding the trading post, he felt the mare dig in, but still held her back. Oh, she knew this game well! It was in her blood. In her very fiber. She wanted to win! He was just getting ready to disobey his father's instructions and let the mare all out early, when something caught his eye among the live oaks to his right.

The entire field had gone by. He had passed every horse that started. Thus his confusion when he looked right and saw a rider closing in on him. His first thought was that he was riding unarmed, to reduce weight. The mare felt his anxiety and craned her neck to see where his eyes looked. Then she caught sight of the rider, and bolted sideways.

The rider had a feather in his hair that fluttered. The pony was a fine paint who was just as excited as any of the racers who had already passed. Jay Blue's eyes looked into the warrior's face and recognized a friend who couldn't be a friend, and yet was. Relief flooded his insides as he realized that the Wolf was alone and unarmed.

The Thoroughbred sensed this calm and settled down a bit, but the jolt had made her really want to run now. Still, Jay Blue held her back and let the Wolf and his horse catch up to them. For several long strides, they paced each other, each admiring the other's fine mount. Now the Wolf looked at Jay Blue, then up the road toward town. He raised an eyebrow and shrugged ever so slightly as if to say, "What are you waiting for? You're losing."

Jay Blue nodded, smiled, touched his hat brim, and let the mare have her head. The Wolf dropped his reins, raised his hands to the spirits, and gave a single yelp that made both horses—pinto and Thoroughbred—burst into yet another realm of speed. The Wolf veered away, putting some timber between himself and his friend, finally galloping among trees that seemed to have grown crowded together there for the sole purpose of whisking him to haunts unknown.

Suddenly, Jay Blue Tomlinson didn't care if he never won another horse race as long as he lived. The Thoroughbred mare who had seen green Kentucky pastures and wild mustang ranges would run the rest of this race as she, herself, saw fit. This wasn't his horse, and it wasn't his race. He was just a fool who owned a saddle.

ABOUT THE AUTHOR

WILLIE HUGH NELSON is the creative genius behind historic recordings like "Crazy," "Hello Walls," "Red Headed Stranger," and "Stardust." His career has spanned six decades and his catalog boasts more than 200 albums. In addition to his innumerable awards and honors as a musician, he has amassed reputable credentials as an author, actor, and activist.

Nelson continues to tour tirelessly, climbing aboard Honeysuckle Rose III (he rode his first two buses into the ground), taking his music and fans on a seemingly endless journey to places that were well worth the ride. He has even produced his own blend of biodiesel fuel.

Born April 29, 1933, in Abbott, Texas, Nelson and his sister were raised by their paternal grandparents who encouraged both children to play music. He began writing songs in elementary school and played in bands as a teenager. After high school, Nelson served a short stint in the Air Force; however, music was a constant pull.

His songwriting career in Nashville took off in 1961 with Faron Young's recording of "Hello Walls" and Patsy Cline's version of "Crazy." In 1962, he scored his first two Top 10 hits as a recording artist for Liberty Records but struggled for a breakthrough the remainder of the decade.

In 1972, he moved back to Texas where the rock and folk music that had become popular in Austin emboldened him. Following his first two albums with Atlantic Records, *Shotgun Willie* (1973) and *Phases and Stages* (1974), his acoustic concept album *Red Headed Stranger* with Columbia Records became one of country's most unlikely hits.

Nelson's convention-busting stardom, combined with the concurrent popularity of maverick Waylon Jennings, prompted journalist Hazel Smith to dub the trend "Outlaw Music." As a result, RCA Records released the multi-artist compilation of previously recorded material *Wanted: The Outlaws*, which spawned the Nelson/Jennings duet "Good Hearted Woman" and quickly became the best selling album country had ever seen.

A fixture on the singles charts over the next several years, Nelson's star rose even further with the 1978 releases *Waylon & Willie*, which included "Mamas Don't Let Your Babies Grow Up to Be Cowboys," and *Stardust*. Nelson's stardom soon translated to another medium with roles in feature films, including *The Electric Horseman*, *Honeysuckle Rose*, and *Stagecoach*. The hit songs kept coming with "On the Road Again" (1981), "Always on My Mind" (1982), and a duet with Julio Iglesias, "To All the Girls I've Loved Before" (1984).

In 1985, Nelson enlisted Kris Kristofferson and Johnny Cash for *Highwaymen*. That same year he founded Farm Aid, an organization dedicated to championing the cause of family farmers. Farm Aid's annual televised concert special raises funds and—along with Willie's annual Fourth of July Picnic—has become a cornerstone of his live touring schedule. He also is currently lobbying against the slaughter of horses for human consumption abroad.

In the 1990s, a $16.7 million bill from the IRS forced Nelson to sell many of his assets, including several homes, and resulted in the release of *The IRS Tapes: Who'll Buy My Memories*. Nelson cleared the debt by 1993, and was inducted into the Country Music Hall of Fame that same year. As the millennium drew to a close, Nelson embarked on another fertile period, releasing *Spirit*, *Teatro*, and an instrumental-focused album titled *Night and Day*.

In 2003, he released *Run That By Me One More Time*, a collaboration with Ray Price featuring new recordings from their combined fifty years of catalog; *The Essential Willie Nelson*, which spans his earliest recordings as well as the celebrated Island/Def Jam Records material; and *Willie Live & Kickin'* featuring guest vocalists ranging from Norah Jones to Toby Keith, with whom Nelson performed his No. 1 single, "Beer for My Horses." *Countryman* (2005), his first ever reggae set, was followed by 2006's *Songbird*, and *You Don't Know Me: The Songs of Cindy Walker*, which earned Nelson a Grammy nomination for Best Country Album. The new millennium also saw the release of Willie's books *The Facts of Life: and Other Dirty Jokes* (Random House, 2002) and *The Tao of Willie* (Gotham, 2006) written with Turk Pipkin.

Nelson's career has been recognized with eight Grammy wins, a President's Merit Award, a Grammy Legend Award, and the prestigious Lifetime Achievement Award. In 2004, the Academy of Country Music bestowed him with the prestigious Gene Weed Special Achievement Award honoring Nelson's "unprecedented and genre-defying contributions to popular music over his nearly fifty-year career."

In 2007, Broadcast Music, Inc. (BMI) named Nelson a BMI Icon, declaring that his "ascendance to internationally-renowned treasure is a singular path marked by self-belief and musical brilliance." That same year he released the two-disc album *Last of the Breed*, a Grammy award-winning collaboration with Merle Haggard and Ray Price that features twenty-two newly-recorded country classics.